DELAY OF GAME

GRAND MARQUEE MANTICORES
BOOK 3

STEF C.R.

Delay of GAME

Delay of Game

Copyright © 2025 Stef C. R.

All rights reserved. No part of this book may be reproduced in any form except for the purpose of brief reviews or citations without the written permission of the author. You may not use this book to train AI, nor was any AI used in the making of this book.

This is a work of fiction in which all events and characters in this book are completely imaginary. Any resemblance to actual people is entirely coincidental.

Cover designed by Lorissa Padilla.
Developmental edits by Kay Morton.
Copy edits by Erin King.

Grand Marquee Manticores

It's a Set Up (#0.5)
The Love Penalty (#1)
Bar Down (#2)

Free Short Story
Tented Feelings

Playlist

Intro – Khalid
Fresh Out The Slammer – Taylor Swift
Slow Dancing – Aly & AJ
Almost (Sweet Music) – Hozier
My Greatest Fear – Benson Boone
the 1 – Taylor Swift
In My Mind – Lyn Lapid
Supercut – Lorde
Simmer – BAYNK, Hablot Brown
If I Go, I'm Goin – Gregory Alan Isakov
All I Wanted – Taylor Swift
Love of My Life – Harry Styles
Too Sweet – Hozier
Until I Found You – Stephen Sanchez
Pretty Slowly – Benson Boone
High Hope – Patrick Droney
Ruined – Patrick Droney
her – JVKE
j's lullaby (darlin' I'd wait for you) – Delaney Bailey
Want U Around – Omar Apollo, Ruel
Ordinary – Alex Warren
Indigo – Kris Allen

To all my anxious bookish girlies—this one's for you.

Author's Note

To my family ... it's that time again.
If you plan to read this book, skip chapters 8, 9, 10, 29, and 30.

As always, my books are filled with humor, spice, and some heavier topics too, such as: anxiety and depression, mentions of pregnancy (side character), mentions of injury and recovery, and PTOA (post traumatic osteoarthritis).

If you are uncomfortable with any of the above, please proceed with caution and prioritize your mental health.

PROLOGUE

Ten Years Ago

JORDAN

THERE'S a strange battle happening in the locker room. The smell of cleaning supplies mixes with Axe body spray and sweat, the latter definitely prevailing. I drop my bag by the bench and take a seat, looking around the mostly empty room.

It's my first day at training camp with the Grand Marquee Manticores but instead of feeling happy and proud of all my accomplishments so far, I feel ... anxious. Like there's something lurking just around the corner, ready to bring me my downfall.

My phone pings with a text and I take a deep breath, hoping that can will my anxiety away. *You got this. Everything will be just fine.*

> Kick ass, baby brother.

I smile at the text from my sister, Tangela, and feel myself relaxing. My shoulders drop from my ears and I roll away the crick in my neck. This always helps. Something or *someone* familiar to ground me when I feel my world is going to shit.

I've always been this walking, talking contradiction. I enjoy my solitude and crave the quiet moments when I'm at home, but I also desperately want to be surrounded by people. I want to go out and make friends, but I dread everything that comes before that. All the awkward conversations and small talk.

I mean, who gives a shit about the weather? It's Michigan, we get six months of winter, get over it. And then there's the Midwest niceness of *How are ya?* and *Ope, not too bad, how 'bout yourself?* Sometimes, I'd rather hit my head against a brick wall than have to talk to people.

"Hey, how's it going?" a deep gravelly voice says, and I look up from my phone.

See, pointless small talk.

I already dread being here—not because I hate Traverse City or Michigan, which has always been home to me, but because my anxiety is holding hands with my introverted side and I'm just a walking mess.

I clear my throat and say, "Good, you?"

The six foot five man in front of me is dripping in sweat. He nods his reply at me and moves to take off his equipment. More players trickle in, wearing their full gear, and I start to panic.

Am I supposed to go to a different locker room?

Did I miss something on the schedule?

Am I late?

A bead of sweat drips in my eye and my hand shakes as I reach down to grab my backpack and hightail it out of the room.

"You're one of the rookies, right?" the same guy asks, and takes a seat next to me.

"Um, yeah. I'm Jordan," I say, voice a little shaky. "Hill," I add, knowing that in hockey, a player is usually recognized by his last name rather than his first.

"First day?" he asks and as much as I hate eye contact, I force myself to be *normal* and make proper conversation. His green eyes are bright, and laser focused on me with so much intensity that I scoot back on the bench a little.

"Yeah," I say, and all but gulp. This dude is huge and hella intimidating.

"I'm Alex Dionis," he says and reaches out a large hand for me to shake. I take it weakly and think the name sounds familiar. Then I realize who this guy is. Not only did he go to my high school, but Dionis is the fucking *captain* of the Manticores. My eyes widen and I try to compose myself. What a poor first impression this must be.

"Nice to meet you, sir."

He pulls his hand back and there's a small smile on his lips as he says, "Sir? What am I, forty?"

"No. I don't know. You're older than me, at least," I say, flustered. *Nice one Jordan. Very smooth.*

"I'm twenty-six, man," Alex complains, shaking his head at me.

"Did you just say he looks like he's forty?" another guy asks, sitting down on the other side of me and flashing me a wide smile. His dark blond hair is damp with sweat, and he looks slightly familiar too.

"I didn't—"

"He sure acts like he's forty. Alex basically lives and

breathes hockey and then do you know what he does? He goes home and watches TV by himself, doesn't come out to celebrate with the rest of us," he says.

"Fuck off, *Robbie*."

My head swivels back and forth between Alex and Robbie, who I now recognize as Robbie Elliot, another guy that went to my school.

"I know he's not actually forty. We all went to high school together, I was a couple years behind you both. I only made the team after you guys graduated."

"Sick, what a small world," Robbie says and presents me a fist. I bump it with a smile that might look more like a grimace, but if he's bothered by my social awkwardness he doesn't let it show.

The two of them continue to take off their gear and after a solid minute of silence I say, "Am I in the wrong locker room? My email said to come in at ten, but not much more."

"You didn't get the full schedule for the week?"

I blink at Alex, more panic gripping at me, making me feel dizzy. "Um, no. I don't think so."

"They probably forgot to attach it," he says, unbothered. "I'll take you to meet the coach, and he'll sort it out."

"Cool, thanks," I say, getting up and throwing my bag over my shoulder.

"Hey, what are you doing later, Jordan?" Robbie asks and for a moment I'm stunned. Is he asking because he wants to hang out or is he just making conversation?

"Nothing."

"Well, you are now. I'm staying at my parents' cabin and we're gonna have a bonfire tonight. Alex will be there too. You should join us. We can reminisce about high school."

I'm not sure what there is to reminisce about since high

school was not that long ago, but maybe I need to socialize. Especially with teammates.

"That'd be cool."

"See you then," he says with a huge smile that reaches his eyes.

ALICE

"MICHAEL!!" I yell after my eldest brother, coughing out the mouthful of water I got when he tipped my kayak over. "I'm going to murder you!"

"Ha, good luck trying," he yells back, swimming towards the small boat launch. Even though my brother is eleven years older than me, he still acts like a teenager. No wonder he's twenty-eight and single.

I flip my kayak upright and get back in, aiming to return to the cabin. The weather is perfect for a bonfire, and I shiver a little in my wet suit. The smoke from the fire pit rises up through the trees and I follow the movement with a smile on my face.

The sky is a beautiful mosaic of oranges and purples, and I wish I had my phone on me to take a picture. I paddle faster and once I reach the dock, I put away the kayak and vest.

Michael says something to me, but I ignore him and angrily walk towards the cabin. My favorite brother, Robbie, jumps out of my path at the perfect time, dodging a collision.

The same cannot be said for his friend that's walking behind him. I see his dark brown eyes widen right as I plaster myself to his body. And oh, what a fine body it is.

The stranger catches me easily and my hands land on his abdomen where they curl into the soft fabric of his baby blue t-shirt. He must be as tall as Robbie—which is to say, almost a whole foot taller than me. My eyes are level with his collarbone and when I look up at his face, my breath catches.

Fuck, he's pretty.

Light brown skin, a dusting of freckles on his nose and cheekbones, thick black eyebrows, and short black hair, neatly trimmed. Fuck pretty, *he's gorgeous*.

"Hi," I manage to squeak out, attempting to still save this first impression.

He opens his mouth to say something back, but then I shift on my feet and my shoes let out an embarrassing squelching sound that the entire Leelanau Peninsula can hear.

The handsome stranger bites back a smile, and mortification slams into me.

Damn it, Michael!

I pull back, wincing at the wet spots I left on his jeans and t-shirt.

"Sorry," I say, avoiding eye contact.

Robbie spins me around and places his hands on my shoulders. At first I think he's going to yell at me for getting his friend wet, but then I see the concern in his eyes.

"Al, what happened? Why are you wet and shivering?"

"Michael tipped me over in the kayak," I say, and it comes out more petulant than I want to sound.

"Michael, what the hell? She could catch a cold," Robbie yells back at our brother, maneuvering me around the stranger and into the cabin. He leads me to the hallway, where he grabs me two fluffy towels before running into the bathroom and turning the shower to the hottest setting.

I bite back my smile. Robbie, always the caretaker.

"You know, I'm not a kid anymore. I can run my own shower."

"You'll always be my baby sister," he says, placing a kiss on my forehead and heading to the back deck, leaving me to my hot shower.

The window in the bathroom is open, and the last thing

I hear before closing it is, "Sorry about that, man. I can get you a dry shirt to change into."

"No worries, I'm okay," the handsome stranger replies.

When I'm done, I take my time getting ready, applying some makeup and drying my hair straight before heading out to the fire pit and properly meeting Robbie's new friend.

"Hi, I'm Alice," I say and offer my hand to him. The breeze ruffles my blond hair and a small strand falls in my eyes.

"Jordan," he says, tracing every feature of my face. His hand is slightly cold in mine, and I rub my thumb over the back of it. His eyelids flutter as he looks down and I swear I see a hint of pink appear on his cheeks.

"Welcome to the team," Robbie says as Alex hands Jordan a drink.

I instantly miss his touch when he lets go, but there's this warm feeling that takes root in my chest and spreads through my body until I no longer feel the breeze.

Welcome, indeed.

PART 1
ALMOST

CHAPTER 1

Nine Years Ago

JORDAN

THE ELLIOTS RENTED out an entire winery in Traverse City for the wedding this weekend. They wanted the best for their oldest son Michael and for my sister Tangela, so that's what they got. The ceremony area is set up on a hill in the back, and it's overlooking the hundreds of rows of grapes, some ripe for picking. The wood structure where the ceremony is supposed to take place is decorated with wildflowers in various shades of pink, orange, red, and purples. All of Tangela's favorites are neatly woven in through sparkling string lights.

I look away from the window and towards Tangela. She looks incredible in her long-sleeved laced dress and pinned up hair. But most importantly, she looks happy. Our gazes meet, and she gives me a smile that brightens up her whole face. And then it drops as my mom arrives to fuss over her veil.

Oh boy. Time to intervene.

I pick up my pace and get there just in time to hear, "Honey, are you sure about this? Say the word and I'll get you out of here, you don't have to marry the white boy."

I roll my eyes at my mother's antics and put my hands on her shoulders, spinning her towards me instead.

"Mom, we've talked about this. No unsolicited advice, please."

Our mom can be a handful sometimes and constantly gets in our personal lives. We've had multiple conversations with her over the years, letting her know when she crosses the line. Like just now. She scowls at me, and her tanned face shows off the wrinkles she's acquired over the years. "Don't get me started on you. Why didn't you bring a date to your sister's wedding?" she says.

Tangela sighs and shakes her head, but before she can intervene, the wedding planner lets us know that guests have started to arrive.

I say, "I didn't bring a date because I'm too busy being in the wedding party. And you should go make sure the guests find the right seats, yeah?"

"Yeah, yeah, I can take a hint," she says, and places a kiss on Tangela's cheek before leaving the room.

The rest of the wedding party files into the room, along with my dad, who looks dapper in his suit and dark red bow tie. My mom always said I was a carbon copy of my dad, but the truth is I could never pull off a bow tie. His eyes are shining, and I think I can see some dried tears on his freckled cheekbones. I need to look away before I start crying too.

As I look around the room, I see Robbie chatting with

one of Tangela's bridesmaids. After I joined the Manticores last year, Alex and Robbie took me under their wing pretty quickly and we've been good friends ever since. Especially Robbie. When he found out my parents retired and moved to the East side of the state, leaving me to spend Christmas alone, he invited me over. Easy as that.

Tangela was in town visiting, and I decided to bring her along. I didn't expect her to be immediately so taken with Michael. I definitely wasn't. He's kind of a doofus in my opinion—almost thirty, working as a bartender downtown, living with his parents. And yet, he must have some good qualities, because after dating for less than a year, my sister said yes to marrying him.

The last of the rain clouds are clearing up just in time for the wedding ceremony and the people are being ushered to take a seat. We all get into position as the wedding planner instructed us during rehearsal, but my partner in crime for the day is missing.

I look around but don't see her anywhere. Before I can ask Robbie where she is, the back door slams open and Alice runs in, wincing at the force, and heads straight for my sister, presenting her the large bouquet of flowers she's holding.

Tangela gasps and says, "You are a lifesaver, Al. I thought I'd for sure have to go out without a bouquet."

"Please, I would have scrounged something up from all these flowers before leaving you hanging."

"Thank you."

"Places, people. We're on a schedule!" the wedding planner yells out.

Alice quickly takes her spot next to me, looping her arm through my elbow, just like we rehearsed. I frown as I look down at her small hand on my forearm. It's covered in cuts and scrapes.

I lean in so only she can hear me and say, "Alice, what happened to your hand?"

She looks up, startled, and her dark blue eyes are glued to my face, roaming around like they don't know what to land on.

"Al?"

"Oh, right. It's nothing, J. I offered to redo the bouquet because it was coming apart."

"You should put something on those cuts."

"I don't have time right now. Later," she says, brushing me off and turning to face the other couples lined up in front of us.

I study her profile for a moment. Alice is five feet, four inches of pure sass. Her dark blond hair is styled half down, with a twist in the back and plenty of hair strands falling into her face and eyes. And the bridesmaid dress she is wearing looks like it's perfectly made for her.

The burgundy material hugs her in all the right places, especially her ass, and I need to shake myself out of it when I realize I'm staring at my best friend's sister, who is six years younger than me at that.

What is wrong with me?

Maybe I should have brought a date.

ALICE

I TAKE a deep breath to steady myself. My hands are itchy and this dress is tighter than I expected, but I got it on the Internet and it came in a couple days ago, so it's not like I had time for a complete re-haul of my outfit. On the bright side, I'm pretty sure I noticed Jordan checking me out a second ago.

Someone yells out that we're next and it's like I've forgotten everything they told us at the rehearsal yesterday. Walk fast to the beat of the music—no, wait—walk slowly to give the people at the front time to get to their assigned places.

My steps pick up without my thinking and Jordan gently holds me back, taking charge of the pace. *Good*. I'm so nervous, I'm a mess.

Michael is getting married. After being an idiot for most of his life, he's finally pulled his head out of his ass and found the perfect girl for him. And I'm so happy. I want this to be the best day ever for them, and if that means taking on some odd chores and fixing up a bouquet at the expense of my manicure, then so be it.

As soon as we get up to the altar, I let go of Jordan's forearm, but he catches my hand back at the last second. My head whips to him and he gives me a small smile and kisses the back of my hand. The whole thing happens so fast that I'm dumbstruck.

Then he's shaking Michael's hand and moving to stand with the rest of the groomsmen. Michael wraps me up in a hug and says, "I know I torture you most of the time, but I love you Al."

"Wow, not even married yet and already you're soft," I say, teasing him and hugging him tight. "I love you too."

I look back to my parents, who are already in their seats up front, and smile. The wedding planner glares at me from across the pavilion and I quickly move over and take my spot on the bride's side.

Robbie and Diana, the bridesmaid he's paired up with,

walk down and my two brothers have a long hug. I look over at the wedding planner expecting her to glare, but she's all smiles.

Rude.

Jordan catches my eye and smiles, subtly running a finger over his throat. It takes all I have not to burst into laughter as he brings up the inside joke from the rehearsal, that the wedding planner is going to murder me for being ditsy.

I don't have the chance to respond to his antics, because the song changes and Tangela and her dad start walking down the aisle.

She looks incredible in her lace dress with long sleeves and pearl buttons. Her black hair is in an updo, with a few strands falling forward, and her smile brightens up the whole pavilion. She waves at me with the hand that's holding the bouquet and I smile, happy that she gets her perfect day.

I expect my idiot brother to make some kind of joke or bad-mannered comment, but when I look over I see tears in Michael's eyes, then Robbie's. And the next thing I know, my vision is blurry too.

No one tells you how emotional weddings are, especially when you're part of the family. I blow out a breath and fan my face, refusing to let the tears fall, and I manage for half the ceremony. But when they get to the vows and I realize how much they love each other and how incredible their life will be together, I lose it.

And I'm not the only one. There's not a single dry cheek in the whole wedding party.

"Ladies and gentlemen, please give a round of applause to Mr. and Mrs. Elliot as they take the dance floor."

"That was one hell of a ceremony," I say to Jordan, keeping my eyes on the couple as they slow dance.

"Could do with fewer tears," he says, and I can hear the smile in his voice.

I scoff, "I think most of those tears were yours."

Jordan laughs brightly and I twist my head to look at him. His tie is looser and he looks more relaxed than he did earlier. "Just don't tell anyone."

"Oh buddy, I got bad news for you," I say, and point across the room at the photographer. "That guy captured it all, it's forever immortalized."

"Hm, any chance we can ask him to Photoshop us out of the pictures?" he says, jokingly.

"It'll be one of those memes, where you ask them to fix the photo and they focus on the completely wrong thing to fix. We'll go viral."

"Good point. Maybe we just keep these in the family then."

"Family," I say, and take a deep breath. "Is that kind of what we are now?"

Jordan shrugs and chews his lip in thought. I'm dying to know what he thinks, and I do my best to keep still but my knee starts bouncing.

Does he see me as a little sister?

That really wouldn't work with the massive crush I have on him.

"In a way," he says, but doesn't elaborate further. I deflate a bit and think of something else to say, but before I can, the emcee asks the wedding party to join the couple.

I stand up quicker than I intend and step on my dress. Before my face can meet the floor, Jordan's hands are there, steadying me against his broad chest.

"Careful," he says.

"Sorry," I mumble.

"Do I need to carry you to the dance floor?" Jordan asks, a little smirk playing at his pink lips.

"I'd like to see you try." It comes out breathier and flirtier than I intended, but Jordan's pupils go wide. I'm worried he might actually do it, or worse, that he'll let go.

Instead, he gently places me back on my feet and takes my hand, leading the way to the dance floor.

His hands find my waist and I step into him, looping my hands around his neck. He's so tall, almost a foot taller than me, and if I didn't have heels on I'd have to stand on my tiptoes to even reach him.

The song is soulful and hypnotic, and I don't take my eyes away from Jordan for even a second. It's like we're caught in this trance, and the whole world around us disappears.

I like him so much.

"Can I ask you something?" I say, quiet enough that he almost doesn't hear me.

Jordan looks away from my mouth where his gaze lingered for a second too long, and he bites his lip. "Of course."

"How come you don't have a girlfriend?"

I don't know why I ask. It's none of my business, and I'm terrified of the answer, but I'm dying to know anyway. Jordan is kind and sweet and perfect boyfriend material. Yet, in the year that I've known him, he's never mentioned a girlfriend. Not even once.

His eyebrows scrunch together, and he looks away from me for the first time since we started dancing. "I don't really have the time for one at the moment," he says, avoiding my gaze.

I gently squeeze the back of his neck and his attention

returns to me. "But if you did, what would you look for in someone?"

Jordan exhales roughly and shakes his head. "Why do you ask?"

"Just curious. You're a really great guy, J. I'm just surprised you don't have a flock of girls following you around all the time."

He laughs softly. "I'm too awkward for that."

"Well, I find it cute," I say, and hold my breath for his response. Jordan looks at me intently and opens his mouth, but he doesn't get a chance to say anything because the song ends. A pop one starts up and everyone else joins, crowding us in.

Jordan lets go of my waist and backs away from me, a solemn look on his face. The crowd swallows him whole as I stand there, stupefied, in the middle of the dance floor.

"J!" I say, but he's already too far away to hear me.

What have I done?

CHAPTER 2

Eight Years Ago

JORDAN

MY PHONE RINGS and I glance at the clock on my nightstand as I reach to answer. Who is calling at three in the morning?

The picture on my phone is a ridiculous one. Alice, crossing her eyes and poking her tongue out at the camera, her hair neatly styled in that half up, half down hairdo she wore at my sister's wedding, her burgundy dress showing off her best features.

I should change it.

I really should, but I don't have the heart to. Not when she sneakily took my phone at the wedding and snapped a bunch of pictures, making this one her caller ID photo. Not when she told me I was cute that night and looked at me like she wanted me. Maybe it was because nobody looked at me like that in a long time, but for a moment I actually considered it—being with Alice, tilting her head back and kissing her. But I didn't; of course I didn't. Not when she's my best friend's little sister.

It wouldn't be right.

Robbie would probably kill me if he knew I thought about his sister like that.

The phone continues to ring as I stare at it until Jess taps me on my shoulder and mumbles, "Babe, make it stop." She whines the last word, and I quickly mumble, "Sorry".

I unplug my phone and take it into the bathroom. "Al, what's wrong??"

The screech from the other end makes me drop my phone from my ear and I fumble with it, catching it at the last second before falling in the sink.

"Jesus, Al, don't scare me like that," I whisper angrily.

"Sorry, sorry, I'm just so excited, J! We're gonna be aunt and uncle!"

I sigh, not knowing why I needed that reminder at three in the morning. "Yes, we've known this for months now, Al."

"No, J. Tonight! We're gonna be aunt and uncle tonight!"

My eyes widen and I scramble out of the bathroom to my closet, tripping in the process. I mumble another "sorry" to my girlfriend and hightail it out of my apartment.

"Which hospital? And isn't it a little early? I thought Tangela wasn't due for another two weeks."

"St. Mary's. And I don't know, my mom just called and said they're at the hospital already. I'm pulling up in front of your building now."

I open the front door just in time to see Alice park her brother's Jeep and wave at me excitedly. I hang up the phone and make my way to the passenger seat, and as soon as I enter, the smell of Alice's floral shampoo hits me. She's wearing a navy sweatshirt with a pretty bow embroidered on the front and black leggings. Her hair looks damp and her face is free of makeup, and the smile she wears is so huge it brings out both her dimples. How did I never notice she has dimples before? She looks beautiful.

"Are you excited?" she asks, and the question brings me out of my haze.

"Terrified," I say, refocusing on my phone and texting Jess to let her know I'm headed to the hospital. How did I not think to tell her?

"Why terrified?"

"I don't know about you, but I don't have much experience with babies. I wouldn't know what to do."

She laughs brightly, "You think Michael knows what to do? If anyone should be terrified, it should be my brother."

I laugh along and say, "Yeah, you're right. I just know Tangela, and she never asks for help, even when she most needs it. So I guess I'm worried about her more. What if she needs my help and I'm bad at it?"

"Oh, J," she says softly, reaching out her hand and grasping my forearm on the center console. "You're gonna be an amazing uncle. I promise."

She can't possibly know that, but the conviction in her words helps soothe my anxiety. I think back on all the times I've been around her in the last year, at holidays and family gatherings. She has this way about her that makes me feel comfortable, more at ease, and I've never understood why.

"Thanks for being here, and for picking me up," I say, my hand twitching to cover hers. "I would have kicked myself if I missed it."

"Of course. I got your back, J," she says with a smile, and

takes back her hand. I bring my arm to my lap and rub at the spot she was holding.

The drive to the hospital is short and I refrain from commenting on Alice's crooked parking, even though she is taking up two spaces. I look back at the car, sighing because that's a huge pet peeve of mine.

Alice turns back and rolls her eyes at me. "It'll be fine, let's go!" She grabs my hand and starts running through the parking garage, and I have no choice but to follow.

ALICE

THIS IS the most exciting thing to ever happen in my life!

Okay, that may be an exaggeration, but I am so thrilled to be an aunt. Ever since I was thirteen and my parents let me get a job as a babysitter, I've loved working with kids. They're so curious, funny, and smart, and I want at least five of them in the future.

I'm buzzing with excitement as we ride the elevator up to the fourth floor and I realize that I'm still holding Jordan's hand, squeezing tightly. He doesn't say anything, just smiles down at me, the same excitement showing in his eyes.

The elevator dings, and Jordan squeezes my hand once more before letting go. I miss the warmth of his hand but recover quickly when I see Robbie walking with a four pack of coffees in his hand.

"Roro," I say, calling him by the nickname I came up with when I was young and couldn't pronounce his name.

He turns around, stifling a yawn and waving at me. "Hey, Al. Glad you made it. And you brought Jordan."

"Hey," Jordan says, fist bumping Robbie's free hand.

"What's the update?"

Robbie grimaces and says, "Well, we might be here for the whole night. The baby is not quite ready to join us. But we've got coffee!"

We nod and follow him into the waiting area, saying hello to my parents when we take a seat.

"I know they live like three hours away and it's late, but do you want to call your parents, J?" I ask, pulling my knees up to my chest on the wide waiting room chair and getting comfortable.

"I'll call them in the morning. If I tell my mom now, she's going to go in helicopter parent mode and call Tangela nonstop."

I laugh and shake my head. Their mom does seem like a handful at times, but she's a sweet woman.

"Besides, Tangela told me she plans on taking a trip over to their side of the state a few weeks after the baby is born."

"Smart," I say, turning my body to face Jordan. He peeks at me from the corner of his eye and his smile hikes up. "What?" I ask, giggling.

"You're going to be the best aunt. Always thoughtful, always considerate."

I can feel the blush taking over my face and I look down, fiddling with my sweatshirt. "Thanks, J."

WE SPEND five hours in the waiting room, our butts numb and glued to the chairs, and just when I'm about to get up and find some coffee and breakfast, Michael comes out.

His hands are shaking and there are tears in his eyes, and for a second I panic that something bad happened. But no, he's smiling like an idiot, clapping his hands to get everyone's attention. I quickly sit up and walk up to him, and he puts his arm around me, tucking me into his chest. "She's perfect," he whispers, and my eyes widen.

They didn't want to know the sex of the baby ahead of birth so this is a surprise to all of us. I hug him back and hear him say to the rest of the family, "Tangela is doing great, and our daughter is here. We're naming her Katie." Mom and I start crying once we realize they're naming her after our grandma Katherine. My dad, Robbie, and Jordan join the group hug too, and we all take a moment to congratulate my brother.

"Thank you for being here, everyone."

"When can we see them?" I ask, and everyone laughs. I'm not sure what's so funny, but whatever.

Michael shakes his head at me, and I deflate. "Not right now. We'll get them discharged first and you can come by later when we get home, okay?"

"Fiiine," I whine, letting him get back to his wife and daughter.

On the bright side, I can go back to sleep now. As my parents and Robbie take off, I hang back and turn to Jordan.

"Let's get you home," I say. I don't know what I expect to see on Jordan's face, maybe the same excitement that's showing on mine, but Jordan isn't looking at me. There's a slight grimace on his face as he looks behind me.

My head turns to look over my shoulder in the direction he's staring and I see a beautiful, curvy blond woman wearing a full face of makeup and a black pantsuit. She's stunning, and she's walking right towards us. My brain doesn't comprehend what it's seeing as she smiles and steps into Jordan's arms, one hand cupping his neck as she kisses him.

And not just a hello peck, but a full on makeout kind of kiss.

My eyes might be bulging out of my head as I stare at them and there's a deeply uncomfortable feeling in my stomach. *I think I might throw up.*

Jordan has a girlfriend? Why the hell didn't he tell me?

I feel more betrayed than heartbroken, because how dare he? We've been chatting for the last five hours, talking about our hopes and dreams, families, careers, and failures. And he couldn't even mention that he's dating supermodel business Barbie over here?

I swallow the tight knot in my throat and walk away from their public display of affection. I don't turn back when he calls after me. I just say, "Looks like you have a ride home. See ya!" as brightly as I can muster.

Jordan has his girlfriend to keep him company now.

He doesn't need me.

CHAPTER 3

Six Years Ago

JORDAN

THE ARCADE MACHINE makes a mocking sound that I take very personally as I lose yet another game against Alice.

Smirking, she flips her long hair over one shoulder and leans in, one hand on her hip, the other extended in front of me, palm facing up. "Pay up, buddy," she says, blue eyes sparkling.

I take a step closer and look down at her, reveling in the way she has to tilt her head up to keep her eyes on mine. I place my hand in hers, palms touching, before pulling her in and twisting her around. She leans into my chest and I lift her up by her middle, my free hand skimming the sliver of skin showing at her waist. Her feet kick up and she honest-to-god giggles, making my insides flutter.

Being around her has started to become a problem because she's everywhere; she comes to all the Manticore games, she babysits my niece, she hangs out with me and Robbie after games.

At first it was a little awkward, and she seemed to keep her distance from me, especially when Jess was around. But after my ex broke up with me, I noticed Alice started hanging out around me more again. And no matter how hard I try, I can't stay away from her. *I don't want to stay away from her.*

"How did you beat me yet again? You don't even like games that much. Is it just birthday luck?" I huff as I set her down. My fingers squeeze her narrow waist once before I notice Robbie making his way to us. I quickly let go and take an involuntary step back. She looks at me, confused, and I try not to stare at how pretty her pink lips are tonight.

"J, are you okay?" she asks right as Robbie pulls up to us and wraps an arm around each of us.

"This place turned out so great," he says, words sounding a bit slurred. We're at Michael and Tangela's new restaurant, The Arcadian, celebrating Alice's 21st birthday.

"Someone's having fun," Alice teases in a singsong voice. I expected her to go crazy tonight and get drunk, but she's been carefully sipping on her fruity cocktail for the last hour.

"Guys, let's do shots together," Robbie says excitedly, and I laugh. It's been a while since he's let loose and had some fun. After Alex left the team to move to Quebec with his professional volleyball player girlfriend, Robbie ended up taking the mantle. He's done a fantastic job at being captain during his first season, but I can tell he's changed. Robbie used to be a lot more carefree, but with the new responsibility on his shoulders, he's become more of an authoritative figure on the team, taking his job very seriously.

Alice giggles again and I swear I can feel the sound of her sweet voice right down to my core. "All right, buddy, just one," she says, and we follow Robbie to the bar. I glance over at Alice and see she's watching me with an intense look that's quickly replaced by a smile. I grin back and almost run into Robbie, not realizing he's stopped.

"Do you think I'm doing a good job?" he asks as he signals to the bartender for three shots.

"What? As a captain?" Alice asks.

Robbie nods and she says, "Of course."

When he looks at me earnestly, I shake my head and smile, saying, "You're the best captain I've ever had." He rolls his eyes and shoves at my shoulder, but I'm not joking. "Seriously, you're the first one in the locker room and the last one to leave the arena. You care about your teammates and make sure they're in top shape physically and mentally before the game, and you're always there when they need someone to talk to. That's huge, man. Alex was good, don't get me wrong, but he had a different leadership style, you know? He led by intimidation, which worked just fine, but you— you lead with your heart, and I think that's more important."

By the time I'm done talking, Robbie picks up the shots, handing us each one. We knock them back and he wraps me up in a big hug, and even though we're the same height and I'm slightly broader than him, it feels like he's giving me a bear hug nonetheless.

"Aww," Alice coos, and slithers inside our arms for a group hug.

"Thanks for being such a good friend. I'm really glad

you're part of the family now," Robbie says, and all I can do is nod, swallowing the lump that's stuck in my throat.

Would a good friend flirt with his best friend's sister? Would he have the kind of thoughts I do?

I nod stiffly as we break the hug. "Yeah, sure. This place turned out amazing," I say, referring to the newly built restaurant.

Robbie's face brightens. "It's so fucking cool. I'm happy they made this happen. This place is gonna be so special, I can feel it." He hiccups and covers his mouth.

Alice meets my eyes and smiles wide.

Yeah, it'll be special, all right.

ALICE

WE HANG out at the bar well past closing time, my parents having brought in my favorite red velvet cake, my brothers popping open the champagne and bringing up stories of us growing up. Tangela and Jordan are the only other people I wanted here tonight for this small celebration. All the people I love, all in one place.

The champagne is sweet and bubbly as it hits my tongue. In my tipsy state, I realize that I can't stop staring at Jordan. *God, he's so hot.*

When my mom presents to me a slice of cake with a candle in it, I blow hard and wish for the same thing I've been wishing for the last few years. *Jordan.*

Maybe I'm too silly to think that anything would ever happen between us, but the more time we spend together, the more I realize that my greatest fear is losing him.

I'd rather have secret feelings for my brother's best friend than have him out of my life.

MY PARENTS ARE the first to leave, then Michael and Tangela, since they have to get back home to my niece. That leaves Jordan, Robbie, and me, and we decide to take a cab back to Robbie's house since none of us is in any condition to drive.

My brother sits up front and chats with the driver while Jordan and I keep our distance in the backseat. Jordan's phone lights up with a text from Jess, his ex, and my stomach churns. Are they back together?

I let my curiosity get the best of me and I nod down at his phone, asking, "So, how are things with Jess? Did you two get back together?" I do my best to sound nonchalant, but my heart is beating a million miles a minute. *Please say no.*

"Nah, we decided to part ways for good. She's looking for something ... more," he says softly, swiping away her text and giving me a half smile.

I mirror it and say, "Not that I knew her well, but—" I swallow hard, trying not to show my jealousy and hurt show at the fact that when I was being flirty with him, he told me he didn't have time for a girlfriend, but then he started dating Jess. "I just think you deserve more too."

Jordan holds my gaze for a moment and I try not to blink, memorizing the way he looks with the streetlights illuminating his handsome face. He looks like he was plucked from one of my romance novels—smoldering eyes, sharp jawline, and all that.

When we get to the house, Robbie manages to pour some water and kibble for the cats and passes out as soon as his head hits the pillow. I smile and close the door to his bedroom, letting him rest.

Back in the living room, Jordan is pulling open the sleeper sofa, but he straightens up when he sees me. "I figured you'd take the spare bedroom, so I'll take the couch."

I nod but walk up to him, helping to set it up. We work in companionable silence and our hands brush every now and then as we lay down a sheet and pillows.

"Did you have a good birthday?" he whispers as Caramel jumps up on the blanket, attacking it ferociously with his little orange paws, thinking there's some monster underneath.

I laugh softly and give him a few pets as he tries to chomp on my fingers. "I had a great birthday. Thanks for coming, by the way."

"Of course, I wouldn't miss it," he says earnestly as his eyes trace every inch of my face. He does that a lot recently—openly studying me, so I take the time to do the same.

Jordan looks tired, but not in an exhausted type of way. His eyes are droopy and darker than their usual chocolate brown color, and his lips are soft.

"Are you ready to go to sleep?" I find myself asking. Jordan contemplates this for a second but shakes his head, and I smile. "Want to watch a movie instead?"

"Sure, birthday girl, I'll make some popcorn while you pick one," Jordan says. He moves to the kitchen, opening up a bag of buttery popcorn.

I put on a '90s romcom and expect Jordan to grumble something about how he hates chick flicks, but he doesn't. He sits down and places the popcorn between us on the sofa bed and we spend most of the movie judging the characters' choices and making fun of their outfits.

Somehow we drift closer together, maybe under the pretense that we need to whisper so that we don't wake Robbie up, and I rest my head on Jordan's shoulder. After a second of hesitation, he lifts his arm up and drapes it across my shoulder so that I can better fit next to him.

He smells woodsy, with a hint of the whiskey he drank earlier tonight, and I close my eyes against the essence of him.

"Thank you for an amazing birthday," I say quietly, and look up at his face right as he looks down at mine. My nose brushes his chin and he freezes to the spot, his fingers tightening on my shoulder. I can hear him swallow, and decide to be a little brave. If anything, I can always blame it on the alcohol.

I place my right hand on Jordan's chest and lift up to bridge the gap, pressing my lips to the corner of his mouth, whispering, "You're the best, J."

When I pull back, I swear I can't even hear him breathe. His eyes are glued to my mouth, and I am begging the universe that he's taking the hint. That he'll kiss me properly.

When he doesn't, I lower my head back down to his chest and return my attention to the movie. Jordan doesn't say anything to me for the rest of the night, but when the movie ends, instead of sending me to the spare room, he repositions us and drags the blanket up to our necks. His arms hold me tight the whole night through and I think I feel him kissing my forehead in the morning before he gets up and leaves the house, quiet as a mouse.

CHAPTER 4

Five Years Ago

ALICE

THE ROOM IS SPINNING. Or is that just me?

I'm not exactly sure how I got to this party, but I think it had something to do with one of my roommates dragging me here in search of her boyfriend. Once they found each other, they ditched me to hook up somewhere in the house. Typical.

I look around the unfamiliar kitchen and try to pinpoint how I got so drunk in the first place. The countertop is littered with empty beer bottles and red solo cups. Ah, it's all coming back to me now—beer pong. Lots of beer pong.

A cute guy with green eyes and dark brown hair roped me into playing and since I had never experienced the game before, I decided to give it a try. Besides, everyone always told me I was the good girl that never embraced the college experience, instead focusing on finishing my bachelor's degree in education as fast as possible. Tonight I decided, I'm in my senior year, so fuck it, we ball.

"I think I might throw up," I tell the cute stranger, whose name I still haven't asked for.

All he does is grimace and point me to the patio door. Lovely. I quickly make my way out and find the nearest potted plant to nourish. *Sorry, little fern. You deserve better.*

Sliding down the nearest wall, I take a moment to feel sorry for myself. This is why I don't drink or party, usually. I *cannot* handle my alcohol.

A text from my roommate comes through telling me her and her boyfriend left half an hour ago to "make up."

I need better friends.

I don't reply to her, and wait for another roll of nausea to pass, while I rest my head back against the wall. I could call one of my brothers to come pick me up, but I don't want to bother them. Robbie is meeting with Alex while he's visiting from out of town, and Michael has two young kids at home now that Lory joined their little family. He's alone with them for the first time ever since Tangela is away for a conference for the week.

There's no way in hell I would call my parents. They've never seen me drunk and with any luck, they never ever will. So that leaves me one other option.

My thumb hovers over Jordan's contact photo and I smile at how cute he is in it—arms wrapped around me, his mouth slightly parted as he sleeps. I managed to sneak a picture the night of my twenty-first birthday. The last time we were that close.

I don't know if our almost-kiss that night made him pull away or if it was something else, but our friendship has been a little awkward ever since.

Blowing out a frustrated breath, I push the call button, silently begging for the universe to swallow me whole. *This is so embarrassing.*

"Hello?" Jordan says in a deep voice, sounding a little distant.

"J, it's me," I say quietly. The sound of video game shooting in the background stops abruptly and I can hear the shift in Jordan's voice as he realizes just who is on the other end of the call.

"Alice? It's two in the morning. What's wrong?"

"I, um—" I mumble, my eyes stinging. I shouldn't have called. He's probably busy too. "I'm at a house party, somewhere downtown. I don't have a ride home," I say, sniffing back my tears.

"Okay, I'll come get you. Can you go look at the house number? Maybe the street name?" he asks gently.

"I don't think I can stand up right now," I huff, annoyed at myself for getting so stupid drunk. "I played beer pong," I say lamely.

Jordan chuckles but then sobers up quickly. "Are you alone? Did you drink from any other cups?"

"No, I don't think so. I'm okay, J, just drunk as a skunk."

"Can you share your phone location with me?"

I place him on speaker, listening to the sounds of his breathing and shuffling as he's getting into his car, and text him my location.

"I'll be right there, I'm only ten minutes away, okay? Go sit on the curb please so I can see you when I pull up."

"Okay, thank you," I say, and make my way to the front of the house.

Eight minutes later, Jordan pulls up, and before I even have the chance to stand up, he's out of his car and slinging my arm around his shoulder, grabbing a firm hold of my waist. The touch of his hand on my bare skin where my crop top rides up is scorching hot, and I take a deep breath so I don't say something stupid about how much I want him.

"Watch your head," he says as he opens the door and helps me into the passenger seat.

"Thank you for coming," I say, giving him a sad smile and tucking my hair behind my ears, silently praying I won't barf in his car.

"Of course. Are you sure you're okay?" he asks again.

I shrug. "I just drank too much. Beer is awful anyway, why do guys like it so much?"

Jordan chuckles and starts the car. "I'm more of a whiskey guy myself, so I couldn't tell you."

The drive to my apartment is slow as Jordan does his best not to jostle me too much, making sure I don't get sick again. I'm still wobbly on my feet as he helps me up the three flights of stairs and into my apartment.

There is no sign of my roommates and I sigh a breath of relief, making a beeline for the bathroom to brush my teeth. When I come out, Jordan hands me aspirin and a bottle of water, making sure I stay hydrated. If I didn't have a major crush on him already, this would be the moment I would develop one.

"Why are you so perfect?" I ask, swaying on my feet.

Jordan's hands easily steady me, his large palms making contact with my waist again. "I'm not," he says, frowning. "Which room is yours?"

I point down to the end of the hall and Jordan guides me to my room, flipping the switch that turns my string lights on. The room is cast in a soft yellow glow, accentuating the cream-colored walls. Stacks of books surround my headboard and nightstands, after I ran out of room on my shelves.

I watch Jordan as he takes in my space and the soft smile on his face warms me up inside. Does he like what he sees?

"This is exactly how I've pictured your room," he says as he gently sits me down at the edge of the bed.

"You've thought about me in my room?" I ask, voice coming out more sultry than I intended.

Jordan sucks in a breath and meets my eyes as he crouches down in front of me, hands on my calf and moving down in a featherlight touch.

"Maybe," he says, dropping his gaze and taking off my high heeled sandals.

I let out an embarrassing moan as the tension in my foot eases and he takes off my other shoe. Then his fingers dig into the arch of my foot, and I collapse back on the bed.

Fuck. All he's doing is giving me a foot massage and I'm a moaning mess. I don't think I've ever been more turned on than this.

"Where do you keep your pajamas?" he asks, standing over me.

"I don't usually wear any."

"Jesus Christ," he huffs. I smile, and even though I'm lying down and my eyes are closed, I can picture the exact shade of pink on his cheeks.

"Okay," he says shakily. "Do you need anything else before I go?"

"Stay," I say, my eyes flying open. Shit, did I say that out loud?

I slowly rise up on my elbows and look at the disheveled sight in front of me. Jordan's white T-shirt is snug, and I let my eyes roam over his broad chest and narrow waist. His hair is longer than usual, missing his usual side fade. The curly black hair makes him look unruly. *Fuck*, he's so pretty.

"I don't think I should," Jordan says hesitantly.
"Please."

JORDAN

IT'S the goddamn *please* that does me in. I don't think I could say no to this girl if I tried.

On the one hand, I'm glad she called me when she didn't know what to do or how to get home. I want her to be safe. But on the other hand, did she have to call *me*? I'm trying my damnedest to put some distance between us, but somehow she always pulls me back in.

Being around her so often has made it hard to ignore the growing crush I have on her. A crush that I know for a fact is reciprocated. The way she looks at me sometimes—like I'm her whole world—drives me crazy. I don't deserve that look.

Even now, laying on the bed in her high-waisted shorts and yellow crop top, Alice looks up at me with those big blue eyes, begging me to stay.

I swallow hard and walk over to her closet, pulling out a soft pair of shorts and a plain white T-shirt for her to change into.

"Okay, but you need to change. You can't sleep in your party clothes," I say, reaching down and helping her stand. She wobbles on her feet and holds on to my bicep to steady herself. My pompous fucking ego decides now is the time to flex. I try to bite back my smile as she stares at the muscles shifting under my short sleeve.

I hand her the clothes and turn to face her bookshelves as she changes. The white shelves are tall enough that they almost reach the ceiling, and each shelf is carefully organized by what looks like genre and author. My eyes snag on a cute cover—blue, with ice skates and headphones on it—and I pick it up to read the back.

"All done," Alice says, and I turn to her with a grin.

"Is this a hockey romance?" I ask, already knowing the answer is *yes*.

The blush that overtakes her cheeks is so fucking cute that I have a strong urge to reach out and pinch her. I grip the book tight in my hands to refrain from touching her. *That would be bad.*

"Careful," Alice says, taking a step towards me and forcing me to loosen my grip on the book by placing her hands on top of mine. "That's the indie edition that is no longer available."

"Sorry," I mumble, and gently place the book back on the shelf. "You have multiple editions of the same book?" I ask, noticing the same title in a different shade of blue.

"Duh," she says, swatting at my chest.

"Why?" I chuckle.

"Because," she groans. "You're gonna think it's dumb."

"I won't," I insist, and follow her to the queen-sized bed, where she lays on top of the comforter.

"If I really like a book, I want to have it in all formats. Special editions especially, but also audiobooks and ebooks," she says, looking up at me and biting her lip, waiting for my judgment.

I lay down next to her even though I don't plan to spend the whole night here. Just until she falls asleep.

"But why do you need the multiple formats?"

"Because I like to reread my favorites, and they're nice to look at on my shelves. My little shrines." She giggles.

"You reread books?" I ask, curious as to why she'd do

that when she always complains about having too many books on her list.

Alice makes a little indignant noise, and I turn my head towards her. Her face is a few inches away from mine and even though she's still a little drunk and tired, she looks so beautiful my heart aches.

"What?" I ask.

"Haven't you ever revisited a favorite movie or video game? How is rereading any different?"

I contemplate it for a second while she narrows her eyes at me. She's right, of course, but I like messing with her, keeping her in suspense. Her button nose wriggles while she waits for my answer and it's the cutest fucking thing.

"I suppose you're right," I say, turning my head back and facing the ceiling, clasping my hands under my head.

"You suppose?" she squeaks, and rises up on her elbow, looking down at me. Her long blond hair falls around her like a curtain and brushes my chest.

I shrug nonchalantly and she purses her lips. I'm hyperaware of how close she is, how sweet she smells, how laserfocused her gaze is on my mouth. But I don't expect what comes next.

Alice grins and leans in, tickling my sides. "Say I'm right, and there's nothing wrong with my book obsession," she says as I laugh uncontrollably, trying to bat her hands away. She's frickin' stronger than I expected, and the more I try to push her off me, the more she tickles me.

"Okay, okay, there's nothing wrong with your book obsession," I wheeze out, but she doesn't let up.

I give up fighting her off and instead grab for her sides, tickling her right back. She yelps and gives in almost immediately, begging for mercy.

"I'm sorry, I'm sorry," she says, a tear falling from the

corner of her eye as she lands on my chest with a thud. My arms move of their own volition and hold her tight against me.

"Hmm, you can give it, but you can't take it?" I tease, reaching out and tucking a strand of hair behind her ear.

Alice's blue eyes flare, distracting me so much that I almost miss her answer, "Oh, I can definitely take it."

My lips part in surprise at the innuendo and my tongue darts out to lick them. I don't have the chance to say anything back as Alice leans in, taking me by surprise yet again.

"Fuck it," she says, right before she crushes her lips to mine. My eyes widen and for a second, neither of us moves. Her lips are soft against my own, one of her hands cupping my cheek, the other resting on my collarbone.

When her lips part against mine, I groan and close my eyes. I keep one arm tight around her waist, fisting the sheet with the other. *Fuck*, I've thought about this for longer than I want to admit, and now that she's kissing me, I can't seem to put a stop to it. Even though I should.

Alice kisses me tentatively, paying attention to every corner of my mouth before finding the confidence to nibble and tug at my bottom lip, asking to be let in all the way. When I open up for her, she becomes an entirely different person, her tongue brushing against mine as she readjusts herself to straddle me.

My control snaps and I dig one hand into her luscious long hair, crushing her to me. Her perky tits press against my chest, and I can feel her hard nipples through both of our thin cotton shirts. *Fuck*.

She moans against my mouth and grinds down on my cock, and I lose my damn mind. In one swift move, she's on her back and I angle her head just right so I can kiss her deeper, wilder.

Her hands claw at my back, roaming over my body as I press her deeper into the soft mattress. I'm hard and needy, but I keep my erection away from her sweet heat. I let her take what she needs, enjoying the soft little noises she makes under me until—

Alice's hand skims down my torso and grips my cock through my jeans. That's when reality crashes over me like a wave.

She was drunk off her ass an hour ago—she'll regret it tomorrow.

She's my best friend's sister, what would our families think?

She deserves better.

I pull back from her mouth and rest my head on her chest. Slowly, I take hold of her hand and bring it up and over her head.

"What—what's wrong?" Alice asks breathlessly.

I pull myself to my knees, looking down at her flushed face, but refrain from touching her again.

"We can't," I say, my shoulders deflating. I don't want her to hate me, but I need her to understand that this can't happen again.

"Why?" she asks, eyes shining with tears. Fuck, I hate myself for putting them there.

"I got carried away, I'm sorry. But this can't happen again, Al. You're—" I stop, not wanting to say the next words.

Alice reaches for me, but I move away from the bed, running a hand over my tired face. "I'm what?" she asks shakily.

"You're like my family. I can't—It would be too complicated, and I can't deal with complicated right now."

When I look back at her, Alice is biting her lip hard, trying not to cry. I look away because I can't risk giving in again, and comforting her would mean just that.

"Just because it's complicated, you don't even want to try?"

I shake my head, not being able to look her in the eyes. "I can't," I say, voice steadier than expected. "I'm sorry."

Alice nods, but everything about her expression is closed off. She lays back down and holds a pillow to her chest, burying her face in it.

"Turn the lights off on your way out."

The dismissal hurts, but I should have expected it. I'm the asshole that just put an end to this crush in the first place. I deserve it.

"For what it's worth, I really am sorry, Al," I say softly, and flip the switch, casting her room in shadows.

CHAPTER 5

Three Years Ago – February

ALICE

I SMILE down at my phone, reading all the birthday texts from my friends and family group chat.

> **ASH**
>
> happy birthday blondie — send me your book wishlist so I can spoil you with smut
>
> **ROBBIE**
>
> Can you not talk about smut and my sister in the same sentence, please?
>
> **ASH**
>
> hey, it's not my fault that's all she reads...
>
> **ELI**
>
> I second the wishlist, though not for the smut reasons. Happy birthday!

> **ALICE**
> Haha. Let's put a pin in the wishlist, I need to update it after Robbie takes me to the bookstore tonight as he promised :)

> **JORDAN**
> Happy birthday!

> **ALICE**
> Thank you :)

> **ASH**
> What's happening at the bookstore?

> **ALICE**
> We're doing the bookstore birthday challenge. I'll have five minutes to look around for books, and a minute to grab as many as I can. He pays for the stack I end up with.

> **ELI**
> How many books do you think you'll be able to grab?

> **ALICE**
> At least ten.

> **ROBBIE**
> You're lucky you're my favorite sister.

> **ALICE**
> I'm your only sister.

> **ROBBIE**
> Still my favorite ;)

I put my phone away and head out of my apartment. The coffee shop at the corner of my street is advertising a lemon scone, and my mouth waters at the thought of it. Even though I don't need any more caffeine, I make the impulsive decision to duck inside.

The sidewalk is slushy from all the melting snow, and I wipe my boots really well on the welcome mat once I go inside.

The barista looks up and flashes me a smile, his nose piercing glinting with the movement. "Welcome in," he says in a deep voice.

"Thanks," I say, a warm smile pulling at my lips. He's cute—his hair is long and black, pulled up in a man bun with a few strands falling out in the front. A few tattoos poke out of his short sleeves, and my eyes jump between the scones and his body, subtly enjoying the view.

I'm rarely attracted to strangers, but there's something about this guy that draws me in.

"What can I get you?" he asks, a full smile overtaking his face. And that's when I notice it—he looks a bit like Jordan, from the shape of his lips to the color of his eyes.

Fuck.

My smile fades as I say, "I'll take a lemon scone and a hot tea, please."

The guy's flirty expression stays in place as he grabs me a scone and hot water, takes my payment, and points to the station behind me where the tea bags are on display.

I want to be bold and ask for his number, but Jordan's face flashes through my mind again. *Why can't I get over him already?*

I stir the bag into my hot water absentmindedly and think back on the last few years.

Even though Jordan rejected me and I kept my distance for a while, I saw him all the time. I still do. It's impossible not to when we get together for family dinner every month and spend all the holidays together. Not to mention, I've been attending more Manticores games this season since Robbie hinted that this might be his last.

Getting over the guy I've been in love with for the past seven years is no small feat. Every time I go on a date, I can't help but compare that person to Jordan—how thoughtful he is, how he's always looking out for me, how he blushes every time I say anything remotely flirty.

After he turned me down that night, I even went so far as to avoid family gatherings, which are my favorite. There's something about the chaos of Sunday dinner, where everyone is chatting, setting the table, and laughing around the kitchen island, that makes me feel at home. Regardless of if we're at my parent's house or at The Arcadian—these *people* are my home.

So skipping out those first few months really put me in a dark mood, but soon after, Ash and Eli joined the team, and Robbie all but adopted them into our family. All of a sudden, family gatherings became more bearable, and I started attending regularly again.

Ash is the world's biggest flirt and he's closest to my age, so the two of us became fast friends, always finding something to talk about or obsess over.

Eli is extremely introverted, and at first I thought he was kind of an asshole, but once he got used to us, he started to open up. We bonded over our love for romance novels, which was a shock to me as he's a six foot three hockey goalie.

Truth is, I can't imagine life without them anymore. Without knowing it, they helped ease the ache of Jordan's rejection, especially since he never brought that kiss up again. While I thought it would be awkward being in his presence, we somehow continued to make polite and short conversations every time we hung out.

But going from nonstop texting and hanging out daily to a

once-a-month conversation—well, it hurt more than I expected. I get that people fall out of touch, but that's usually when a major change happens: someone moves away, they get a new job, they start dating. But in our situation, the distance was intentional. He made it clear he didn't want to give us a chance.

I can't deal with complicated right now. I've thought about his words so many times, analyzing them until they drove me crazy.

Complicated. I suppose he's right, there is a lot at stake if we were to date. Especially if it didn't work out—I would hate to be the wedge between our two families.

Right now. Did he mean there was a chance for us later? If so, when?

At some point I realized stressing over his words was pointless. He stopped texting, stopped hanging out, so I kept my distance too. But more importantly, I made my peace with letting him go, even though my feelings never really went away.

And I was fine. At least, I told myself I was.

Until a couple of months ago, I got an out-of-the-blue text about a book recommendation. Jordan wanted to know what to get for Tangela's birthday, and what should have been a quick text turned into a late-night phone call, which then turned into a trip to the bookstore to find all the right presents to make her a bookish gift basket.

Since then, I've gotten the feeling that he might want to reconnect. That maybe—just maybe—he might want to give this *complicated* thing a shot.

A splash of hot water lands on my finger as I stir, and it breaks me out of my reverie. After throwing the tea bag away, I add a little honey and place a lid on my drink. I turn and wave at the barista on my way out and balance my hot drink and scone in one hand, while I pull my phone out to check the newest text.

> **ELI**
> There's a special screening of Pride and Prejudice tonight at the downtown theater. Want to go after dinner?
>
> **ALICE**
> OMG yes, how is that even a question??!

I squeal in delight and head back to my apartment to wait for Robbie. After the bookstore trip, we're going to my parents' house to help them prepare for my birthday get together. I can't imagine a more perfect ending to this day than watching one of my favorite movies with one of my favorite friends.

Though, there is one person missing—Olivia. I wish she could be here tonight, but she's back home in Minnesota, where she has to referee a hockey game. As soon as Robbie told me about this new friend of his, that just so happened to be a woman, I was so excited. As much as I love the boys, there's only so much testosterone in our family that I can handle.

As soon as I met Olivia over Thanksgiving, I knew she'd be the one for Robbie. There was something in the way she looked at him, like he was a bright and shining light in her life, that made me bold enough to outright ask her what her intentions were. One might argue that it was too soon, but I think that was the push she needed to confess her feelings.

Since then, they've been inseparable, constantly texting and calling since their crazy schedules keep them apart most of the time. I'm excited for our group trip to Northern Michigan next week, and to get to know her better. I already know we have similar taste in books and songs, but I want us to be friends.

I take a seat at my dining table, moaning around a bite of the delicious lemon scone, and send Robbie a text, letting him know I'll be ready soon. He's usually quick to answer, but this time, it sits unread.

ROBBIE IS an hour late and won't answer his phone. I pace the apartment, trying not to panic over all the possible scenarios of why he's not here on time. This is so unlike him. Another call goes to voicemail, and I decide to text the group.

ALICE

Anyone know why Robbie is AWOL?

ELI

I was trying to get ahold of him but he didn't answer me either.

JORDAN

I thought he was with you at the bookstore?

ALICE

He never showed up at my place.

JORDAN

He ditched you?

ASH

maybe he and Olivia are having a little video chat if you know what I mean...

> ALICE
> Ew, no Ash. Why would you give me that visual?

I try to wipe away the mental image of my brother and Olivia doing god knows what over a video call when my phone rings.

"Robbie?" I ask, my vision blurry with tears.

"Hey, Al. I'm sorry, I completely spaced out on time. I've been trying to get a hold of Olivia but I think something happened with her phone, it keeps sending me to voicemail."

"Oh, do you think she's okay?"

"Yeah, I'm sure it's nothing. I just worry about her, you know? She went out last night with some coworkers but she didn't give me any more updates."

"I can try giving her a call too. But, Robbie, are you still coming to get me?" I ask, feeling stupid. Here I am, worried that he won't take me to the bookstore, when he's worried about his girlfriend not making it home safely.

"She's calling me back now. Al, I'm sorry, I have to take it. I don't think we'll have time to go to the bookstore before dinner," he says hurriedly.

I bite my lip and nod, even though he can't see it. "Yeah, that's okay—"

"I gotta go, I'll see you later," he says, hanging up on me.

JORDAN

I STARE at the group text from Alice. Did Robbie ditch her? She was so excited about that bookstore trip and has been talking about doing that silly trend since the summer. Would it be weird if I took her instead?

Without giving it too much thought, I call her.

"Hello?" she answers, voice hoarse, like she's been crying.

"Alice, it's Jordan. Is everything okay?"

"Hey," she says in a wobbly voice. "Yeah, I'm good. What's up?"

"Have you heard from Robbie?" I ask, not liking the sound of her voice one bit. I don't care that Robbie is her brother, I'm gonna smack the shit out of him for hurting her.

"Yeah, he's got something going on with Olivia. He's fine though, sorry I freaked out over the group chat." She sniffles, and I swear to god it physically hurts me to hear her so dejected. This girl is nothing if not sunshine and rainbows.

"Wait, so he did actually ditch you? What the hell?" I ask hotly. My fingers are already on the keys and I'm grabbing my jacket off the hook as I say, "I'm coming to get you. You're getting those books today no matter what."

"Really?" she asks, her voice filled with surprise and what sounds like wonder. Fuck, doesn't she know I'd do anything for her? I guess I've hurt her badly enough keeping my distance the past couple of years, but that doesn't mean I stopped caring about her. If anything, I cared *more*, knowing she was right within reach, and yet so far from me.

I really hated myself for making her miss family gatherings, all because she didn't want to be near me. If anything, I should have been the one to stay away. But I didn't. I couldn't. Because deep down, I still wanted her friendship. I wanted to be around her and hear her sweet laugh and listen to her ramble about her most recent book obsession. I just didn't want to add the pressure of a relationship, not when I wasn't sure that something between us would last. She's my best friend's little sister. *Complicated.*

"I'll be there shortly. Bring your biggest tote."

Alice giggles on the other end of the phone and my smile grows wider. When Eli and Ash joined the team, and Robbie started inviting them to family dinners, I was jealous. Not because of the attention they got from the Elliots, but because Alice started attending more and more again. And she was making genuine friendships with them, getting Eli out of his shell and flirting with Ash.

And I realized that I wanted that back. I wanted to be the one that made her laugh. I wanted to be the one she confided in when she was struggling with her career choices.

I wanted to be the one.

I wanted to be hers.

I PULL up to her apartment building, trying hard not to think back to the last and only time I was here. Because if I think too hard about that night and what an idiot I was, I might actually lose my mind and ask her to kiss me like that again.

Alice comes bounding down the steps with a cute beige beanie on her head and a large canvas tote on her shoulder. I squint at the words on it that say: *Came for the books, stayed for the smut.*

I roll my eyes and try not to blush when she opens the door to my SUV and hops inside. Her eyes are still a little red from crying, but her smile is blinding.

"I hope you brought your wallet, because books ain't cheap," she says, looking me dead in the eye.

I grin back at her and say, "Don't hold back on my account, I want to see how much damage you can do in sixty seconds."

"Oh, it's on!" She laughs and throws her arms around me. It's awkward since I'm only partially facing her and there's a center console between us. But when her signature floral scent envelops me, I automatically put an arm around her, pulling her close.

I missed her.

We stay in each other's embrace for a moment longer than necessary, until someone honks at me for blocking the sidewalk.

Alice pulls back, startled, and I inwardly curse at the stranger for ruining the moment.

"We should get going," she says, fiddling with her tote and adjusting her hat. Could she be nervous to hang out with me again? Just the two of us?

This isn't the first time we've been alone together since the night of our kiss. There was the time she helped me pick out birthday presents for my sister, Tangela. We wandered the aisles for hours in the search for the perfect book, which then turned into a whole basket, as Alice suggested we get bookmarks, annotation kits, tea, mugs, and even a blanket for it.

Who knew girls were making this book thing into such a hobby?

She seemed more shy around me at Thanksgiving and Christmas, sneaking glances from across the room and rambling any time I asked her something. And then there was New Year's, when I drove her home at the end of Robbie's party and we listened to Hozier and talked about how wonderful Olivia is and how fun our trip to Northern Michigan will be.

My mind is still racing with thoughts about Alice as we park the car. The independent bookstore she likes is rather small, but it does have two stories. I hold open the door for her and get a whiff of her floral perfume as she enters. My hand shakes with the need to touch her, to land on the small of her back, but I restrain myself.

This is unchartered territory for us, and the truth is, I'm still not sure what I want from her. Friendship, definitely, but beyond that, I'm torn. Everything is still complicated. Still messy. All I know is that I don't want to be the one that hurts her feelings.

And yet you did just that by rejecting her.

I shake myself out of my own thoughts and look around the quaint bookstore. The lighting is warm and the music transitions from Hozier to something by Noah Kahan. I smile, realizing how much Alice likes this song and how we spent so many summer nights around a bonfire, listening to her indie playlist that sounded just like this. Her eyes find mine and there's a soft gleam there, like she remembers it too.

With a small smile, she turns her gaze away from me, perusing the shelves. I grin to myself and take a few steps closer, blocking her view of the books.

"Hey—"

"Alice Margot Elliot, this is cheating," I say in my most serious voice, though the corners of my lips betray me.

She gasps and brings both her hands to her chest. What a drama queen. "Did you just call me by my full name? What did I do to deserve that?"

"You said you'd get five minutes—timed—to look

around, followed by a minute of book-grabbing. So what are you doing looking at books already?"

She groans and throws her head back. "But I can't not say hi to my favorite books."

My eyebrows go up and I smile down at her. She's so fucking cute in her pink puffy coat and hat with a giant pom-pom on it.

"Are you telling me you're looking at books you already have?"

"That is exactly what I'm saying," she says, walking over to one of the display tables and running her hand over a book titled *Divine Rivals*. "I miss you so much," she whispers.

A laugh escapes me at the way she wistfully talks to the books, and Alice pins me with a glare.

"Don't laugh at me," she chides, but I can tell she's not hurt by my laughter by the way the corners of her mouth pull up in a small smile.

"No, keep talking to your fictional boyfriends, it's cute," I say, and bite my bottom lip.

Alice watches the movement and I try my best to compose myself. *You're here for a reason, dumbass.*

"Ready to peruse?" I say, getting my phone out and setting a five-minute timer.

"I was born ready," she says, pulling off her coat and leaving it with her tote on one of the high-back chairs in front of the cozy fireplace.

As soon as I tap the start button, she's off, all but running from one section of the bookstore to the other. She starts in the general fiction, skimming the shelves and nodding to herself.

"When you nod, does that mean you saw something you want?" I ask, following her around the store, smiling politely at the people around us as she speed-walks to the next section.

"Shh!"

"No interrupting, got it," I say. I can only imagine she's mentally cataloging where each book is located on the shelves so she can come back to it later.

She spends most of the time—three minutes to be exact—in the contemporary romance section, and I'm about to remind her there's a whole other story of the building when she takes off running up the stairs.

I laugh and follow her up two steps at a time, my long legs allowing me to catch up with her. Her short sleeve tee rides up, giving me a glimpse of skin above her high-waisted jeans, and I do my best not to stare at the spot. Except the only other place to look is down—at her ass.

Groaning, I look anywhere but at her as soon as we reach the top of the stairs. Alice heads for the fantasy section and nods to herself a few more times. She's about to turn to the YA section when the timer goes off.

"Damn, that was five whole minutes already?" She looks at me, eyes wide and cheeks a little flushed.

"I guess so," I say, blushing a little and trying not to think of how great she looks in that tight little yellow T-shirt with the words "romance girly" on it.

"Okay. I think I got it handled, I know where most things are," she says, rubbing her hands together and grinning like the little villain she is.

I shake my head and reset the timer to one minute. "So how do we do this? Do you want to start up here or go back down?"

"We'll start here, there's not much I need to grab from this area anyway."

"Okay, and … go!"

Alice zooms past me, grabbing three fantasy books from the shelf and bounding down the stairs, giggling. I smile as I continue to follow her and snap a few pictures, careful not to disturb the timer.

Fifteen seconds left on the clock, and she's already got a stack of books from her hip all the way to her neck. But my girl is determined to get more as she balances the stack and reaches up to grab a couple more, tucking them under her chin.

"And ... time," I say, right as the alarm goes off. Everyone in the store is looking at Alice with impressed expressions on their faces and it makes me beam with pride.

"Little help now?" she squeaks, and I hurry to put my phone away, easily grabbing the stack from her hand and taking it up to the register.

"This is—wow. You got fifteen books," I say, impressed.

Alice looks up at me, expression beaming with a smile. It dies down as the cashier starts to scan the books and she says, "You know, I don't have to get them all. It was fun to do it, regardless."

"What are you talking about? You're getting them all," I say, brows furrowing at her words.

"That's just—a lot of money, and I didn't actually mean to put you out ..." she trails off, biting her lip in the process.

"Hey, I don't care about the price. I wanted to do this for you, okay? So just accept it, please," I say low enough only she can hear me and bump her shoulder with mine.

Her eyes shine when she looks back at me and says, "Thank you, J."

My heart skips and I wrap an arm around her shoulder, bringing her into a side hug. *I missed her calling me that.*

"Happy birthday, Al."

CHAPTER 6

Three Years Ago – All Star Break

ALICE

THE CAR RIDE to the Leelanau Peninsula started off awkward and tense as we navigated the worst of the storm in Robbie's truck, but somewhere past Cadillac, Jordan started to relax more. The whole time, he made sure I stayed alert, watched for accidents on the highway, and fed me snacks, not to mention he played my favorite Taylor Swift songs. It was ... unexpected.

This week is turning out completely different than I thought. Robbie and Olivia were supposed to join us for a week of snowboarding and fun at the cabin, but instead, Olivia's plane was delayed from Minnesota. With how much snow was coming down in Grand Marquee, Robbie suggested that Jordan and I go ahead without them and try to make the best of it. I expected Jordan to bail almost immediately, but he quietly helped pack up the truck and has been mostly silent throughout the ride.

Ever since my birthday a few weeks ago, our friendship has been getting better, back on track. At least that's what I thought. Although I can't stop thinking about that night when I kissed him. The night he rejected me.

I shake the memory away and reach for my water bottle in the center, but before I can wrap my hand around it blindly, Jordan springs into action and hands it to me, our fingers brushing with the movement. I take my eyes off the road for a second to glance at him and my heart skips a beat just like all the other times I'm near him.

Am I always going to be destined to love Jordan, only for him to never feel the same way about me?

"Thank you," I say, and hand the bottle back. He quickly takes it, almost like he's been watching my every move, anticipating what I'll do next.

"Thanks for driving," he says quietly. "Never been a huge fan of driving in the snow. I'd much rather navigate."

I flash him a big smile and decide to tease him a little, lightening up the mood. "You just want to be a passenger princess."

Jordan makes a little indignant sound in the back of his throat and says, "What is a passenger *princess*?"

My laugh gets him to turn his body towards me, giving me his full attention. "You know," I say, shaking my head and laughing again, "it's when the front seat passenger gets to be pampered, enjoying snacks, being in control of the music, and not doing the hard work of driving."

Jordan smiles and I can't help but bite my lip, enjoying the fact he's letting some of his walls down and showing me his playful side again.

"You know, I think you would make a perfect passenger princess," he says, gaze locked on my profile.

"Yeah?" I ask, blushing a little.

"You just have that vibe about you."

I hum, "Maybe when we get back to the city, you can drive me around every now and then."

"Maybe," he says, still looking at me.

Oh, what I wouldn't give to be Jordan's passenger princess.

"Any last supplies you think we'll need for the week? We're about to pass the last grocery store for a bit."

"I'm all set. Robbie packed for four people, so I think we'll make it," he replies.

"True. I hope Olivia made it okay. I want them to have a good time even if they couldn't come."

"I'm sure they will," he says reassuringly, and taps his fingers on the center console, his body still partly turned towards me.

"So," I say lamely, and drum my fingers on the steering wheel and blow out a breath.

"Yeah?" Jordan prods, like he's looking for something, anything, to make conversation with me as well.

"What do you want to do this week?"

He half shrugs and I can't help but look over at him. He looks so damn cute in a cable-knit cream sweater and dark blue jeans that look a little tight over his strong, muscular thighs. His face looks cleanly shaved, and his brown eyes take on a chocolate hue in the light of day.

I feel a tightness in my chest and remember to breathe as I maneuver the truck through the small unplowed roads of the peninsula.

The cabin looks as good as ever when we pull into the driveway. My parents were here a month ago and they decorated the wraparound porch with wreaths and left the holiday lights up. The garage door is blocked by half a foot of snow, so I park to the side of it and turn the engine off.

"I'll go through the garage side door and open it. We should have some shovels in there, if you don't mind helping," I say, batting my eyelashes.

"Of course, I've been pampered enough on the ride," Jordan says with a smile, and puts his gloves on.

After thirty minutes of shoveling, the driveway doesn't look much different than when we started, which only shows how much snow keeps coming down. But at least the garage is unobstructed so we can pull the car in and start unloading.

As soon as we enter the cabin, I'm hit with the smell of sandalwood and patchouli, and I smile at my mom's choice of essential oils. This has always been her favorite and I can't deny that it smells divine.

Jordan makes a few trips to the car and brings everything we need inside as I put food away in the fridge. When I'm done, I step away from the large kitchen island, and into the living room. My eyes take in the place that's been a stepping stone for every single core memory I have. Birthdays, Christmases, New Years—they all happened right here at this cabin.

The fireplace has seen better days, but there is dry wood next to it. No doubt my dad paid someone to stop by and stock the place up for us. The pictures on top of the mantel show all of us Elliots over the years, but the one that snags my attention is a family picture from Michael and Tangela's wedding. We were all in our best attire, but towards the end of the night, when everyone had let loose not just their ties and shoe straps, but also their inhibitions. We look like one big happy family, everyone laughing and smiling, clinking together champagne flutes.

"That has to be one of my favorite days," Jordan says from behind me, and I startle. His hands land on my shoulders as he steadies me, and I blink up at him. He's so cute, with a dopey smile on his face as he reminisces about that night. Does he remember how we danced together that night, and how I called him cute?

"Why is that?" I ask, finally finding my voice.

"All our friends and family were there, and we were celebrating love. I'll never forget it," he says, gaze moving from the picture to me. The chocolate hue is gone now, but his eyes are just another lovely shade of brown. They get darker as his eyes roam over my face and his thumb moves back and forth on my navy blue sweatshirt, near my collarbone.

I shiver and he stops the movement, but he doesn't pull away. Jordan steps in and gives me a tentative hug, and I'm so stunned that for a moment, I just stand there, arms at my sides.

But then the sweet scent of him envelops me and I lose all train of thought, melting into him, wrapping my arms around his waist.

"You're cold," he says, pulling back and rubbing my arms up and down. "I'll start a fire."

I nod but don't let go of his waist right away, basking in his closeness for a moment longer, my cheek pressed against his heart.

"I'll make us some hot cocoa," I say when I finally step away.

JORDAN

. . .

WHEN ROBBIE SAID we should go ahead without them, I thought it was a terrible idea. I almost bailed. *Almost*. It was the sight of Alice bundled up in her favorite leggings and navy blue sweatshirt with a pink pom-pom hat on her head, ready to go to the cabin, that stopped me.

The weather was worse than I expected, and I made sure not to distract her while she drove us, even though all I wanted was to finally talk to her and see how she was doing after her birthday.

The truth is, I want to spend time with her constantly because she's funny and a great conversationalist, and even though I might have some unresolved feelings for her that I could never act on, that doesn't mean I should ignore her.

I tried keeping my distance, but that never seemed to fucking work in the past. Not until she kissed me that night two years ago and I completely freaked out. My biggest regret was not explaining why I needed to put some distance between us. I was so terrified of letting her in.

And yet, I can't help but feel drawn to her like a moth to the flame.

I *like* her.

Even though I have no right to, I want to be the person she confides in, the one she's not afraid to ask for help. I want to be there *for* her.

Maybe that's why I hugged her. The urge to hold her in my arms as she shivered was so strong, I couldn't help myself.

Outside, the snow is still coming down, blanketing the backyard and the frozen lake in a thick layer of white. Inside, the fire is roaring as we unpack more things, stocking up the pantry with breads and muffins, chips and various snacks. As Alice makes us hot cocoa with mini marshmallows and caramel syrup, I pull out a few board games from the shelf near the fireplace.

"Do you want to play card games or strategy games?" I ask, holding up Power Grid and Exploding Kittens.

Alice wrinkles her nose in the cutest way and I'm so dumbstruck, staring at her pretty face, cataloging her bow-shaped lips and small button nose, that I miss her answer.

"Sorry, which one?" I ask.

She giggles as she places our drinks down on the coffee table, and even that small little noise gets me all flustered. *What is wrong with me?*

"I said, maybe we can play later. We should get some dinner started soon, since it seems like we're kind of stuck here for the rest of the day. It's snowing too much to hit the slopes," she says with a sigh.

I frown, looking out through the window to the front of the cabin and notice how much snow there really is accumulating on the roads. "Think we'll be fine with the truck tomorrow?"

"Probably. They'll plow the roads at least, but we'll need to take care of the driveway in the morning. There's a snow blower somewhere in the garage as well as shovels."

"Should be fine, then. Are you excited to snowboard?" I ask, and take a seat next to her on the couch as we both sip on our hot cocoa and look at the fireplace, the faint smell of smoke and burning wood permeating the air.

Alice grins and fiddles with her hair with one hand, cradling the mug with the other. "So excited, can't wait to kick your ass racing down the slope."

I scoff, bumping her knee with mine as I bring it to the couch to face her more. "Yeah, right."

"Oh, I'm serious, I need my rematch from a couple years ago."

"Didn't realize it was a competition," I say, giving her a smile.

"It's always a competition, J."

God, the urge to kiss the smug smile off her face right now is so strong.

"What do you want for dinner?" I ask to change the topic, even though all I want to do is keep on teasing her, talking about everything and nothing in particular.

"Grilled cheese and soup?" she asks, looking at me with big blue hopeful eyes.

I chuckle at her favorite comfort food choice and say, "Sounds delicious."

"SHOULD we also make some mulled wine?" Alice asks, pulling out the Crockpot. The soup is ready and the sandwiches are almost done as we work together in the kitchen to get dinner ready.

"Sure," I say, moving to feed the fire again. It's much warmer inside the cabin now and I pull my cable-knit sweater over my head and drape it over the back of the couch. When I turn back, I find Alice staring at me, blue eyes blazing.

"Oh, good idea," she says, swallowing hard and reaching up to take her navy sweatshirt off. It snags on the claw clip in her hair and for a moment she's left flailing around the kitchen, arms up, face covered, and her baby blue undershirt riding so high up that I get a glimpse of her belly button and ... is that a *piercing*?

I stare longer than I should at her silky-smooth skin and the tiny floating stud on her navel, having to adjust my cock as I approach her. *Fuck*, how am I this affected by a glimpse of skin?

"Wait, stop moving for a second," I say, steadying her with a hand on her waist, my thumb sweeping over her warm skin. *Bad idea. Very bad idea.* My cock twitches and I will myself to think about anything else—kittens, my grandma, my teammates naked in the shower. Yep, that does it.

I let go of her waist and gently take her sweatshirt all the way off. Her face is flushed and her hair is messy from the struggle, but fuck—she looks perfect. My mind is in the gutter once again as I imagine her sweaty and flushed under me, hair messy from my hands instead.

"Thanks," she says, breathing hard, her chest brushing mine with an inhale.

Okay, time to put some distance between us.

"I'll get the wine out," I say, clearing my throat and heading down the hall to the garage. I realize I'm still holding her shirt and in a moment of pure lust-induced insanity, I duck into my room and stare down at it like it's a fucking lifeline. I bring it to my nose and take a deep inhale of her signature floral scent—peony, I think—and close my eyes.

Fuck, fuck, fuck.

I'm so fucking fucked.

CHAPTER 7

Three Years Ago – All Star Break

JORDAN

THE NEXT MORNING, I wake up in the cold room of the cabin, the plaid comforter pulled up all the way to my chin. I regret sleeping in nothing but my underwear last night, and I shiver as I rip the comforter off me.

After eating dinner and playing a few rounds of games, Alice headed to bed in the loft upstairs, and I retreated to my room. I couldn't stop thinking of how good she felt in my arms when I hugged her, or how soft her skin was as I helped her lose a layer. Eventually, the thoughts of her smiling face and soft laugh lulled me to sleep.

I throw on the nearest sweatshirt, not bothering with pants, and rub the sleep away from my eyes as I head to the bathroom and splash some water on my face.

When I step back into the hallway, Alice's gasp startles

me and I stop dead in my tracks. I turn around slowly, aware that I'm wearing nothing but boxers and a sweatshirt and my hands fly to my crotch, trying to cover up the boner I'm sporting.

Her blue eyes are wide as she takes me in. I expect her gaze to be on my hands, but instead they're glued to my chest and the too-tight sweatshirt.

Wait, why is it tight?

I blink quickly and look down at what I'm wearing and—

"J, are you wearing *my* sweatshirt?"

Fuck, this is so embarrassing.

"Jesus, Al, I'm so sorry," I say, making quick work of reaching behind me with one arm and pulling it off me, one hand returning to cover my crotch. I close the distance between us and hold it out to her, my cheeks burning hot.

I'm such an idiot. Why did I even have it in my room?

"It's okay." She giggles and takes it from my hands, pressing it to her chest. I can't bring myself to meet her eyes, but I sneak a glance at her mouth. Her bottom lip is trapped by her teeth and she's trying not to laugh.

"I'm gonna go die of shame now, thanks," I mumble, and half turn to walk away when she stops me with a hand on my forearm.

Her hot pink nails dig into my skin, and I stare at the indents she's making.

"Don't, it was cute," she says, pulling me into a hug. I welcome it and wrap my arms around her shorter frame, tucking her nose into my collarbone. Her hands are warm on my naked back, and I let myself relax against her.

I'm all too aware of my morning wood so I keep some distance between us. She giggles again and the puff of breath tickles my chest. "You know, the color looked good on you, but I think it's a size too small," she teases, and I spring back from her.

Her laughter follows me down the hallway and past the closed door as I get dressed for the day.

ALICE KEEPS REFRESHING the ski resort's website as we stand around the kitchen counter but the same message from earlier rolls at the top of the page: *Closed due to inclement weather*.

"This is such a bummer," Alice whines as I top off her coffee mug. She gives up on refreshing the page on her phone and grabs the mug with both hands, blowing on it before bringing it to her lips and taking a sip.

I can't say I'm complaining. While this trip was supposed to be for snowboarding and outdoorsy activities, I wouldn't mind spending the day with Alice by the fireplace. I swallow hard at the image of us curled up on the couch, wrapped up in blankets.

"Maybe we could watch a movie," I offer lamely, hoping I can cheer her up.

"Yeah, I guess. I was just so excited to go out in the snow," she says, bottom lip sliding in a pout. My gaze stays rooted on her lips and I will myself to look away, but I can't. It's physically impossible.

"We can always shovel the snow," I say eventually, a teasing smile playing at my lips. Alice rolls her eyes at me and pulls her hair up in a messy bun at the top of her head, letting a few strands of hair fall softly around her angular cheekbones.

"That sounds like work, and I'm here for fun," she says, eyes gleaming with mirth.

"I can be fun," I say, blatantly lying. Since when do I consider myself fun? My idea of it is playing board games and video games and hiding indoors for most of my time. Most women, like Jess, have found that to be ... not so fun. But I can't help it that I get anxious almost every time I go out in public, or that I dislike large crowds.

"Of course you're fun, J. I just meant there's not much to do indoors," she says, smiling at me and looking around the room. "Do you want to start with a movie or a game?"

"Do you even have to ask?" I smile down at her, enjoying the fact that she so effortlessly gets me.

"I'll set up Power Grid," she says with a grin over her shoulder as she heads for the game shelf. "And grab some snacks, please."

"You got it," I nod, already pulling out chips and guac, and Alice's favorite—gluten-free Oreos.

ALICE

JORDAN ALWAYS WINS THIS GAME. No matter how hard I try, my strategy never comes close, but I don't mind. I love seeing the way his brain works when he gets laser focused on something. He's so much smarter than he ever gives himself credit for, and I don't often get to see this side of him, but when I do, it's magnificent.

Jordan bites his lip in thought, planning his next move to take over my side of the board and I smile. Propping my chin in one hand and taking a bite of my Oreo with the other, I keep my gaze on him the whole time. God, how I've missed hanging out like this. I've missed his wit and his beautiful face and his smile.

My lips twitch thinking about him in my sweatshirt and how flustered he was. I don't know if hugging him was the right move, but I just *needed* to feel his skin, peppered with goosebumps from the cold. He felt so good and solid against me, and even though he was trying to hide his erection from me, I could still catch a glimpse of the bulge in his boxers.

I wonder if he thought about me once he went back to his room. I wonder if he laid in bed thinking of me. I wonder if he touched himself. That mental image has me wriggling in my seat.

"Al?"

I swallow hard and break out of my daze. Here I go again, fantasizing about the man that's been nothing but a friend to me these last seven years. The man that made it clear we can't pursue anything because things would get too complicated.

"Sorry, what?" I say, taking a sip of sparkling water.

"It's your turn again. We're almost done, I'm sorry it's taking so long. You must be bored," he says, looking down at the table with a frown.

"No, I'm not bored, I promise. I just spaced out for a second, I'm sorry."

"All good." He smiles and I beam back at him. I really need to put all these horny thoughts away. Maybe I need to charge my vibrator and use it before I go to bed so I stop drooling all over one of my closest friends.

Once we take a few more turns, it's clear that Jordan has once again beat me. I shake my head as we pack up all the pieces and put the game away. "How do you always win? Is there some secret to it?" I ask.

Jordan smiles and says, "I just really like thinking about

all the strategies and potential outcomes. It comes naturally, for some reason. Plus, it helps that I know my opponent so well. It makes it easy to anticipate what your next move might be."

My mouth drops open and I gasp. "That's so devious."

Jordan laughs and takes our snack plates away, rinsing them and adding them to the dishwasher.

"What do you want to do next?" I ask, pulling my sweatshirt sleeves over my hands to keep me warm.

"How about I start another fire and we can read together?" he says, and I immediately perk up. Jordan is not a huge reader, and when he does pick up a book, it's either fantasy or nonfiction, so I'm intrigued by his proposal.

"Really? You want to read with me?"

"Well, it wouldn't be the same book. I have Bobby Orr's autobiography."

"Of course you do," I sigh, making my way to the stairs that lead to the loft.

"What? He's one of the best defensemen in hockey," he yells after me.

"I believe it." I chuckle. "I'll go grab my book and be right back."

I make quick work of grabbing my latest romance book and plugging in my vibrator, for good measure. I'm sure once I finish this smutty romance I'll be turned on and in need of some release.

When I return downstairs, Jordan is crouched down in front of the fireplace, and I take a second to admire how good his ass looks in the black sweatpants he's had on since morning. The muscles in his back shift under his snug gray long-sleeve waffle shirt and I bite my lip, thinking about how good it felt to have my hands on him. That night in my room, the way he kissed me back and took control—I keep replaying that moment over and over again. I fantasize too often about how that night would have gone if he hadn't put an end to it.

Jordan stands, stretching, lifting his arms high above his head, shirt riding high enough to give me a glimpse of light brown skin and a smattering of black hair trailing down into his sweatpants. I want to run my hands down that path and feel him—all of him. I want—

"You're back," Jordan says, giving me a soft, lopsided smile.

"Yeah," is all I manage to get out before I tear my gaze away from him and take a seat on the couch.

"Want to share a blanket until the fire gets going?" he says, unwrapping one of the king-sized sherpas we keep in the living room.

I nod eagerly and he chuckles. "Stand back up for a second," he says, offering me a hand. When I take it, a little spark of electricity courses through me, and I doubt it's only static. My body is so wired up every time I'm around this man, it doesn't know how to function properly.

Jordan lays the blanket on the couch and we sit on top of it before he pulls one corner around my shoulder and the other around his, cocooning us both in so that we're sitting close, legs touching from hip to thigh. I try to sit still, not wanting to break out of this moment. Does he realize how close we are?

"This okay?" he asks, dragging the ottoman over so we can both put our feet up.

"Yep," I squeak, clutching my book to my chest.

With our feet up and the blanket pulled over and around us both, we settle in and crack open our books. The faint smell of smoke from the fire mixes with Jordan's citrus and honey cologne, enveloping my senses.

I read the same page again and again, the words not quite making sense as I'm overwhelmed by Jordan's proximity and warm body. Our shoulders brush with each movement he makes to get to the next page, and even though I'm wearing a long-sleeved sweatshirt, I feel like my arm is on fire where we touch. Scooting lower, I tentatively rest my head on Jordan's shoulder and get into a more comfortable position for reading.

"Here," he says, shrugging his arm out and putting it around me so I can lean into his chest instead. My heart beats wildly as he keeps that arm around my shoulder and readjusts his book in his lap so he can keep flipping the pages with his free hand.

It doesn't take long for me to melt into him and make progress on my book. I fly through a quarter of it, but start to get squirmy when I make it to one of the sex scenes. I usually don't shy away from reading smut in public—in fact, I read it with a straight face—but being surrounded by Jordan's smell and his hand wrapped around me, brushing my shoulder, well, I can't not think about him as the hero in my book.

I picture *his* hands cupping *my* breasts, kneading until I'm writhing and begging for him to touch me where I need him the most. I picture him kissing me wildly, fucking me with his tongue, pumping his fingers inside me.

"You okay?" he asks and I shut the book, trapping a finger inside so I don't lose the page number.

"Hm?"

"You seem tense. Everything okay?" he asks, bookmarking his page and offering me all his attention. *Shit.*

"I'm fine," I lie through my teeth, keeping my eyes closed and my head resting on his chest. He sees through me and sits up enough to peer down at me.

"Are you falling asleep?"

"No," I say, opening my eyes. Which is a mistake because now I'm met with Jordan's eyes peering down into my soul.

"Your eyes seem droopy," he says, and leaves room for me to respond. When I don't, he narrows his eyes and asks, "What were you reading just now?"

"Nothing," I say, sitting up fully and clutching the book to me.

"Okay," Jordan says, and I let out a deep sigh, happy I wasn't caught. "I'm going to add a few more logs to the fire. Do you need anything while I stand?"

"No, I'll run to the bathroom while you do that," I say, placing the book face down on the coffee table.

I all but sprint down the hall and splash cold water on my face, hoping I can break out of this lust induced daze. When I return to the couch, Jordan is back to reading his book and I re-enter the cocoon before reaching for my book. Except—it's not there. I could have sworn I left it on the coffee table. Patting down the blanket and the couch, I try to think where I could have set it down.

"Looking for this?" Jordan says breezily, waving my romance book in his large hands. My *open* book.

I give him a wide-eyed, panicked look and carefully so as to not spook him, I say, "What are you doing with that?"

"What does it look like I'm doing? I'm trying to find out what made you so flustered."

"Mm-hmm, right, right. How about you give that back to me, and I'll tell you?" I say, not knowing how to get out of this.

"I don't think so. I'm quite enjoying how Madison here is writhing and whimpering under Jonas's touch and 'pumping fingers'," he says, referring to the exact chapter I was reading earlier.

My cheeks turn a flaming hot shade of red and I bury my hands in my face, groaning. "J, I can't handle you making fun of me. Please give it back."

Warm hands take a hold of my wrists, gently pulling my hands from my face. I grimace but look into Jordan's eyes, expecting him to laugh at me or think what I'm reading is stupid.

"Why would I make fun of you?" he asks softly, pulling my hands in his lap and stroking his thumb across my wrists.

"I don't know," I say meekly, feeling embarrassed, but not for the reason he may think. I don't care that he caught me reading smut, I feel bad that he caught me reading smut while I was thinking about *him*.

"There's nothing wrong with the books you read, and I'm not going to make fun of you."

"Of course there's nothing wrong with them," I huff, and he frowns at me.

"Then why are you acting so weird? I'm pretty sure I've seen you fly through one of these books in a single sitting at Christmas."

I laugh and shake my head. I can't tell him. Can I? Will he find it weird?

Jordan's open expression makes me wonder if I should just tell him. He must know I never got over him, even though he didn't want me, even though he said it's too complicated. I never stopped wanting him.

"I was just reading that scene and—" I say, biting my lip. Jordan's brown eyes are reflecting the gold from the flames, and I give in a little more. "I couldn't help but picture you instead."

CHAPTER 8

Three Years Ago – All Star Break

JORDAN

MY HEART STUTTERS for only a moment before it kicks back into gear, beating wildly. *I couldn't help but picture you instead.* Alice's cornflower blue eyes are piercing as she holds my gaze, not backing down, not taking back her statement.

Fuck. I want her so much.

"Why?" I hear myself asking, heart in my throat. Could she be messing with me? Teasing me just because I stole her book?

"Why what?" she asks, eyebrows scrunching together in confusion. She's so fucking cute with her messy bun and light brown sweatshirt drowning her small figure. All I want is to pull her in my lap and run my hands all over body.

"Why couldn't you help it?"

She blinks at me a few times, her confused furrow turning into a scowl. Even when she's trying to look annoyed, she's still as beautiful as always. Alice purses her lips and says, "Because, J."

"Because what?" I ask, leaning in almost involuntarily, barely realizing that I'm still holding her wrists and that my touch turns pressing. *Tell me, please.*

"Because I never got over you," she says tiredly, pulling her hands back. I miss their warmth and softness right away, but she surprises me in the best way by grabbing my face with both hands, her thumbs sweeping over my cheeks. Leaning in, she whispers, "I think about you all the damn time."

My eyes close and I try to breathe, try to think, but I can't. I'm too fucking weak when it comes to this girl, and no matter what comes of this, all I know is that I think about her all the damn time too.

When I look at her again, her lips are inches from my own and she's staring at me like she can't believe I'm real. There's no denying it—I'm so fucking gone for her.

"Fuck the consequences," I say right before capturing her lips with my own. I swallow down her surprised gasp and devour her mouth, chasing her sweetness.

Alice's hold on my face shifts so that her thumbs dig into my jaw, angling me as she lifts up onto her knees. My arms clasp around her waist and I fist her sweatshirt, trying to find my control. It must have gone out the window earlier when she told me she never got over me. I was such a fucking fool, keeping my distance, when I could have had this—*her*—this whole time.

"Are you going to push me away again?" she asks breathlessly.

I shake my head, pulling her down to straddle me. Alice

gasps at the contact, feeling my hard and throbbing cock through my sweatpants. Eyes wide, she assesses me, waiting for a verbal reply. "I don't think I could say no to you a second time," I rasp, running my hands from her back to her hips and thighs, kneading the soft flesh there.

"What do you want?" she whispers softly. It's a stark contrast from the way she grinds herself on my cock and I hiss out a breath.

"I haven't wrapped my head around what this means yet," I say, cupping her cheek and brushing a strand of hair behind her ear. "All I know is ever since you called me cute at that wedding," I say, nodding to the framed picture, "you've had my feelings all knotted up. But—" I bite my lip. "For now, all I want is you." I expect her to pull back and demand more from me. The last thing I want is just a fling. Especially with her.

Except Alice gives me a smile so big it lights up her whole face, so I stop over-thinking everything and just give in. I grab the back of her neck and pull her in, letting our mouths do the rest. Her much smaller hands land on my chest and she lightly pulls at the fabric as I nibble on her bottom lip. Her hips move at a torturous pace as she grinds and circles them on top of me.

The fire crackles but I barely hear it over the little moans Alice makes as I kiss every inch of her mouth. My hands make their way under her sweatshirt, roaming up her back and finding—nothing. No bra. I pull back in surprise and the little minx above me grins down at me.

"Yes?"

"You—there's—" I say, flustered.

"Is there a problem?" she says sweetly, shifting her weight above me and teasing the head of my cock with her mound. Fuck, I want these layers off.

"You're such a bad girl, aren't you?" I say, voice low and gravelly with lust. "You wore nothing but this sweatshirt all day just hoping I'd notice, didn't you?"

Her eyes widen and she lets out a small whimper. My hands flex around the skin of her back and I drag my fingertips around her sides and under her breasts, brushing my knuckles against her perky tits.

"J," she moans, and I close my eyes for a brief moment, trying to not blow my load in my pants like a fucking high schooler. I let my hands caress down her torso and bring them back to grip her plump ass with both hands, kneading each cheek as my mouth finds hers again.

She feels so soft and good against me that each kiss brings me closer to the edge. Using all my willpower, I push her away, just a little, so I can lean forward and wrap her legs around my waist.

"What are you doing?" she asks.

"Taking us somewhere more comfortable," I say, standing up in one swift movement and holding on to her tightly. Her arms fly around my neck and she bites her lip, hiding a smile.

When I start walking to my bedroom she stops us. "Let's go to the loft."

"Why?"

Alice's blue eyes are swallowed up by her black pupils and I kiss her again, swiftly. Because I can't help myself, apparently.

"Because," she mumbles against my lips. "I have condoms."

I groan and smack her ass, which only increases the friction on my cock. "Naughty girl." Taking the steps two at a time with her in my arms, I bring her to the loft, looking around the large room. The bed is fluffed up with a ton of decorative pillows and a plush-looking comforter.

I make a beeline for it, dropping her down in the middle of the bed and pressing some of my weight against her, stealing another kiss. When I pull back, Alice is smiling at me with a soft look on her face, more of her blond hair coming out of her bun and fanning across the pillows. I stare down for a second longer before rasping, "Condoms?"

She bites her lower lip and blushes, and I swear I could come just from watching her, she's so fucking stunning. "On the nightstand."

I smile back and kiss along her jaw before pulling away and taking a step towards the nightstand.

"Wait," she says, quickly sitting up and grabbing my wrist. But it's too late. I've already seen it.

Right there, on the nightstand, is a purple vibrator.

ALICE

MY CHEEKS BURN with embarrassment and I grimace as Jordan gently lets go of my hand and picks up the vibrator.

Why did I leave it out in view? Not only did he catch me reading smut, but now he knows about my best friend, Thanos. There's nothing special about it by any means—it's a standard purple vibrator, but it gets the job done, hence why I've kept it around for so long. The fact that it's somewhat big for me and purple is the reason I've named it Thanos, after the infamous villain.

I watch Jordan's face closely, but I can't get a good read on what he might be thinking. Just when I think he might say this whole thing was a mistake and that we should stop, he says, "Is this what you normally use?"

Taking a deep breath, I say, "Yeah. Why?"

He gives me a lopsided grin and takes a step towards me, unplugging Thanos in the process. "Just wondering," he says, looking down at it and turning it this way and that. "Can I use it?" he says and my eyes all but bulge out of my head.

"*You* want to use it?" I ask, shocked.

Jordan frowns at me, but then his eyes widen. "No, I—I didn't mean on me," he sputters, and I smile at how easily flustered he got when he was so confident a second ago. This man is a walking contradiction and I freaking love seeing him come undone.

"I mean, I wouldn't judge if you did," I say, biting my lip and scooting closer to the edge of the bed. My fingers find the waistband of his sweatpants and I pull him toward me, feeling him up through the thick fabric.

Jordan laughs and throws the vibrator on the bed next to me. "Never say never, I guess, but I'd rather focus on you for now," he says, cupping my cheek and stealing another kiss. I melt into him but keep my hand on his bulge, rubbing him.

His hand gently takes mine and pulls it away from his cock. "What I meant, before you so rudely interrupted me," he says, panting against my mouth, "is that I want to use it on you. Trust me, you'll need the warmup."

My brain doesn't register what he means, but a second later, Jordan takes off his waffle shirt, followed by both his pants and boxers, and my jaw is on the floor. He's ... fucking *huge*. Way bigger than my stupid-ass vibrator. And definitely much bigger than either of the two guys I've ever been with.

I swallow hard and stare at him. A few freckles mar his chest where he sports a little bit of black, curly hair. My eyes roam over his chiseled abs and to his defined Adonis belt, where a strip of hair runs down to his cock. I don't think I've seen anything more perfect in my life.

Licking my lips, I grab the vibrator and bring it next to Jordan's cock, comparing the two. Let's just say Jordan's is thicker. By a lot.

Choking on a laugh, I manage to say, "Yeah, I think I'll need the warmup."

CHAPTER 9

Three Years Ago – All Star Break

JORDAN

THIS GIRL MIGHT BE the death of me. She's on her knees, at the edge of the bed, her small figure still drowned by that damn sweatshirt. Her pink nails stand out in contrast to the brown skin of my dick, where she's gripping me, comparing my size to her purple vibrator.

I groan when she squeezes the base, trailing her fingers up and down, revealing the head, which is leaking with pre-cum. I need to do something, anything, to take this slow before I explode all over her fingers.

"Stand up," I rasp, my voice deep and dripping with need.

Alice looks at me with wide eyes but obeys. *Good girl.* I take a step back, making room for her as she gets down from the bed, throwing the vibrator down on the comforter nonchalantly.

The things I want to do to her with that toy should probably stay locked up in my brain, never to be revealed.

"Are you gonna boss me around?" she asks with a smirk, reaching for my cock again. I swat her hand away and she frowns.

"Take your clothes off," I say, sidestepping her and sitting at the edge of the bed, my legs spread wide enough for her to return to my cock if she wants. Though I'd much rather explore her body.

Alice's smile turns shy as she drags her sweatshirt slowly over her head, exposing her navel and the ring I caught a glimpse of the other day. Biting her lip, she continues to drag the material up her body and revealing her perky tits, nipples hard and pointed at me.

Dropping the shirt to the floor, she moves her hands to the waistband of her leggings, pulling them down along with her underwear and socks.

My hand drifts down and I pump myself once, twice, my eyes never leaving her perfect body. Alice's gaze is glued to my hand, and she bites her lip hard, a small shiver running through her.

"Can I touch you?" she asks, taking a step further and looking down at me.

"Yes," I rasp right as she leans in and steals a kiss. Her lips are bruising and when I open up to her, I'm lost to the sweetness of her mouth. Biting my lip, she reaches down and replaces my hand with her own, matching my grip and movements. Almost like she was studying what I was doing and understanding what I like.

I groan and she takes it as the encouragement it is, pressing her body into me, her nipples grazing my chest. My hands land on her waist and I dig my fingers in, slowly moving to her backside. Her plump ass is soft as I knead it, drawing moans from her sweet mouth.

She stops pumping me for a second and I pull back, making sure everything's okay. Alice gives me a devious grin and reaches down between her legs, coating her fingers with her wetness before bringing her hand back to my cock. There's something so raw and dirty about the way she just used her own arousal as lube and I groan, letting my head fall to her chest.

"Fuck, you're so hard," she moans into my hair, twisting her hand and running a thumb over my slit.

"How can I not be when I've got the girl of my dreams naked and touching my cock?"

Alice whimpers and pulls my head back, kissing me hard and biting my lip. I didn't mean to say that out loud but I'm happy with the result.

"I've wished for you so much—and thought about *this* so many times. How you'd feel, how you'd make me come," she says, hand moving faster and faster. My abs clench with each squeeze of her fingers and I think I need to slow this down again.

"Tell me," I say, stopping her movements and standing up. Leaning in, I kiss her cheeks, her jaw, down the column of her throat. "Tell me what you fantasized about."

"You—your mouth—between my legs ..." She pants when I find a particular soft spot right below her ear. The mental image she's giving me makes me want to be buried in her pussy already.

So I gently lead her to the bed, laying her down as I keep kissing every inch of her. I press my lips to the tips of her breasts before taking a nipple in my mouth, sucking and licking as she writhes under me. My other hand finds the other tight bud and I pinch her lightly.

"J, fuck, I need—more" Alice moans and all it does is spur me on, biting down gently and reaching a hand down, caressing her folds. She jolts under me and digs her fingers into my back as I keep devouring her small breasts, my middle finger circling her clit, adding the smallest amount of pressure.

"More?" I ask, kissing down her body and flicking her belly button ring with my tongue while I bring a finger to her entrance.

"Fuck, yes," she says, shifting and widening her legs for me.

"Good girl," I praise her, my mouth finding her swollen clit and sucking hard while my finger slips inside her hot, wet cunt.

"Oh god," she screams out, throwing an arm over her eyes and arching her back.

"No baby, it's just you and me in this room," I say, blowing on her pussy and adding another finger, pumping faster while pressing down on her lower belly. I smile and bite down on her inner thigh at the string of curses she screams out at me.

It doesn't take long for her first orgasm to hit. Alice's legs start to shake, and her chest is heaving. And when I suck her clit again, adding another finger and curling them inside her, she explodes, her walls clenching around me and her hands grabbing at my short-cropped hair, nails scraping against my scalp.

"Fuck, you taste so good," I say, slowly pulling my fingers out and wiping my mouth with the back of my hand.

"J, how am I supposed to move now?" she pants out, chest red and splotchy, a soft, satisfied smile on her face.

"Oh, that was just part of the warmup," I say, reaching over on the comforter.

My fingers close around it right as Alice asks, "What do you mean?"

With a smirk, I lean down and steal a quick kiss before I turn the vibrator on, the buzzing noise drowning out her gasp.

ALICE

MY EYES widen and I watch Jordan's devious smirk as he brings the vibrator to my sensitive clit. He's got it on the lowest setting, but even that's too much right now. This has already been more than I've ever experienced when it comes to sex.

No one's ever gone down on me before, and *fuck,* it felt so good. I should feel embarrassed at how fast I came once his mouth was on me, but I can't bring myself to care about that right now. Because Jordan is kissing me, devouring me whole, and he's pressing the vibrator inside me at a torturous slow pace.

The string of curses that comes out of my mouth is filthy, but not as filthy as the sight of Jordan as he buries the toy all the way inside me, pulling back and looking at my naked body.

"Does it feel good?" he asks with a smirk, and all I can do is nod and breathe through the pressure and build of my second orgasm.

"What would make it better?" he inquires, flicking his tongue against one of my sensitive nipples.

"Fuck, I don't know," I say, chuckling and throwing an arm over my eyes.

Jordan doesn't let me get away without an answer though. "Tell me, how do you like it?"

My cheeks burn at the fact that I've never explored much in bed—I usually just press the vibrator to my clit and imagine Jordan's mouth on me and that does the trick. But now he's asking me what I like, and the reality is, I don't know.

One gentle hand grasps my arm and pries it off my eyes. Jordan's brown eyes are soft and a tad concerned. "Everything okay?" he whispers, leaning in and kissing my cheek. His other hand stops pumping the toy inside me and I let out a small whimper. I don't want him to stop.

"I just—" I say, closing my eyes tight against my own frustration. "I don't have a ton of experience, so I'm not sure what to say. I don't know how to tell you to make me feel good."

When I open my eyes again, I find Jordan staring at me, lips parted. The freckles on his cheeks stand out in the low light of the room, and I run my thumbs over them. He kisses me then, a slow kiss that promises to lead to more.

"How about I do my best to make you feel good, and if there's something you don't like, you just tell me?" he asks, some of his earlier confidence dissipating. I can't imagine anything not feeling good when he's involved. He's all I see. He's all I want.

I nod, taking his plump bottom lip between my teeth and pulling until he follows, pressing his cock into my thigh and returning one of his hands to the vibrator, pumping in and out until he's got me panting under him.

"J, I'm close," I say, fisting the sheets as he trails kisses down my body, returning his mouth to my clit. One hand holds me down as the other turns the vibrator to a higher setting, fucking me slowly. And when he sucks on my clit again, I scream out his name, my legs shaking, the tight feeling building and building until my vision turns spotty and my thighs clench around Jordan's head.

"Fuck, that was so hot," he says, pulling the toy out and continuing to leave slow, languid kisses to my sensitive cunt.

"J, if you keep doing that, I won't be able to take you. It'll be too much."

He chuckles against me. "I better hurry then." Stepping back to the nightstand, he grabs a condom and rolls it onto his thick length. I lean up on my elbows and admire all six feet, two inches of him in his naked glory. I can't believe this is really happening. *Finally.*

When he returns to the bed, I sit up and guide him to lay down against the mountain of plush pillows. He lets me roam his body with my hands, feeling every muscle, every inch of light brown skin, until I reach his cock, gripping the base and guiding it to my entrance.

Jordan's hands grip my waist as he oh-so-slowly presses into me. It takes me a moment to adjust to his thickness, but he kisses me through it, kneading my flesh, squeezing my ass and telling me what a good girl I am. How well I'm taking his cock.

My eyes roll back in my head and I finally, blessedly, sink all the way down. Jordan's fingers tighten their hold on me, and I moan into his kiss. "Fuck, you feel so good," I mumble, nipping at his jaw and circling my hips.

"I might not last long, you're so damn tight," he gasps, burying his face in my chest and tentatively snapping his hips up. I throw my head back in pleasure and lift up so that his tip is the only part that's inside me. Then I slam back down, enjoying the sound of slapping skin and Jordan's groans.

I do it again and again, until Jordan's had enough. His palm comes down on my ass cheek in a loud slap and I let out the most embarrassing loud moan. He smacks my other cheek and takes control, pinning me to his chest and fucking me hard enough that I bite his shoulder.

His hips stutter and I pick up the pace, fucking him through his orgasm, my lips finding his again. And when he reaches between us and presses his thumb to my clit, I come undone once more.

CHAPTER 10

Three Years Ago – All Star Break

JORDAN

THE SNOW FINALLY STOPS. It takes us two hours to clear the large driveway and pack up the truck, and my body happily accepts the workout I get from shoveling the snow. The sun is out and after being stuck inside the cabin for two days, the light is blinding.

Alice is bundled up in her thermal sweater and snow pants, the pink overalls making her look adorable. Her dark blond hair falls in two perfect French braids and she sports a blue headband to keep her ears warm. Our eyes connect as she looks around, backing us out of the driveway, and for a moment my heart stutters. She's so effortlessly beautiful.

Her lips have a tint of red to them, and I can't tell if it's from the cold or if she put some Chapstick on. I'm dying to press my mouth to hers and find out if she tastes like her favorite cherry lip balm.

After what felt like the best orgasm of my fucking life last night, we took a quick shower and cuddled in her bed until we both fell asleep. I knew if I let myself get this close to her, I wouldn't be able to stop these feelings from flooding in. And I was right.

All morning, I couldn't stop touching her as we got dressed and ready for the day. Couldn't stop kissing her between bites of breakfast and sips of coffee. Even now, I want her to pull over so I can drag her to my lap and kiss her, touch her, hold her. Anything.

Instead, I keep my hands firmly clasped in my lap, trying not to distract her from driving us to the ski resort.

"Excited to finally do what we came here to do?" Alice asks with a smile.

"I'm not complaining about our other activities," I say with a grin. Alice blushes and bites the corner of her lip, and I watch with rapt attention, wishing that was my teeth digging into her plump red lip.

"Me either," she says a little breathlessly, giving me a coy look out of the corner of her eye.

"But snowboarding will be nice. Then maybe we can fire up the sauna back at the cabin," I say, my mind racing with thoughts of Alice in nothing but a bikini. Or better yet, naked.

"I have some ideas of things we could do in the sauna," she says, and I inhale through my nose and beg my erection to go away.

"You'll be the death of me," I say, focusing on playing her favorite songs for the rest of the drive.

The resort is not as busy as previous years, likely because of the snowstorm that passed through this week, so we grab our lift tickets and get to the top of the mountain in record time.

I help Alice clasp her helmet tightly and kiss her—just once—before pulling back and pulling the goggles over her eyes. The smile she gives me is blinding and I force myself to step back from her before I ask her to ditch the mountain and head back to the cabin.

"Ready?" I ask, adjusting my own goggles and securing my bootstraps.

Alice does the same, sitting down next to me and saying, "I was born ready."

I chuckle and tell her, "Last one down has to buy the hot cocoa." Then I push myself up and glide down, getting a head start.

"You traitor!" she yells after me, laughing. I look back for a second and see she's following close behind. I angle myself straight down the mountain to get some speed and watch my edges so I don't flip myself face-first into the snow. Even though this is only a Blue Square intermediate slope, I still want to be careful, not only because of my career, but because I want Alice to be safe too. I know how competitive she can get, and the last thing I want is for her to get hurt.

I cut across the slope a few times as we approach the bottom of the hill, slowing down enough before coming to a full stop in front of the fire pit and the food truck that sells hot cocoa.

"No fair, you always beat me," she huffs, reaching down and unclasping her boots. I do the same and rest my snowboard against the wood beams near the fire pits.

"Get good, noob," I say, and it earns me a slap across my bicep. Not that I can feel it with how little force she puts behind it and all the layers I'm wearing to ward away the cold.

"Go grab us a couple seats by the fire. I'll get the cocoa," she grumbles, shuffling away to the food truck.

I do as she says, finding two available spots and moving the chairs closer to the fire pit. Grabbing a couple logs from the basket nearby, I throw them in, keeping the fire going. I wish the rest of our friend group could have come too. I snap a picture of the fire and mountain behind it right as Alice photo-bombs it, poking her tongue out at my phone. I smile and send it to the group.

> **ELI**
> I wish I was snowboarding instead of sweating in California.
>
> **ASH**
> That's not what you said last night after winning the All Star mini game.
>
> Hi Al, cute braids!
>
> **ROBBIE**
> Hope you two have fun snowboarding. Olivia and the cats say hello as well.

"Hot cocoa, as promised," Alice hands me a paper cup with no lid, the steam billowing out in the cold weather. I blow on it and take a small sip, instantly enjoying the velvety chocolate taste and the warmth it brings me.

"Take a seat," I say, motioning her over with a tilt of my head. She shuffles between me and the fire pit, but before she can make it to her chair, I gently wrap an arm around her middle, mindful of our drinks, and pull her to sit in my lap.

Alice gives me a small grin, a small dimple popping in her right cheek. I lean in and kiss it, my hand squeezing her waist as she melts into me, and we rest against the back of the wooden chair. Careful not to spill her drink, she presses a sweet kiss to my mouth, gently tugging at my bottom lip with her teeth. I open up to her and the instant her tongue touches mine, I groan. Fuck, I want her again.

"Someone's eager today," she whispers, taking a long sip of cocoa and licking her upper lip, enticing me. What I wouldn't do to have those lips on my cock.

Jesus, I need to slow down. What is it about this girl that makes me act like a high school virgin, excited for any bit of physical attention?

"Hm, should I not be?" I say, leaning away from her. "We can go back to just snowboarding," I say, smirking.

Alice narrows her eyes at me and says, "Maybe we should, then I can have my way with you in the sauna."

I down the rest of my cocoa as she giggles and does the same. Then I scoop her up and carry her to the beam where our snowboards rest.

"Hurry up already, sheesh."

ALICE

JORDAN and I race down the mountain two more times before we finally relent and head back to the cabin. Even though I planned to buy the cocoa *again*, Jordan insisted it should be his treat. The fire pit was taken so we took our drinks and fresh churros to go.

"Hit me," I say, opening my mouth and leaning towards the passenger seat as Jordan carefully breaks off a piece of churro and brings it to my mouth. I'm careful to keep both hands on the wheel and not take us off the road.

The cinnamon sugar hits my tongue and I moan around the bite of the delicious dessert. Jordan seems to choke on air in the face of my reaction and I smile to myself. I bet he's all flustered again, maybe even sporting an erection. Fuck, I love how quickly he gets turned on. *By me.*

Jordan feeds me another piece and I eagerly take it, biting the tip of his finger in the process. "If I could pick a dessert to eat for the rest of my life, it would be these churros."

He laughs then says, "Don't you have a gluten intolerance?"

"Don't remind me," I pout. Yes, technically I *do* have an intolerance, but sometimes the pain is worth it.

"I'm curious. What else would you pick if you had to only eat one meal for the rest of your life?" he asks, and I ponder it for a moment while we listen to a Hozier song.

"That's a tough one. Maybe … tacos?"

"Really? What is it with you and Mexican food?"

"Hey, Mexican food is delicious. Why? What would you pick as your only meal?"

Jordan shakes his head, tapping his fingers on the center console. "Lasagna."

"That's—not bad, actually. I've always wanted to take an Italian cooking class. They seem fun. You know … I expected you to say something basic like chicken."

"There's nothing wrong with chicken. Throw it in some marinade and you have yourself a great option for salads, wraps, or the grill."

My stomach rumbles and I groan. "Okay, maybe we need to stop talking about food."

Jordan laughs and the sound makes me feel lighter, somehow. I bring a hand to the console and thread our gloved fingers together. His chocolate brown gaze is locked on my face as he gives me an intense look. One that promises he's not done with me yet. I shiver in anticipation and welcome what's to come.

"Maybe we can take a cooking class together," he says, voice taking on a shy note. Does he think I wouldn't jump at the opportunity?

"We definitely should," I say, squeezing his fingers.

It's dark by the time we make it back to the cabin, and we all but sprint out of the truck to get inside. Jordan's hands are on me the second we take off our snow pants and thicker layers and drop them to the floor of the hallway.

One of his hands cups the back of my head, angling me just right so he can devour my mouth. He presses long, languid kisses to my lips and groans against me, mumbling something that sounds like "I knew it was cherry."

I take a step back and Jordan follows, pressing me into the wall, letting go of my head to lift me up. My legs lock at the small of his back and he presses his hardness into me. We both gasp at the same time and hold on tight to one another. Our noses brush and I take a deep inhale as he exhales against my lips. He tastes like churros and hot cocoa, and I never want this day to end.

"We should probably find some food," he says but doesn't put me down yet.

"Probably. We should also warm up the sauna."

"How about you start that and I'll make us some sandwiches?"

I smile and press another kiss to his lips. "Deal."

When I return from the basement, having gotten the sauna ready, Jordan offers me a BLT. I smile, noticing he even made it on my favorite sourdough bread. We eat standing around the kitchen island, sharing a bag of cherry potato chips in the process.

As he puts away our plates, I grab one of the Laffy Taffy pieces from the bowl and unwrap it, popping the strawberry candy in my mouth.

"I love the puns they have," Jordan says. Slowly, I look at the wrapper and chuckle to myself.

"What kind of bear has no teeth?"

Jordan looks at me, an amused smile on his lips and his eyebrows raised.

I smirk and say, "A gummy bear."

He laughs and wraps his arms around me, pressing a kiss to my neck. "C'mon, *gummy bear*, let's go enjoy the sauna."

"Last one down there has to get naked," I yell, taking off towards the stairs. Jordan follows close behind me but right as I open the door, he picks me up around my middle and plunges us into the dry heat of the sauna.

"Oh no, now we both have to get naked," he whispers in my ear as he sets me down and closes the door. His hands find me almost immediately as he peels off my shirt and sports bra, his thumbs brushing over my already hard nipples as he kisses me again.

My hands delve under his shirt and I rake my nails up and down his hard abs, drawing the hottest reaction from him. Jordan moans against my lips and pulls me close, grabbing my ass with both hands and kneading it, pulling my leggings down as I lift his shirt up. We both stop and chuckle at the ridiculousness of our situation.

Pulling back, I take the rest of my clothes off and he does the same. We waste no time as Jordan picks me up and carries me to the wooden bench. He sits and I straddle him, rubbing myself on his cock.

"Condom?" he asks, and I shake my head.

"I'm on the pill, so if you want, we can skip the

condoms." Jordan groans, then takes one of my nipples in his mouth and flicks it with his tongue, sending shivers down my spine.

I feel like I'm on fire, and it's not just the sweltering heat of the sauna. It's *him*, it's the magnitude of us and the realization that this is happening.

I don't know what I expected last night, but it wasn't for Jordan to wash my hair in the shower and hum against my neck as he held me before sleep took over. Maybe deep down I was worried he'd reject me again. That he'd have a part of me and decide it's still not enough. That this is too complicated.

But he's still here.

He still wants me.

And *fuck*, do I want him too.

He holds me tight, palms flat against my shoulder blades as he drives his cock inside me. I gasp and clench around him, finding his lips with mine.

"So fucking tight," he whispers, our tongues mingling.

I pull back and catch a bead of sweat off his forehead with my lips as Jordan fucks me at just the right angle, pulling a cry from my lips.

"You feel so good," I whisper against his temple as he paws at my breasts and brings a free hand to my clit. "Faster, J!"

"Yeah?" he smirks, pulling me off and turning me around. I lean forward, holding myself up on his spread knees as he pumps into me at a merciless pace.

The heat is making me dizzy and it's somehow intensifying the pleasure. When he slows down, I pick up the pace myself, bobbing up and down on his thick cock.

Jordan circles my clit again with two fingers and hits a spot deep inside me and the pleasure that was slowly building erupts in a flurry of cries and curses as I spasm and clench around his cock.

I'm limp, fully satiated, and I can tell Jordan is getting close just by the way his breathing becomes more stuttered.

"I'm going to come. Where do you want me, baby?"

I don't give him a reply, but I do find the will for my legs to move. I pull myself off his cock and kneel down in front of the wooden bench, taking him in my mouth as deep as I can, and gripping the rest of him with both my hands. Jordan rests his elbows on the bench above him and drops his head back. I whimper at the fucking masterpiece in front of me and watch the veins in his neck pop as he tries to hold back his release.

I rake one hand down his stomach, digging my nails in, and force myself to take more of his cock until I'm deep-throating him. I've never done that before, but I can tell it's the right move as Jordan grabs the back of my head, holding me there as he shudders and comes down my throat.

I choke and sputter, but swallow down every drop. When I look back up at him, Jordan is watching me in wide-eyed awe.

"Fuck, you're perfect," he says.

I wink and grin back at him. "Right back at ya, hotshot."

CHAPTER 11

Three Years Ago – March

JORDAN

THIS GAME IS FUCKED. We're in the second period of this godforsaken game, and so far it's been full of penalties and fights. One of the Vortices, Mitchell, has been harassing Olivia the entire game, and it's getting on all our nerves.

The moment Mitchell trips Ash is when it all goes to shit. Ash drops his gloves so fast, none of us have time to get to them and break them up. Ash lands a few punches to Mitchell's face, and while it's deserved, it also means we're going on a penalty kill.

Robbie and I have different shifts, so while he's out there with another defensemen, I'm on the bench, contemplating what I could do better to help us out of this situation and get us back to winning the game.

I get the opportunity for a shift change with only

twenty seconds left in the penalty kill. I manage to snatch the puck away and attempt a breakaway, but Mitchell comes out of the box and heads towards me at full speed. Retreating, I look around for someone to pass the puck to. Ash is still in the penalty box for fighting, but I see Trip out of the corner of my eye. I don't get the chance to pass because Mitchell charges at me and I angle myself against the boards, hoping to dodge the check.

Except—it doesn't come. A whistle blows and I look around confused. Where is Olivia?

Looking down where Mitchell is laying on the ice, I realize—he wasn't charging at me.

There's nothing worse than seeing someone unconscious on the ice. The fact that it's Olivia makes this ten times worse. One moment she's skating backwards and the next she's checked so hard that her helmet flies off, her head hitting the ice.

Panic grips at me as I notice blood on the ice, but I drop my stick and gloves and move quickly. The whole arena is quiet, waiting with bated breath to see what's happening.

"Get the team physician," I tell Trip, pushing him towards the bench. I notice Robbie jumping over the wall and skating over, so I make quick work of lifting Mitchell off of Olivia.

"You fucking piece of shit," I yell in his face, pushing him away from her. More players have come to surround Olivia, not letting the people see her current state. *Fuck, I hope she's okay.*

The team physician comes over and we make room for him to assess her. When I turn around to look at the commotion behind me, I see Robbie pummeling the hell out of Mitchell. *Shit.*

"Hey, whoa, that's enough," Ash says, helping me get Robbie away.

"You need to calm down," I say, using both my hands to hold him back.

"How the fuck am I supposed to calm down when she's fucking bleeding and unconscious because of him?" Robbie exclaims, and my heart breaks for him.

The whole game gets delayed as a stretcher is brought out and Olivia is taken to the hospital, Robbie leaving the game to follow her.

"How much trouble do you think he'll get in?" Ash asks me as we watch Robbie take off down the tunnel.

I blow out a breath. "A few suspensions, at least."

"Do you think she'll be okay?" he asks, blue eyes worried as he looks at me.

With a hand on his shoulder pads, I say, "Yeah, she's a tough cookie, she'll be just fine. I saw her talking as they rolled her out, so that's a great sign."

"Right," Ash mumbles, looking over at Eli. Sometimes it's like they communicate telepathically, and this look says *All will be fine.*

ALICE

I THINK my heart stopped beating the whole time Olivia was down. I blink back my tears and take a few deep inhales, pulling out my phone and texting my brother.

> ALICE
>
> Which hospital are they taking her to?

He doesn't reply right away, which only heightens my

anxiety. I leave the lower section of the arena and pace around the concourse area until my phone buzzes with a text.

ROBBIE

St. Mary's.

I rush down the stairs and jog a few blocks away to the hospital, looking for the emergency room. A middle-aged nurse is the only person at the check in desk and I walk up to her, panting a little.

She looks at me with a raised eyebrow and narrows her eyes on me in what might be recognition.

"Hi, I'm looking for Olivia Wilson, she was brought over not too long ago. Am I in the right spot?" I ask, glancing down at her name tag that reads *Janice*.

"Let me guess, you're her fiancée too?" she says with an amused expression.

"Pardon?" I ask, confused.

"Olivia is getting an MRI. Her fiancé is in there keeping her company and getting his hand checked out," Janice says, looking at her computer. I frown but then realize Robbie must have told her he's engaged to Olivia so they could let him in.

I smirk and tap the counter a few times. Janice raises an eyebrow at me and I shake my head, smiling. "That's my future sister-in-law right there, take good care of her," I say, and retreat to the waiting area. Janice laughs and winks at me and I immediately feel better, knowing they're both okay and looked after.

Hospital chairs, as I've found out over the years, are notoriously uncomfortable. Nevertheless, I find a position that works best, pulling my knees up to my chin and resting my phone there. I type a message to the rest of my family and the friends group chat with the hospital name and floor number and settle in, opening up an ebook to pass the time.

AN HOUR LATER, my parents show up with Michael and Tangela in tow. My nieces are nowhere in sight and while I'm bummed because I haven't seen them in a while, they probably shouldn't be out this late at night anyway.

"Any news?" my mom asks, and I shake my head no.

"Robbie mentioned they're waiting on some results and that for the most part she's okay."

"That's good," Mom says, squeezing my forearm. I pull her into a hug and smile to myself, wondering if I should tell her the whole "fiancé" bit. She'll probably go ballistic and pester Robbie to actually propose soon, so I hold my tongue.

"I'm glad you could all come. I'm sure this will mean the world to Robbie," I say, walking over to Michael where he sat down in a chair. Just to be a menace, I ruffle his hair like he used to do to me when I was a kid, and he playfully swats me away.

"Robbie will be just fine, it's Olivia I'm worried about," Mom says, tucking her silver-streaked blond hair behind her ears in a familiar gesture.

"Hey, did we miss anything?" a voice says from behind me, and I turn to see Ash and Eli standing shoulder to shoulder.

"No news yet, waiting on them to come out or for Robbie to text with updates." I give each of the boys a hug.

"I brought them clothes," Eli says, gesturing to the plastic bag he's holding.

"Good, I'm sure they'll appreciate it. Where's Jordan?"

"Parking."

I nod and pace around the corridor, checking my phone to see if Robbie sent updates. When I get back to the sitting room, Jordan is in one of the chairs, his back to me. It takes everything in me not to rush over and hug him. That game was brutal and I'm sure it couldn't have been easy to see that hit up close.

I look down at the jersey I'm still wearing and bite my lip, making my way over and walking by him to take a seat. When our eyes connect, I can tell he's affected by my choice in attire.

I've had his jersey for years, usually only wearing it to games when I know he won't see me in it afterwards. But tonight, I dug it out and planned to surprise him at his apartment, wearing nothing but the jersey with number 20 on it. *His jersey.*

Jordan swallows hard, his nostrils flaring and eyes turning a dark shade of brown. If my entire family weren't here, he'd probably maul me.

I listen to the chatter around me and pull out my phone, sneaking glances at Jordan. He looks hot in his post-game attire, wearing a dark red button-up shirt with the sleeves rolled up and slacks that show off his muscular thighs. His hands grab the arms of the chair and he flexes, knowing how much I like the muscles in his forearms.

Blushing, I peek at his face and find him smirking at me. *Hot nerdy bastard.* I focus on my phone instead and text him.

ALICE

> If you keep looking at me like that, you might give our secret away.

JORDAN

If you keep wearing my jersey, I might bend you over right here in this waiting room.

ALICE

Ooh, are you a bit of an exhibitionist?

The tips of Jordan's ears turn pink, and he bites his lip as he contemplates a reply. I love flustering him, especially when it comes to sex.

JORDAN

No. I just really, really like you wearing that damn jersey. I'd do anything to get my hands on you right now.

ALICE

Are you getting hard just watching me?

I bring a hand to the collar of the jersey and play with the laces, crossing one leg over the other. The material rides up my thigh and Jordan follows the movement with dark interest. I've never been this turned on in a public setting, but there's just something about this man that makes me absolutely lose my mind.

Jordan fidgets in his seat and I notice him subtly adjusting himself and covering his crotch with his coat.

ALICE

You are, aren't you? Thinking of all the ways you could have me.

JORDAN

Fuck, you're torturing me.

ALICE

Not yet, but I could be.

He groans loudly and every head in the silent waiting room turns towards him.

"You alright there, Jordie?" Ash asks with raised eyebrows.

"Fine," Jordan mumbles, his cheeks pink from embarrassment. "And I told you to stop calling me that."

Ash grins and winks at him. "Aw, but it fits you so well." Jordan rolls his eyes and flips him off, but Ash just smiles wider and blows him a kiss.

Just as I'm about to send another text, I see Robbie coming out, his arm around Olivia. They stop by the front desk to check out, and we all make our way over to them, eager to make sure they're okay.

"Olivia, honey, how are you?" mom asks, clutching at her necklace and looking her over in concern.

"Is your middle finger broken?" Ash asks Robbie with amusement on his face. I whip my head around to look at my brother's hand, and he does in fact have a splint on his middle finger. I stifle a laugh and shake my head.

"Do you have a concussion?" I ask, bringing my focus back to Olivia, who is smiling at us with tears in her eyes.

"Guys, slow down," Robbie says.

"Thank you all. I'm fine, but two of my ribs are broken and they'll take about six weeks to fully heal. As for my head, I did get a few stitches, but the concussion is not severe."

"Here, I brought you both some clothes," Eli says, and hands them the bag. Robbie throws a hoodie on first and then helps Olivia with hers. I watch the two of them and tear up at how perfect they are together and how horribly wrong this night could have gone.

The rest of my family gives them hugs and heads home, the rest of the guys wanting to follow.

"Here, I need to use the restroom, so you guys can head to the car," Jordan says, handing his car keys over to Ash.

"Thanks. Get well soon, all right? We're gonna need you to keep us in check," Ash says to Olivia, and pats her shoulder. Eli waves at us and the two of them head out.

"I will." She chuckles, slumping further into Robbie. I can tell she's getting tired.

"I'll drive you both home and take the truck back to my place," I offer, and Robbie smiles at me in gratitude.

As we wait for the elevator, I see Jordan heading out of the bathroom.

"I forgot, I need to use the restroom, why don't you two head down first?" I tell them.

"Okay, we'll see you down there," my brother says.

As soon as the elevator doors close, I turn and sprint over to Jordan, jumping in his arms. He catches me easily and I wrap my legs around his waist, intertwining my fingers at the back of his neck and holding tight.

"I offered to drive them home, so I won't be able to come by the apartment," I pout, touching my nose to his.

Jordan's arms tighten around me as he pulls me closer. He leaves featherlight kisses on my cheek and nose and says, "That's okay, you'll just have to wear that jersey another night."

I chuckle and find his lips, capturing them with my own. He softly moans when I sink my teeth in his bottom lip. We kiss for longer than we should until we hear the nurse clearing her throat.

Jordan quickly sets me down and takes a big step back from me, flustered that we were being watched. I bite back my smile and say, "All right hotshot, another time then."

CHAPTER 12

Three Years Ago – April

JORDAN

I WAKE UP WITH A START, breathing hard as I try to shake off my nightmare. I usually get them when I'm stressed, but I've never had this specific one before—we're all at Robbie's house, hanging out and playing board games, when all of a sudden an earthquake starts. I'm glued to my seat, unable to move, unable to help. I just sit there, watching everything around me crumble to dust. Then I blink, and everyone is gone, and I'm alone on a pile of rubble.

My heart beats fast and I try to calm down, but my mind is running in a million different directions. Maybe it's the realization that we've clinched the playoffs and we're about to give it our best and make this the best season. Or maybe it's the stress of my performance, because I've felt off ever since Robbie suddenly retired at the beginning of the month—like I'm missing a limb.

I asked him to reconsider, mostly because we were so close to the end of the season, but also because I didn't want to lose one of my best friends. Without him as captain, I feel like we might drift.

But in the end, Robbie wanted to focus on his new passion project—the youth foundation nonprofit—and spend more time with Olivia, helping her through her injury and recovery.

I close my eyes tight and try to regulate my breathing, but it still comes out in stuttering waves. A cold hand on my naked back jolts me and I turn to face her.

Alice squints at me, her blond hair fanned out on my pillow, her thumb brushing back and forth on my back. "J, what's wrong?" she asks, sitting up and placing her head on my shoulder.

I relax a bit, pulling her into my embrace. "Just a bad dream. I'm sorry I woke you," I say, kissing her forehead and running my fingers through her wavy mussed-up hair.

Ever since we got back from the cabin, our time together has exponentially increased. Alice has been at my apartment every night, except when I was gone for away games. We still have not put a label on what this is, but it's clear that we're not anywhere near being done with each other.

That night at the hospital, as we were waiting for Robbie and Olivia, I realized that all I wanted was to hold her and be close to her. I just wish I didn't live in constant anxiety about how her family will react when they find out about us.

Hugging her closer, I inhale the faint scent of her coconut shampoo and let our bodies fall back against the mattress. "Do you want to talk about it?" she whispers against my shoulder, in the same spot she's burrowed herself every night she's been at my apartment. She fits so effortlessly into my arms, and I don't know what to do with that information.

"I won't be able to fall asleep if I think about it too hard." I sigh and hold her closer to me. Her hand lands on my collarbone and she rubs her thumb in soothing circles.

"Okay, J," she mumbles, and relaxes in my arms, falling back asleep almost instantly. I'm jealous. I wish I could shut off my brain like that.

I spend the rest of the night overthinking everything.

What are Alice and I doing? Do we have a future together?

Am I going to get my shit together before the playoffs start? Or will I fail everyone?

MY ALARM GOES off and Alice jumps off me, eyes wide and hair askew. I smile fondly at her rumpled state and reach over to silence my phone.

"Shit, what time is it?" she asks, trying to untangle herself from my sheets and almost falling off the bed in the process. I catch her around the middle before she can face plant and pull her back into my arms, kissing her.

"It's 6:30 a.m. You still have plenty of time before you need to get to work," I say, knowing she has to get going soon and get back to teaching middle schoolers.

"I badly need a shower, someone made a mess of me last night," she mumbles against my jaw, and I smirk.

"Maybe you should think twice before enticing me with

that jersey," I retort, and she laughs, blue eyes sparkling with mischief.

"Enticing, huh?" she asks, eyebrow quirked, her hand trailing down my stomach, and grabbing my cock through my boxer briefs. It twitches at her touch, but I pull her hand back. If we have a repeat of last night, she'll definitely be late.

"Very," I say, and press one more kiss against her lips before jumping off the bed and starting up the shower.

Alice follows me inside the bathroom, rubbing the sleep away from her eyes, my T-shirt she's wearing riding high on her creamy thighs.

Maybe we do have time for a quick round—

The phone rings and I frown. Alice startles and places a hand on her heart. "That scared me. Who is calling so early?" she says.

"No idea, I'll check it out and join you in a second," I say, pressing another kiss to the top of her head.

My heart drops when I see Coach Brian's name on my phone. Our last game of the season is tonight, and we've already clinched a spot in the playoffs. What could he possibly be calling about?

ALICE

I'M SORE *EVERYWHERE*. Not that I'm complaining about it. When I showed up to Jordan's apartment last night in nothing but his jersey and a trench coat on top, I didn't expect him to lose his mind over it, bend me over the couch, and fuck me senseless. And when I could barely walk, he carried me to the bedroom, grabbed my overnight bag from the car, and spent an indecent amount of time going down on me, apologizing with his tongue.

This past month has felt surreal. I let the hot water spray over my skin and smile as I think about the little bubble we've been under since coming back from the cabin. Maybe it's wishful thinking, but I think all my dreams might be coming true. I've carried a torch for Jordan for so long, and now that I finally have him, I can't imagine letting him go.

"J?" I call out, realizing it's been a while and he hasn't joined me. I turn the shower off and step out onto the mat, grabbing a clean towel off the hook. I don't bother to wrap one around my hair, but instead I walk back into the bedroom, seeing what the holdup is.

"Jordan?" I ask, but I don't get an answer. His phone is gone from the nightstand so maybe he's taking a call somewhere else. Curiosity gets the best of me, and I step out into the living room.

There's nothing here except for the jersey on the couch and the sound of complete and utter silence. When I look for Jordan's car keys on the hook by the door, I don't find them.

He's gone.

THE CLASS BELL rings while I'm in the middle of explaining to Joe, one of my sixth-grade students, why he needs to improve his writing skills, and more specifically why he can't get away with "The book was fire" as his literary analysis for *The Hobbit*.

I sigh and pinch the bridge of my nose as the little shit

smirks at me and throws his backpack over one shoulder. "Great talk everyone, happy to continue this discussion next time," I mumble, and plaster on a smile for the rest of my class.

There's always that one kid—smart as a whip but determined to make the teacher's life a living hell. That's Joe. He could be so much more if he applied himself, but instead he chooses to spend his time making wise-ass remarks and avoiding any conversation about his home life. Not that I try too hard to pester him, after all, it's not my job to be his counselor. But it still nags at me that I haven't been able to get through to him all year.

I grab my phone from my purse and check to see if Jordan called or texted while I was busy, but there's *still* nothing. I pull my bottom lip between my teeth and gnaw at it in concern. What could have been so important that he had to run out of his own apartment so early in the morning?

And why is he avoiding me?

I shake off the uneasy feeling. I'm sure it's fine, it's nothing bad. If something had happened with his sister or parents, I would have found out by now, either from him or my own family. It's probably something hockey related.

Taking a sip of my iced brown sugar latte, I try to focus my attention on my next group of students, ready to talk about *The Hobbit* all over again. Good thing it's one of my favorite books.

A knock at the door has me spinning towards it, my hand flying to my chest.

"Didn't mean to startle you," Megan says, taking a few steps forward. I've known Megan since I started working as a substitute English teacher at Rowen Elementary last year. We both started on the same day, and we struck up a friendship pretty quickly, being the youngest two on the teacher roster.

"Sorry, I'm just jumpy today," I say, tucking my hair behind my ear nervously. I don't have a lot of female friends outside of Olivia, and while I adore her to pieces, we're not yet at that level in our friendship to share *everything*. She's very perceptive and guessed that I had a crush on Jordan, but I haven't told her yet about the cabin and how we've been sneaking around this past month. I especially didn't want to bother her as she's recovering from her nasty injury on the ice.

Megan, on the other hand, is a great listener. She's already heard me pining after Jordan countless times, and maybe I just need to tell someone, anyone, that we're finally together.

"Jordan and I finally took the next step," I say vaguely, rolling my lips inward and swaying from side to side.

Megan's pale blond eyebrows fly up her forehead as she says, "Really?"

"Yes," I squeak out, followed by a bunch of word vomit. "We went to the cabin a month ago, and he caught me reading smut and then he read some of it and I thought he was gonna make fun of me, but he was actually really cute and sexy about it, and I admitted that I still have a crush on him, and then he kissed me. And then we did a lot more than kissing, and when we got back, it's just been nonstop. I mean, I knew he was gonna be good in bed, but *hot damn*, the man has stamina. And last night was so unbelievably perfect, but then he got a call this morning and I haven't seen or spoken to him since, and I'm getting a little worried."

Megan wraps me in a gentle hug, and I relax against

her. She towers over me, as she's nearly six feet tall, and when she pulls back, she cups my head with both hands.

"I'm so happy for you. I know you've carried a torch for him for so many years, I bet it feels nice to give in and explore this new thing. Just—be careful, okay?"

"We use protection," I say. "Well, mostly."

Megan chokes on a laugh and her ring-clad fingers land on my shoulders, shaking me a little. "I meant be careful with your heart and feelings, but good to know, you little nympho."

"I am careful," I say, a touch defensively.

"Okay," Megan nods, a small dimple popping in her angular face.

"Seriously," I say, peeking around her, making sure no kids are in sight. "I've been in love with him since I was seventeen, I think I know my own feelings."

"I'm not saying you don't. Just—" She hesitates briefly, tilting her head in thought. "You, my friend, like to wear your heart on your sleeve and I just don't want anyone to take advantage of that. I'm sure Jordan is lovely, and I want you both to be happy. Just make sure you two are on the same page about what this is."

I ponder her advice, knowing she's never led me astray, and I realize that she does have a point. Jordan has never brought up the fact that we are a couple now. He hasn't labeled us in any way, not even as a hookup.

"I guess you're right," I say, taking a seat and taking one more look at my black phone screen before the bell goes off again.

"Al, I love you. I'm sure everything is fine, and I'm glad you finally got your dream guy. I can't wait to meet him," Megan says, retreating to the door and giving me a wink.

Right. If only my dream guy would answer the phone, I would love to talk about where we stand.

CHAPTER 13

Three Years Ago – April

JORDAN

I BLINK BACK tears and push myself to run another mile. I've done nothing but run myself into the ground on this treadmill all morning, ever since Coach Brian called to give me the news.

I'm being traded to another AHL team in Texas.

Traded.

I don't know what I'm supposed to feel, but I'm numb to it all. It doesn't feel real. It can't be real. Not when I've given this team everything for the last seven years. The Manticores have been my home since that day when I showed up to training camp late and scared shitless of my own future. If it hadn't been for Alex and Robbie, who knows where I would have ended up. They were like my brothers—we did everything together, from working out, to going to brunch together, to spending late summer nights at the cabin around a fire pit.

It was a shock to learn that Alex requested a trade and followed his girlfriend to Quebec, but at least I still had Robbie. And then Eli and Ash came along, and they quickly wormed their way into my life too. But now, Robbie's retired, and I'm getting traded, and everything is such a fucking mess. I can't help but ask myself what happened? How did I get here?

I used to be the one to get called up to the NHL whenever there was a need, but not this year. I've made some good defensive moves, but my game has been off. I'm not at my best, and somehow I lost track of that.

Is it my anxiety?

Is it the stress?

Is it Alice?

I wince at that last thought and press the cooldown button on the treadmill. I shut my eyes tight and try not to think about the fact that I'll have to confront her at some point today and break the news.

I can't help but feel like I've failed everyone—my friends and the team for not being a good enough player to the point they had to trade me; Alice, for starting something only for us to have to call it quits; and myself, for not giving it my all.

The cold shower at the gym is eye-opening, but I choose to wallow in my self-pity a moment longer. I know exactly how I got here. *I wasn't good enough.*

And I can't keep dwelling on the past. I need to look forward and move on. As soon as I'm out of the gym and in my car, I call my sister and tell her everything.

"Jordan, honey. Hold on a minute, what do you mean

you want to leave tomorrow?" she says gently, like I'm a spooked animal.

"I can't do it, Tangy. I can't stick around until next season, watching my friends go on without me, while I have nothing left here."

"Ouch, that's not fair. You have me," she says, and I can hear the sadness in her voice. I'm hurting her too, but I can't fucking stay another minute here. "You have your nieces who love you and look up to you. And what about Alice?"

I close my eyes and rest my head against the steering wheel. I don't want to think about Alice right now.

"She won't want to be with a loser who's about to move thousands of miles away."

"You don't know that," Tangela says in a frustrated voice. She's always so softspoken and kind that I'm taken aback by her tone.

"Look," I say, swallowing hard. "This is my decision. I need to do what's best for me and right now that means getting on a plane to Texas and finding a place to live." Maybe that makes me a coward, but the truth is, I don't want to face any of it. I'm not strong enough to handle it.

"You'll regret it, little brother."

"Maybe," I whisper. "Please don't tell anyone. I'll handle the goodbyes myself," I say, and hang up.

ALICE

BY THE TIME I get to my apartment, I've started to worry. I haven't heard anything from Jordan or the rest of my family when I texted the group chat.

My phone chimes and I rush to get it out, dropping a bag of groceries on the floor of my kitchen.

"Shit," I mumble, taking inventory of the key limes that are rolling around. Those are supposed to go in a pie, not on the floor.

When I look back at my phone, I see it's a text from Olivia.

> OLIVIA
>
> How are you holding up?

I frown. What is she talking about? I start typing back a response but Jordan's caller ID pops up on my screen. I quickly swipe to answer and bring the phone between my ear and shoulder, crouching down to pick up the limes.

"Hello?"

"Hey. I'm downstairs. Can you buzz me in?" Jordan says in a flat voice, and I instantly know something bad has happened.

"Yeah. Are you okay? I've been worried, you didn't answer me all day and—"

"I'm fine," he says. It's short and clipped and my heart stutters. Is he mad at me?

Abandoning the limes, I make it to the front door and buzz him in, waiting with the front door open and the phone still at my ear. The line goes silent, and I slowly blink at it. What is happening right now?

Jordan makes it up the stairs and walks towards me with a quick stride, but it's all wrong. He doesn't wear the smile I got so used to the past month, the one that says he's happy to see me. And he definitely doesn't greet me with a scorching kiss and his hands all over me. In fact, he avoids my gaze altogether and walks past me into the apartment.

I swallow the lump in my throat and slowly close the door, taking my time to turn around and face him.

"Have you heard yet?" he asks, staring at my plush pink carpet.

"Heard what, J? What is going on?"

Jordan purses his lips and shakes his head, and I can't tell if he's irritated with me or with himself.

"I'm leaving," he says, matter-of-fact.

I sigh, having no goddamn clue what he's talking about. "Okay, like on a trip? Don't you have some time until the playoffs start?" I ask, confused.

"No. *Fuck*," he says, his deep voice booming in the quiet of my apartment. "I'm being traded."

I blink and shake my head, not certain I heard him right. Did he just say *traded*?

"I'm moving to Texas. Tomorrow," he repeats, more firmly this time.

My breath comes out in a rush, and I try to speak, but words fail me. I'm like a fish out of water. Jordan paces the floor of my apartment, his shoulders broad and imposing, his hands planted on his hips. I'd laugh if it wasn't for the fact he just told me he's leaving.

"Okay, so you're getting traded," I say, nodding to myself, making sense of it all. I could get another teaching job somewhere else. I could go with him. Unless ...

"Why didn't you tell me this morning when you got the call?" I ask, crossing my hands over my chest. That must have been what got him so freaked out he had to leave his own place.

"What?" he looks at me, bewildered.

"Why did you wait all day to tell me?" I ask stubbornly, already knowing the answer, but needing him to say it.

"Because," he groans impatiently, "I had just found out I'm moving thirteen hundred miles away. I needed to process and find a way to—" He stops, biting his cheek.

There it is.

"To what?" I ask, blinking back tears, but not backing down from this challenge. He should have told me sooner, damn it.

"To tell you."

"And you think that distance matters to me?" I say with a shaky smile, taking a step forward. "It doesn't. I think we can make this work."

"Make what work?" he asks, incredulous, pinning me with his dark brown eyes. There's none of his usual kindness showing now, just pure anger. "Alice, we're not *together*!"

I instantly recoil, my face falling as I drop my arms from my chest. I try not to let my tears fall but my lip trembles and everything is blurry now anyway.

"Do you mean that?" I ask in a small voice.

Jordan pauses and my heart soars. He's just angry about the trade, he didn't mean it, he—

"Yes."

His resolute answer feels like a punch in the stomach, and it takes everything in me not to fall to my knees and cry. I fiddle with the sleeves of my cardigan and use it to wipe the tears off my face.

"Then leave," I manage to say in a steady voice.

"Alice," he tries to say, taking a step towards me. "This is for the best. Let's not make this complicated and messy over a crush."

A crush.

That's all I am to him. After *everything*. I'm fucking

furious at him for making me fall head over heels in love only to leave me behind.

His expression shutters when he sees my face, hot tears still falling. But I don't give him a chance to say anything else.

"I said, leave."

PART 2
IF I GO, I'M GOIN'

CHAPTER 14

Three Years Ago – November

JORDAN

FOR THE FIRST time in my life, I spend Thanksgiving alone. The walls of my small studio apartment in Austin are bare as I haven't bothered to decorate or buy any furniture besides the essentials. I've lived here for seven months now, and this place still doesn't feel like my new home.

I hate everything about this place—the sweltering heat, the traffic, the fact that I have no friends. I stab around at the store-bought mashed potatoes and rotisserie chicken on my plate, but I quickly give up on my meal. Nothing tastes the same as the Elliots' cooking. I even miss Robbie's focaccia, for fuck's sake.

I'm sick of the quiet in this apartment and I'm sick of being lonely. I didn't realize how hard things would get once I moved away. I knew I was putting distance between myself and everyone else, but I figured I'd be okay, that maybe I'd make some friends during the off season. Instead, I joined a team of hotheaded assholes, none of whom have bothered to connect with me. Training camp was gruesome, but my game has been better than last season, and I even got called up to play for Dallas once so far.

And yet, I don't feel any sense of fulfillment. Not in my career or my personal life. I just feel ... miserable.

Tangela was right, I do regret leaving Grand Marquee in April. I should have stayed and supported my friends as they made it to the Calder Cup playoffs. When I found out they were in the finals, I bought a ticket to the last game and flew into town without telling anyone. It was a fucking amazing game and Ash and Eli crushed it, bringing home the Cup. I should have stayed and told them how proud I was of them.

I should have offered to help Robbie and Alex with the nonprofit they started after Robbie retired and Alex moved back to Grand Marquee. I'm sure they wouldn't have turned me down. I should have spent more time with my sister and my nieces. And most importantly, I shouldn't have lied to Alice.

Every time I think about her, I can't stop seeing the hurt and tears and pain I caused her by brushing us off as nothing but a crush. I didn't want to say it, but I just couldn't stand the way she was looking at me. Like she believed in me, like she'd follow me if I asked—like I was worth it.

I wasn't, and I didn't deserve her dedication. So I ended it. And I regret that the most. We could have had more time to figure things out. We could have stayed friends.

My phone buzzes with a notification and I open the

group chat that I'm still a part of but rarely respond to nowadays.

> **ROBBIE**
> Happy Thanksgiving!

I know Robbie's message is aimed at me, but I don't respond. A few minutes later, a picture comes through of the whole family. Robbie's parents are standing behind the couch, one holding Katie, the other holding Lory. Both my nieces are smiling brightly and my heart hurts with how much I miss them. Even though Tangela and Michael took a trip here this summer, a week wasn't enough time to spend with them.

My friends look cozy sitting together on the couch, Ash's arm around Eli's shoulder. I zoom in on Ash's face and wince at the massive black eye he's sporting. The game last night must have been intense. Next to him, Alice is sitting with her knees pulled up, an open book in her lap. I smile at the sight and take a screenshot of the zoomed in picture of her. She looks so pretty with her hair in a messy bun and wearing a sweatshirt with a pumpkin on it. *God, I miss her.*

Olivia is seated next to Alice and she's holding hands with Robbie, who is more preoccupied with watching her than the camera. It can't be easy for him to be back in Grand Marquee, working on the nonprofit all the time while Olivia is traveling all over the Midwest as a referee. I don't know how they do it—and look so happy doing it. Tangela and Michael are sitting on the floor, and he has his arms wrapped around her.

I should be there too.

I quickly close the message and look up the next flight to Grand Marquee. It's twice as expensive as usual and there are two layovers, but it should get me there by tomorrow. It's impulsive and stupid since I have to be back Sunday for a game, but I miss my family too much.

My duffel bag is packed in record time, and I take a cab to the airport. I text Tangela on the way too, since I'll need a place to stay for a couple nights.

JORDAN

> Making a quick trip home. Do you have an extra ticket to tomorrow night's Manticores game?

TANGELA

> Yay! I miss you, little brother. Michael is taking the girls to a movie tomorrow so there are spare tickets if you want them.

JORDAN

> Thanks. Don't tell anyone yet.

TANGELA

> You and your secrets...fine.

ALICE

ASH WAS on fire tonight as the Manticores won 4–1. It was strange to sit next to Robbie and Eli at a hockey game—every other time I've attended, they were on the ice.

The truth is, I haven't been to many hockey games since Jordan left. I came to the home playoffs because I wanted to support my boys, but this is my first game of the new season.

With Robbie being retired, and Eli currently being up at the NHL temporarily, Ash is the only one of the group that's left playing for the Manticores, and he doesn't actually care if I attend the games or not.

"I'm surprised by your choice in attire," Eli says as we wait by the players entrance for Ash and Olivia, who was a ref in tonight's game.

I swallow and look down at my #20 jersey. "I couldn't find my other ones," I mumble and cross my arms. Eli doesn't believe me, but that's okay. The truth is, ever since I moved into Eli's apartment as he got called up to Detroit as a backup goalie for two months, I haven't been able to find my hockey jerseys. I know they're in a box somewhere, and I destroyed my entire closet trying to find them tonight, but I couldn't.

The only reason I had Jordan's is because it was packed separately in my "things that remind me of him" labeled box. The one I try not to open under any circumstances, unless it's an emergency, like tonight, or when I get a little too wine drunk and cry about him until the early morning.

"What's going to happen now that Nadison got hurt again?" Robbie asks Eli, bringing up the reason for our friend's call to the NHL. During training camp two months ago, Nadison suffered a pretty nasty injury, taking him out for six to eight weeks. Lucky for Eli, he was called to step in. When Nadison came back from injury reserve two days ago, he got hurt again, but no details have been shared.

"Sounds like another six to eight weeks, from what I heard," Eli says, running a hand over his pale blond stubble. I sigh, feeling bad for Ash. I'm sure he was excited to get his boyfriend back.

"That's great," Robbie says. "For you, of course. Sucks for Nadison."

I chuckle. "Smooth."

"Does Ash know yet?"

"Yes," Eli says, disappointment written all over his face. He doesn't want to be apart from Ash. I know how he feels.

Though he's not a touchy-feely person, I wrap my arms around Eli's waist anyway in a tight hug. He sighs and hugs me back, resting his head on top of mine. "Thanks, *lapsi*."

I roll my eyes at his nickname for me and squeeze him even tighter. Eli just laughs and a throat clears behind us.

"Trying to make a move on my man, Al?" Ash says low enough for just us to hear and I punch his arm. "Ow, what was that for?"

"Stop being an idiot," I say.

"You're just ticked cuz I know you have a thing for hockey players."

"Ash, seriously," I say more firmly.

"Wait, what do you mean?" Robbie says, eyes narrowed on Ash.

The dumbass just smirks and shrugs.

"Al, what does he mean?" Robbie asks again, focusing his blue eyes on me this time.

"Nothing, I don't know," I say, flustered. I really don't want to think, let alone talk about Jordan. I spot Olivia coming our way and I make my way to her, wrapping her in a hug, whispering, "Please save me, they're teasing me about being into hockey players."

Her deep laugh calms my nerves and she pats my back in acknowledgment. "I'm starving," she says loudly for the guys to hear. "Can we get some food now?"

The Arcadian is packed, but our reserved table is nestled at the back of the restaurant, by the kitchen. We all order our favorite burgers and appetizers and catch Eli up on the latest news. Robbie is planning a fundraiser over the holidays and Ash and Eli immediately respond by wanting to donate signed items.

"Can I donate one of those giant cardboard cutouts of myself?" Ash mumbles through a bite of his sandwich and we all look at him with incredulous expressions on our faces.

"What?" he asks, swallowing.

"Why do you have a giant cardboard cutout of yourself?" Robbie asks, his eyes lighting up with amusement.

Eli reaches over and wipes aioli off the corner of Ash's mouth with his thumb. The two of them are trying to keep their relationship under wraps so we're all a bit slack-jawed in the face of their PDA. When he realizes we're all staring, Eli blushes and leans back in his chair.

"I don't have one, but it would be a good reason to get it," Ash says, wiping his mouth with a napkin and looking at his boyfriend adoringly.

"Sure, man. If you can order a cardboard cutout of yourself and sign it, you can donate it to the auction," Robbie says on a laugh.

"Challenge accepted." Ash smirks and wiggles his eyebrows.

I laugh and joke, "While you're at it, can you get me one too? I could use it for my bookish social media posts."

I don't get a reply, and when I look in the direction everyone else is staring, I see Tangela approaching the bar.

Robbie looks around, confused. "That's weird, Michael isn't here tonight. He said he was taking the girls to a movie."

"Maybe she's just grabbing some food," I say, frowning.

"But would she drive twenty minutes away just for some food?" Olivia asks.

"No, that's weird," Robbie says. "Maybe I should go talk to her and see—"

He stops, halfway out of his seat and stares over at the bar, mouth open. I follow his line of sight and suck in a sharp breath.

What is *he* doing here?

I look around the table and see everyone's confusion and disappointment mirrors my own. He didn't tell anyone he was visiting.

Robbie puts his head in his hands and Olivia rubs his back, whispering, "Do you want to go over and talk to them?"

He shakes his head no, but Ash says, "Fuck that, he owes us at least one fucking conversation." The chair scrapes loudly on the floor, and before Eli can stop him, Ash is across the room tapping Jordan on the shoulder.

My heart beats wildly, but I force my attention to my phone. I don't need this. Not now. Not when I'm wearing his goddamn jersey.

But fuck, my eyes betray me anyway, glancing up at him. He looks so good in a light green cable-knit sweater. Damn him.

CHAPTER 15

Three Years Ago – November

JORDAN

WHEN I TURN AROUND, I'm met with a very angry looking Ash. My eyes widen as I spot the rest of the group at the table. I didn't expect them to be here.

"Ash—"

"No, Jordan. What the actual fuck, man? You don't call or text back for months, and now you're back in town and you don't even tell us? Why weren't you at Thanksgiving?"

I realize that we're probably making a scene and that I should table this conversation for another time, but my gaze catches Alice and the jersey she's wearing. My old jersey. My stomach churns with the feeling of guilt and hurt and I don't know if I'd rather throw up or cry over the sight of her right now. Does it mean anything that she's wearing it? Does she still care about me? Or has she moved on?

I take an involuntary step forward. The thought of her with anyone else makes me irrationally angry and I take a deep breath, cracking my knuckles.

Ash blocks my path and murmurs, "Don't even think about it."

I finally look back at him and nod in understanding. "I'm sorry, Ash. You're right, I've been a really shitty friend."

Looking down at my feet, I try to reign in this feeling of being miserable—of feeling sorry for myself.

"I've been dealing with a lot, honestly, and that shouldn't be an excuse, but I really needed to focus on my mental health."

"Oh, okay," Ash says, some of his ire fading. "Look man, I know how that is, and I get it, truly. Just—we're here for you, even though you ditched us for Texas."

I laugh and push gently on his shoulder. "Yeah, like that was my choice."

"I know, I'm sorry. If it's worth anything, our defense kinda sucks without you, man."

"Yeah, that'll make me sleep better at night," I say with a snort.

"Do you wanna join us?" Ash asks tentatively.

I look back at Tangy and she nods at me, already grabbing her purse. "I'll see you tomorrow for brunch," she says, giving me a quick hug.

"Well, come on," Ash says, smiling over at the table.

I blow out a breath and follow behind him. For a moment, everyone is silent and I dread the anxiety and awkwardness that my actions have led to. But then Eli stands up and offers me his hand to shake.

I swallow the knot in my throat and take it, pulling him into a hug. He grunts out a laugh and hugs me back.

Robbie follows suit and hugs me. "Good to see you, man."

"Yeah, you too," I manage to say. It's an understatement. Even if things are tense right now, seeing him is still a relief. I've missed him more than I expected.

I finally let him go and I wrap Olivia in a quick hug. She gives me a small smile and sits back next to Alice.

Seeing her up close has my stomach twisted up in knots. She's so pretty, and I want her to smile at me like she used to. Before I fucked everything up.

"Hey, Al," I say, taking a tentative step towards her.

"Hey," she says, giving me a wave and returning to her phone, all but ignoring me. I deserve it, I do. But it still fucking hurts.

Eli brings me a chair and I move to sit between him and Alice. My shoulder brushes hers as I readjust my chair and I feel her stiffen next to me. That's not the kind of reaction I ever want to draw from her, so I lean back as far as I can without making it obvious I'm giving her space.

The conversation picks back up and besides the fact that Alice so clearly hates me now, it feels like I've never left, like not much has changed. Except, I watch as Eli puts his arm around Ash's shoulder and whispers something in his ear. Ash smiles and puts his hand on Eli's thigh, and I can't help but stare at them, impressed that they actually acted on their feelings.

A smile takes over my face and I say, "You two finally figured it out, huh?"

"What do you mean 'finally'?" Ash says, indignant.

"Please, you two were always crushing on each other, it was really obvious."

"Says the most oblivious guy ever," Alice mutters loud enough for the whole table to hear.

When no one says anything for a beat, she lifts her eyes up from her phone and glances at me. I try to catch her meaning, but she quickly glances back away from me and I frown.

As Olivia excuses herself for being tired, she offers Alice a ride home. Robbie stands up too and the three of them are ready to head out.

"Jordan, how long are you in town?" he asks me.

"I head back on Sunday."

"How about you come over for dinner tomorrow? Ash, you're invited too."

"Gee, thanks for the afterthought, grandpa," Ash says.

I look between Robbie and Olivia who are smiling at me and glance at Alice. She still won't fully look over at me and my shoulders drop in defeat. She likely won't attend this dinner, so what the hell.

"Sure, that would be nice."

"Great, we'll see you then," Olivia says. They say goodnight and head out, and I'm left staring after Alice ... and my last name embroidered on the back of her jersey.

Ash and Eli catch me up on the last few months and tell me the story of how they got together and their fateful trip to Finland. I'm happy for them and I do my best to tell them about Texas without giving away how much I hate it there.

By the end of the night, I'm back in my sister's guest house, all alone once more, thinking about ways I could make things right by Alice. I should explain or apologize at least. Would she even forgive me?

ALICE

. . .

I TRIED to get out of dinner, I really, really did. But I already skipped on the tree farm tradition, knowing that Jordan was going to join. And when Robbie spent the whole morning chopping down trees for the family and bringing one to my apartment, setting it up in the stand for me, well —I couldn't say no to my favorite brother.

So I threw on my favorite sweater dress, a green one with flowy sleeves that makes me look like I have a skinny waist and a perky ass, and I took extra time to curl my hair and do my make-up. I told myself I was dressing up for me, but in truth, I just want to show Jordan what he's missing out on. If he's going to just show back up in our lives unexpectedly, the least he can do is suffer a little.

I sing along to one of the carols—us Elliots are always starting Christmas celebrations right after Thanksgiving— and add some decorations to Robbie's living room. I freeze at the sound of the doorbell and will my nerves to go away.

What right does he have to make me nervous? I scoff to myself and shake myself out, my sleeves billowing with the movement. *Get it together, Al.*

"You okay?" Olivia asks, walking over to me as Robbie heads for the front door. She's wearing a red sweater with a fluffy white and black Santa hat on it, and I smile at how quickly she embraced our crazy ass traditions.

"Yeah, better now that I'm seeing you in this sweater. I need to take a picture."

"Ugh, you're the worst." She laughs and smacks my shoulder lightly. I snap a quick picture and send it to the group chat.

"What do we want to start with? Dinner? Drinks?" Robbie says, walking up to us, Jordan trailing close behind. My eyes land on his chest and the expensive-looking sweater he's wearing. It's a nice charcoal gray color and it fits him just right, showing off his broad chest and perfect biceps.

I grit my teeth. Couldn't he wear sweats for once? An image flashes in my mind of the time he wore nothing but sweats at the cabin after we went into the sauna together and how good he looked with sweat gleaming down his— nope, not going there. I make a beeline for the kitchen counter, pouring myself some orange juice and champagne in a flute.

Robbie comes over and says, "Wait, I have just the thing to make that perfect." He opens the fridge and takes out a cup of cranberries, dropping one in my drink, then carefully placing a slice of orange on the lip of my glass.

I raise my eyebrows at my brother as I watch him proudly admire my drink. "Wow, are you switching careers once more? Going into mixology now?"

"Oh, shut it. You know you like it," he says, making one for himself and clinking glasses with me.

Olivia comes over and checks on the pot roast in the oven. The whole place smells incredible and if it weren't for the giant six foot three elephant in the room, I would actually be excited to hang out with my favorite people. But my stomach flutters and I can feel Jordan's eyes on the side of my face from where he came over to stand by me.

I just wish Ash could get here already. He always has something random to talk about and would make this awkward silence dissipate.

"When's Ash coming?" I ask, taking another drink and rubbing the side of my neck, willing Jordan's gaze to land somewhere else. I feel like he might set me on fire with his looks alone.

"He's not," Robbie says, putting on oven mitts to take the food out.

The mimosa tastes bitter all of a sudden. How am I supposed to make it through dinner now?

"Oh, is he okay?" Jordan asks, gripping the counter.

"Yeah, he got called up to play in Detroit tonight. Sorry, I forgot to mention it," Robbie says, placing the pot roast on a board in the center of the kitchen island, followed by the potatoes and honeyed carrots.

"That's amazing," Jordan says, reaching for a beer and pouring it in a glass.

"I'm so excited for him, I can't wait to see him on TV," Olivia says, and smiles at me. Our eyes hold for a second and I'm sure she can sense my panic about this being essentially a double date. She takes in a deep breath and lets it out, never taking her eyes off me. I mirror her and do the same, relaxing a bit, knowing she's got my back.

Out of everyone in our group, Olivia is the only one that knows the full extent of what happened between me and Jordan. Eli and Ash have hinted at knowing bits and pieces, or at least that they assume something happened that week at the cabin, but Robbie has been pretty oblivious.

Dinner is thankfully pretty quiet as we talk about the upcoming holidays and plans. Robbie fills us in on the progress for his nonprofit, Blue Line Brigade, and talks about how grateful he is that Alex and Malia moved back to Grand Marquee last year and that they decided to start the nonprofit.

I briefly mention that teaching is going well still and that my bookish social media account continues to grow. Olivia tells us how excited she is to have her grandma move to Grand Marquee to have the last member of her family closer.

Unsurprisingly, Jordan plans to be in Texas over

Christmas and New Years, but he hints at returning over the All Star break when we plan to take a cabin trip.

I take another sip of my drink, trying to erase all thoughts of the cabin from my mind. I haven't been there since two months ago, when we all went up to visit Ash and Eli at training camp. That was the first time we found out they were in a relationship as we literally caught them kissing in the backyard.

I squeeze my eyes tight, hiding them from view. *Stop thinking about that week. Stop thinking about his hands on you. Just stop.*

"Al, everything okay?" my brother asks.

"Yep," I lie. "The mimosas are getting to me, I should go sit on the couch," I say, standing and moving to the living room, picking Beans up on the way, plopping the chunky little black cat in my lap. He squirms for a moment, but then fully sits down and starts to purr. I give him gentle pets on his fluffy little head and he tips his nose up, mouth open in satisfaction.

I smile and lean back, letting my hands roam over his fur. The couch dips next to me and I square my shoulders. Looking back to the kitchen, I don't see Robbie or Olivia.

"They went to take the trash out and turn on the Christmas lights," Jordan supplies, and I nod, deciding that's enough of an answer.

"Can we talk?" he asks after a few minutes of silence.

I debate giving him the silent treatment, but I'm better than that. I can handle this as a mature adult. "There's nothing to talk about."

"Sure there is," he says, almost pleading. I turn my head, finally looking at him head-on, and find that he's already watching me, a mixture of regret and sadness in his brown eyes. Whatever—he's the one who hurt *me*, he's the one who left.

I hold his gaze, keeping any emotion off my face. "No, there's really not."

He sighs in frustration and a muscle in his jaw ticks. "Al, I'm so—"

"Don't," I snap, spooking the cat, who jumps off my lap and runs to his cat tree. "Can you just keep pretending like nothing happened? It's what you've been doing this whole time, cutting everyone off."

Jordan winces and shakes his head, "Will you let me apologize, at least? Or explain."

I tilt my head, pondering it for a second. "No, I don't think I will. I think you said precisely what you needed to that night and then your actions and disappearance from our lives spoke the rest."

"That's not fair," he says, pinching the bridge of his nose.

His wish for a heart-to-heart is here a little too late and I'm pissed that he would corner me like this when he clearly could tell I didn't want anything to do with him. "No, Jordan. You know what's not fair? It's not fair that you left me like I was *nothing*. I wasn't even worth a full explanation from you. It's not fair that you treated me like garbage and didn't even talk to me about your issues or decisions. I was just an afterthought at the end of the day.

"It's not fair that you got to walk away with a clean slate. And it's definitely not fair that you're back now and want to act like none of that happened—like you didn't break my heart." My voice wobbles on the last word and I wipe the single tear that escapes me. Jordan looks at me, mouth open like he might respond. But he doesn't. His eyes shine with tears, and my first reaction is to console him. Apologize for being so harsh.

Fuck that. I can't do that when I'm still so fucking angry about his actions.

"Al," he says in a hoarse voice.

"Let's just get through the rest of tonight so we can get back to our own lives and only interact when we absolutely need to. Okay?"

He doesn't respond, but when Robbie and Olivia come back inside, he moves to the chair as we settle in to watch Eli and Ash play against Boston.

CHAPTER 16

Two Years Ago – June

JORDAN

"THIS IS A REALLY STUPID IDEA," Ash tells me as we get ready for the rehearsal dinner. I fix the dusty pink tie around his neck and narrow my eyes at him. He might be right, but I'm not backing down.

"It'll be fine. If she wants to go out of her way to avoid me, so be it. But I'm not going to make it easier," I mumble.

Ash sighs and fidgets with the sleeves of his shirt, rolling them up to expose his forearm tattoo. "Can you two just get along? You already bickered over Christmas," he says, looking at me disapprovingly.

"That's because she brought some random date and he was a dickhead."

"True, but you didn't have to crush the guy so hard at

Uno. And what about the All Star break?" he counters, and I cross my arms over my chest.

"What about it?"

"You guys turned everything into a competition that week. Board games, pond hockey, even snowboarding. To be honest, man, you were both kind of annoying."

"Yeah, well. She's the one that won't accept my apology. I've tried to make things right but she's stubborn," I say morosely.

"Pot, meet kettle," Ash scoffs, sitting on the couch to put his shoes on. "You did the same thing over Easter too. I just —I don't want you guys to ruin this weekend. Robbie and Olivia don't deserve that."

My shoulders slump and I sit next to him, sinking into the couch. I rub both hands over my face and groan. "I know, I swear I'm not trying to be difficult. I'm just frustrated that she won't talk to me."

Ash leans forward and clasps his hands, resting his forearms on his knees. "That's tough, and I get it. I would be heartbroken and mad too if Eli never wanted anything to do with me after I fucked up." He looks over at me with keen blue eyes and I can't believe I'm getting sage advice from Ash. "I just think this particular weekend might be the right time to let it go," he says.

I swallow, not wanting to admit that he's right. I nod, but deep down the truth is that I don't want to let *her* go.

"There you are," Eli says, walking into the living room, dressed in black slacks, the same white button up that all of us are wearing, but wearing a dusty blue tie, indicating he's part of Robbie's wedding party. I pull at my matching one, loosening it up a bit.

"Here I am," Ash says with a smirk, lifting up on his knees and pulling Eli down by his tie. They meet in a kiss over the back of the couch, and I check my phone just to give them some privacy. With all of us bunking up at the cabin, there's not much of that to go around.

"You look good in pink," Eli tells Ash, running his hand down the fabric of the tie. His own tattoo of a sailboat peeks out of his sleeve and I smile at these two idiots, happy they got their shit together enough to admit they're in this for the long haul. I wouldn't be surprised if they decided to tie the knot next.

"Is everyone ready?" Robbie asks from the hallway, fixing up his green shirt, opting to go without a tie.

"How come you don't have to wear one?" Ash asks, frowning.

"Because I'm the groom."

"So?"

"Take it up with the boss," he says, chuckling.

"Olivia!!" Ash yells, and a moment later, Olivia steps out in a green dress that matches Robbie's shirt, her dark brown hair flowing in waves around her shoulders. She's barefoot and wearing very little makeup, but the smile on her face makes her look radiant.

Robbie gravitates toward her and kisses her forehead, whispering something none of us can hear. She blushes and squeezes his hand in acknowledgment.

"Do I have to wear a tie?" Ash whines, and she shrugs.

"That's not up to me," she says, returning to the hall and putting on a pair of sandals.

"Who is it up to then?" he asks, flailing his hands around like a toddler. We all chuckle and shake our heads, but then Alice comes down the stairs. She's wearing a pink dress and her dark blond hair is pinned half up in a bun, strands of hair falling around her face.

"Me," she says, smirking at Ash. "And that tie stays on no matter what."

"Ugh, you're no fun," he says.

"Well, someone has to keep you all in check," she says with too much sweetness in her voice. "And we need to head out or else we'll be late."

"Can I talk to you for a second?" I ask quietly as everyone heads out the door.

"Must we?" she sighs, turning back to look at me.

"Look, I just want to say that—" I start, thinking of ways to make her listen to me, that I'm not looking for a fight. But then I notice the circles under her eyes, and the way she's clutching the clipboard too tightly, and her bitten cuticles. All at once, I understand the pressure she's putting on herself and the anxiety she must be feeling, wanting this to go off without a hitch.

So instead, I smile and say, "You're doing an amazing job, and everyone is having a blast." Her mouth opens in surprise, but I keep going. "I know you don't trust me much right now, but if you need anything—a break or some help—let me know, okay?"

She looks at me for a long moment, her blue eyes assessing my honesty. Finally, she nods, her shoulders relaxing. "Thanks."

ALICE

WHEN OLIVIA ASKED me to help her with the wedding planning, I thought she meant picking out color schemes and going dress shopping. It turns out she needed a lot more help than that. Not that I'm complaining, I'm genuinely excited for her to officially be my sister-in-law and I cried big fat happy tears when she asked me to be her maid of honor.

Even though my mom helped find a venue in Traverse City and did the seating arrangements, seeing how we have a lot more of our side of the family coming, I still took on more than I could handle. I've been stressing out, wanting to make this wedding perfect for them. With Blue Line Brigade taking off and all but doubling the number of kids in attendance since last year, he didn't have much time to plan the wedding. And Olivia has been traveling around the country, reffing not only the regular season, but the playoffs too.

So it's been mostly me and my mom pouring over all the details and logistics. Olivia's grandma, who moved to a nursing home in Grand Marquee recently, has also helped a little, to the best of her abilities. She's the sweetest old lady, and she very much approved of the pink and blue color scheme we chose.

Thankfully the rehearsal dinner went swimmingly. Everyone remembered their positions and timing for walking down the aisle, and the dinner itself was delicious, being held on the patio of a restaurant overlooking the bay.

I expected Jordan to pester me, wanting to apologize again for how he left things between us. Maybe I've been too stubborn, not hearing him out, but at the same time, I'm just trying to protect my heart. Especially from him.

What I didn't expect was for him to be helpful. Not only did he tell me I was doing a great job, but he looked out for me throughout the night, bringing me water and appetizers. It was nice and thoughtful and infuriatingly kind of him. Especially since I've been giving him a hard time for the better part of the last year.

Ever since he reconnected with us after Thanksgiving, he's been more active in the group chat, sending us updates and video-calling Robbie more, which is especially annoying when I'm around and have to listen to them being besties.

I've done my best to ignore him every time he comes to visit, but it's hard. He's so damn sweet and likeable. And yet, I can't get over the fact that he just left me behind like I meant nothing.

I take another sip of my coffee as I look out at the lake and mentally prepare myself for today. I love weddings, but I'm never planning one again. Unless it's my own.

"Hey," Olivia says from behind me. I startle, having not heard the sliding door open. "Sorry, didn't mean to scare you."

"Oh, it's okay," I smile at her, patting the spot next to me. Olivia joins me and rubs sleep from her eyes, leaning her head on my shoulder.

"Last night was amazing. You've truly outdone yourself," she says, squeezing my knee. I place my coffee down next to me and wrap my arms around her.

"You deserve the world, my friend. I'll make sure today is perfect, don't you worry."

She chuckles. "I'm not worried. I do think you missed your calling; you'd make a terrific wedding planner."

I groan and let her go, grabbing my coffee once more. "You're lucky I love you. I was just thinking how I'm never doing this again, unless it's for my own wedding."

"Fair enough, it's a lot. I'm sorry we've put it all on you."

"Don't be. I'm glad you trusted me with this."

"Of course," she says. We sit in companionable silence and listen to the rustle of trees as we wave at the few neighbors out kayaking on the lake.

After a while, Olivia says, "Are you and Jordan okay?"

"I think so. I've been really harsh on him, but he was really helpful yesterday."

"Maybe it's time to hear him out," she says, her green eyes watching me closely for a reaction.

I sigh and nod. "Yeah, maybe."

WHEN I ARRIVE at the vineyard ahead of everyone else, the venue is a disaster of massive proportions.

Okay, maybe it's not *that* bad, but the balloons are not set up around the arch by the entryway like I was promised they would be. And the tables have nothing on them except for linen. All the decorations I brought over yesterday are still in bins. The venue coordinator was supposed to set them all up. The guestbook is missing too, and I'm on the verge of tears.

I hold my breath, trying not to panic. This will set me back long enough that people will arrive and the tables won't be ready. Nothing is going as expected, and I can't focus enough to formulate a plan. I need help.

I bite my lip and pull out my phone, calling the one person I've been doing my best to avoid this week. He did offer to help. I just hope he's up for the challenge.

"Al?" he asks in that deep voice of his.

"I need help," I cry, my tears giving in almost instantly.

Jordan patiently listens to my rambling and calmly says, "I'm on my way."

CHAPTER 17

Two Years Ago – June

JORDAN

WHEN WE GET to the event space at the winery, my first priority is to find Alice. The space has a few people setting up the stage and instruments for the band, but she's nowhere in sight.

"Okay, let's split up," I say, looking at the group of people I dragged out here early to help. All of us are in the wedding party, so I'm hoping we can wrap up in time for the pictures.

"What do we need to do?" Eli asks.

Shit, I don't know. She mentioned something about the decorations and balloons on the phone, but I really just need to find her.

"I'm assuming those balloons need to be tied to the

arch," Alex says, pointing at the balloons on the table and all the supplies laid out.

"We can take that task on," his wife, Malia, says, already marching over there.

"Okay, thanks," I blow out a breath, nodding appreciatively at Alex. He gives me an imperceptibly small smile back and follows his wife. Thank god. I wouldn't even know where to start on the balloon arch.

"There are boxes near that wall," Ash points out, taking off his backpack.

I frown at him. "Why did you bring a backpack?"

"For supplies," he says matter of fact, reaching in and pulling out three walkie-talkies.

Eli laughs and says, "Where did you even find those?"

"What? Alice had them in her room, I figured she wanted to use them." He hands me one and runs over to Alex, handing him the other.

He keeps the third one for himself and speaks into it. "Operation Save the Wedding is a go." Ash smirks at me, and Eli shakes his head at his boyfriend's antics. He presses the button once more and says, "This is the Love Guru. Over. And. Out."

We all laugh, and I let Ash and Eli handle the decorations while I go looking for Alice. I knock at the women's bathroom door and look around the entire building before finding her outside, sitting on the ground with her back against the building.

"Hey," I say gently, lowering myself next to her. Alice wipes her cheeks and looks at me, her bottom lip wobbling.

"I'm fucking this up, aren't I?" she whispers, and I shake my head, bringing my arm around her, pulling her into my side.

"Never. This is not your fault and you're doing amazing. We'll get it all sorted out," I say, tucking her head under my chin.

"Promise?"

"Yeah, baby, I promise," I say, kissing the top of her head. Alice stiffens in my arms, and I mentally kick myself for letting the pet name slip. What is wrong with me?

I expect her to shove me off, tell me to leave, but she's quiet. I hold my breath, hoping she lets me stay. Eventually she relaxes again, and I move my arm to her lap to clasp her hand. "Let's go. I brought reinforcements," I say, squeezing once before helping her up.

"You did?" she asks, looking up at me with hope. I reach out and brush her tears away with both my hands, letting my thumbs linger on the apples of her cheeks just a moment longer.

Of course, that's the precise moment that Ash's voice comes through the walkie-talkie in my pocket. "Love Guru here, we got all the decorations out of the boxes but need assistance with visuals. Over. Out."

I bite my lip, suppressing my smile and watch as Alice's face lights up. "Did he just call himself the Love Guru?"

With a vigorous nod, I say, "Absolutely, he did. He's taking this job very seriously."

A laugh breaks out of her, and I want to bottle it up and keep it for myself. It's light and bubbly and everything I remember her to be. I can't help the grin that takes over my face as she laughs again and again.

"Oh, Ash," she says, wiping another tear—this one of joy.

"Would you like the walkie-talkie?" I ask, holding it out.

She gasps, and I raise an eyebrow at her. "I would be honored," she says, her fingers brushing over my palm and sending a jolt of electricity through me.

"Love Guru, this is Hitchin' Crew Leader. Rendezvous at the patio door in T minus one minute. Over. Out."

"Fuck yeah, let's gooo!" Ash says, followed by his signature call out.

"Let's get this wedding back on track," I say, leading the way to the rendezvous point. As soon as Alice sees Ash and Eli, she immediately goes into planning mode, giving us all tasks. Alex and Malia continue to work on the balloon arch, and it looks way better than what any of us could have conjured up.

By the time we need to go back and get dressed for pictures, the whole place is ready and we all have code names. Ash is the Love Guru, Alice is the Hitchin' Crew Leader, Eli got nicknamed Checklist Crusader by Ash, and Malia came up with Glam Squad for her and Alex. As for me, I chose Fellowship of the Ring.

"Thank you for this. I couldn't have pulled it off without help," Alice says, stopping me with a hand on my forearm.

I swallow down more pet names and sweet nothings, refraining from telling her I'll always answer when she calls. I know that's not what she wants to hear. She's made it clear she wants to put our past behind us. I smile instead and say, "Of course."

Her blue eyes trace my face, and she takes a step towards me. I inhale a mix of her coconut shampoo and sweat and somehow manage not to grab her and kiss her. *Fuck, I miss her so much.*

She takes another step, then another, until her eyes are level with my collarbone, and she wraps her arms around my waist, resting her cheek on my heart.

I'm sure it's beating wildly for her, and after a moment of shock at her embrace, I bring my own arms around her and pull her even closer. I should keep this a friendly hug, but my fingers find the back of her head and tangle in her hair there, massaging her scalp. Alice's breath is hot against my thin T-shirt, and I think it's time to put some distance between us, before I completely lose it and do something stupid, like kiss her.

My control slips anyway, and I kiss the top of her head instead, reluctantly letting her go. "C'mon, we don't want to be late," I say, leading us to the car.

ALICE

THE REST of the day went off without a hitch. I managed to only cry three times during Robbie and Olivia's vows. And if I happened to look over and see Jordan crying too, well—that was just a bonus. I wanted to keep on hating him, but the truth is, I can't. Not after being there when I needed him most today.

Ash and Malia stood to my right as Olivia's other bridal party members, while Jordan, Eli, and Alex stood by Robbie. The pictures will no doubt look incredible, especially as half the guests are hockey players and coaches. I've never seen a room so full of beautiful people.

Michael, Robbie's old Manticores coach, brought his son Josh, who is working over the summer at Blue Line Brigade, and his wife, Jen, who volunteered to take the pictures today. She worked for the Manticores for the longest time as their team photographer.

I tear up just thinking about what an incredible family Robbie has had in this team, in these *people*, over the years.

After Jordan and I give our speeches, along with Grams

and my mom, the party begins and people are mingling both indoors, grabbing food, and outdoors, watching the sunset and enjoying a glass of wine. My job is done, and I can finally, blessedly, enjoy the night too.

I grab an entire tray of shots from the bar and make my way to our bridal party table. I wave Robbie and Olivia over, and they join us. The eight of us gather around the table and I hand out the shots, giving Ash a water cup, since he's been sober for a year.

When I get to Olivia, she says, "None for me." I do a double take and look between her and Robbie, seeing matching smiles on their faces.

Holy shit.

"Are you serious?" I ask, looking around the table, seeing everyone's shocked expressions, the shots long forgotten.

Olivia nods and I scream, jumping up and down with joy. I'm going to be an aunt—again!

"Shh," Robbie shushes me, placing a hand over my mouth. "No one else knows yet."

I tamp down my excitement and hug my best friend. "I'm so happy for you guys," I say, crying for the fourth time.

BY THE TIME I'm done dancing, my hair is a sweaty mess, I'm two drinks in, a little tipsy, and having the time of my life celebrating love.

"Love Guru, thank you for this dance," I say, dropping in a curtsy in front of Ash.

He laughs and picks me up, spinning me around. "Anytime."

A slow song starts up and everyone finds their partner, ready to sway together. I look towards the table, thinking I can maybe sit down and talk to Jordan, but a hand captures mine and gently pulls me back. I steady myself on his chest and can't help the smile that shines for Jordan.

"May I have this dance?" he asks, leaning in to whisper in my ear.

I nod and bring both my hands around his neck, letting him lead me throughout the slow melody. His hands are warm as they land on the small of my back where the cutout of my dress is. Jordan's thumbs sink into the flesh there, and I press myself closer to him. He smells like red wine and a little hint of smoke from the bonfire that was started out back, and I revel in the feeling of having him this close again.

We could have had so many moments like this if he hadn't broken up with me and moved so quickly. We could have found happiness in every text, every call, every conversation, and I don't understand why he chose solitude. Maybe it's time to hear him out.

"J, why did you leave so suddenly?" I ask, looking up at his clean-shaven face and twinkling brown eyes.

He blows out a breath and musters up a smile, but I can tell it's weighed down by regret. "Are you sure you want to know now?"

I swallow and nod, so he continues, pulling me closer and whispering in my ear. "The trade announcement messed with my head. It caught me by surprise, but the truth is, I already knew I wasn't playing up to my potential. I just expected a talk from my coach, not a trade at the end of the season. I felt like I was letting everyone down and taking the blame for a lot of missed plays. And the more I thought about it, the more I realized that I had nothing to offer you—and that scared me the most."

"That's not true, though," I say, looking up at him again. How could he think that? "All I wanted was you, just as you are."

Jordan sighs and our steps slow enough so that we're just standing in the middle of the dance floor. "I was too scared to be in a relationship with you, especially when I knew—" He pauses, biting down on his bottom lip and shaking his head. I want him to tell me everything he's thinking. I want him to be honest. "I knew that I wasn't good enough and I was scared that if we did long distance, I would find a way to fuck it up, just like I fucked up my career."

"J," I sigh, my heart hurting for him. He's more than good enough.

"I'm sorry for how I ended things, and I'm sorry for pushing everyone away. I hate it there and I'm so fucking lonely, all the damn time. I miss my family, and I want to come back."

I nod, slowly trying to tease out his deeper meaning. Perhaps he does still have some lingering feelings for me, but I can tell he's not in a good place, mentally, to be in a relationship right now. I lean my head on his chest and take a deep breath. "Maybe someday," I say, low enough that I'm not sure he hears me.

CHAPTER 18

Two Years Ago – September

JORDAN

I saw this bookstore today on my drive back from Dallas. It was all pink. I'll send you a picture.

ALICE

OMG, that is adorable. When can I visit so you can buy me all the books?

JORDAN

Season is starting soon, but you can sleep on my couch anytime. ;)

ALICE

Wow, you won't even offer up your bed? That's kind of rude.

JORDAN

I'm a professional athlete, I need my comfortable Tempur-Pedic mattress.

> **ALICE**
> LOL. Fine, I'll see if I can swing a trip sometime soon if the couch is still available.

NOVEMBER

> **ALICE**
> Are you coming home for Thanksgiving this weekend?

I got called up to Dallas, so I have to play Saturday. :(

> **ALICE**
> Look at you, hotshot! So proud, can't wait to see you on the big screen. <3

> **ALICE**
> THAT GOAL WAS PURE FIRE!!

JORDAN

:D Thanks, Al. Feeling like I'm getting back to my old self.

> **ALICE**
> I'm really happy, J. I hope you know we're all rooting for you. See you at Christmas?

DECEMBER

JORDAN

My flight got canceled. Looking for alternatives, but everything is booked. :(

ALICE

NOOO! Want me to call and yell at people for you?

JORDAN

I'm on hold. I'd love to see you yell at some poor airport worker, but we both know you're all bark and no bite.

ALICE

Yeah, fair. I would politely ask them for a refund and then cry when they tell me no.

JORDAN

Looks like I won't be able to make it.

ALICE

ALICE

Merry Christmas, J.

JORDAN

Merry Christmas, Al.

JANUARY

ALICE

Olivia's due date is at the end of the month. Please tell me you're coming!!

JORDAN

I would not miss it for the world. I should have a road trip to the Eastern Conference around that time.

ALICE

YES! I'm so excited. We get to be aunt and uncle AGAIN.

JORDAN

I wish I could be there all the time. I miss you guys.

ALICE

I miss you, J.

Good luck with your game tonight :) Wish I could watch it but I'm in the hospital with Olivia and Robbie.

JORDAN

Is she having the baby today?

ALICE

Doctor said it will take most of the night before our niece gets here.

JORDAN

I'm only a four hour drive away, I'll rent a car after the game.

ALICE

Can't wait! ;)

Are you on the way? I saw you guys lost, I'm sorry.

J, are you still coming?

She's here!! Where are you??

Jordan, what the hell? I thought you said you wouldn't miss this.

Whatever, I should have known you'd let us down. Were you even planning on showing up?

Guess not.

PART 3
PRETTY SLOWLY

CHAPTER 19

Now – August

JORDAN

A CAR HONKS behind me and startles me enough that I jump and hit my head on the trunk of the car. With a muttered "fuck" under my breath, I drag the last box out of the new SUV. It's not like I wanted to make the twenty-hour drive from Texas, but plans changed, and I wasn't able to ship my belongings in time and fly back to Michigan like I initially intended.

I heft the heavy ass box in my arms and fumble for the keys, locking the car in the process. Another honk is aimed at me, and I spin around, ready to give whatever asshole is behind the wheel a piece of my mind.

I'm about to do just that when I realize I know the asshole behind the wheel. The fucker is wearing the biggest smile on his face as he hops out of the car and runs at me, enveloping me and my box in a big hug.

"Jordie, my man, you're finally back," he says, running a hand through his dark red hair. Ashton fucking Meyers: former teammate, current best friend, and a constant pain in my ass.

"I told you never to call me that. And what are you doing here, shouldn't you and your boyfriend be enjoying the last few days of peace and quiet before the new hockey season starts?"

Ash reaches out and takes the box from me, and I don't miss the way his muscles flex as he easily maneuvers it. I frown at his biceps and say, "Did you get bigger?"

"I put on about twenty pounds of muscle in the last year," he says smugly, walking towards the apartment building.

"Jesus, man, the other NHL teams better watch it. You're gonna be a beast out there."

"Damn right," he says, and winks at me.

We take the elevator to the third floor, and I let Ash carry the box for me. I enter the code on the keypad and unlock the door to the apartment. Ash catalogs my stuff and looks at me, head tilted. "Is this really all your stuff? Just two suitcases and some boxes?"

I grab one of the suitcases and roll it inside, using it to prop the door open. "You told me the apartment is mostly furnished, so I got rid of a bunch of stuff. Figured I'd start fresh anyway."

"Well, yeah, you've got furniture and kitchen stuff, but you still need some decorations. Things of your own to make it home, ya know?" Ash says, placing the box on the kitchen island and heading out to the hallway for another one.

"I'll figure it out. Thanks for letting me sublet the place, by the way. You and Eli are welcome to stay here anytime you're back in town, if that wasn't clear."

"Of course. Did I tell you we're looking at buying a house in Grand Marquee?"

"Really?" I ask. I'm not surprised that they're looking at houses since they already rent a condo in Detroit, but I'm surprised they're looking in Grand Marquee. "Wouldn't you want a house closer to where you play?"

"We're going to keep the condo during the season, but we're thinking about moving closer for the off-seasons. I hear the house across the road from Robbie is up for sale."

"Ah, so that's the real reason you're in town. It's not to help me move into your old place. It's to get closer to Robbie."

"It's a double whammy," Ash says, bumping his hip against mine as he walks by. My steps falter and I wince at the pain that shoots through me. I try to recover quickly but Ash notices and his eyes go wide as saucers. "Jordan, shit—I'm so sorry, I totally didn't realize that was your injured hip."

"It's fine," I say, walking over to the island and gripping the counter.

"I'm such an idiot," Ash says, quickly coming over and pushing the bar stool towards me. I shake my head and ride out the pain. It's been months since my career-ending injury, and it still follows me around.

When the doctors told me I had a hip fracture, I didn't think much of it. People come back from that, right? Well, not me. Because of the direct acute trauma to my hip joint, I developed post-traumatic osteoarthritis, also known as PTOA. I was hopeful that it would go away after a few months, but even with physical therapy, exercise, and lifestyle changes, the doctors told me it could stay with me for the rest of my life. Not only was I devastated to lose my hockey career over a stupid injury, but I've had to come to terms with my chronic issue.

Some days are great, some days are manageable, and some days even the smallest thing like getting out of bed feels excruciating. I thought I was in a good spot, getting back in touch with my family and friends. Texas was a little more bearable. I had plans to visit Grand Marquee more often, but this injury took me right back to the darkest, most miserable place in my head.

I take a shaky breath and muster a smile. "You're not an idiot. It was an honest mistake, don't beat yourself up over it."

Ash gives me a gentle hug and I want to make another joke that he got soft since dating Eli, but I don't. I give into it instead, hugging him harder. The truth is, I don't know if I'd be here if it wasn't for Ash. While I was at my darkest, I pushed people away. *Again.* My own family and friends.

I'm not proud of it, and I know I have a lot of work to do to gain back their trust. But Ash—he was the one that pushed me to get better. I kept most of the details of my injury to myself because I didn't want my friends to pity me, but Ash flew down to Texas after a few months and made sure I was going through therapy—physical and mental—and that I was taking care of myself.

"How are you doing with everything? Are you sure you don't want to take more time to get better before starting the new job?"

I squeeze his shoulder and plead with him to understand. I need this. "I can't sit around all day, man. I'm gonna go crazy if I do."

"Just don't push yourself too hard, okay?"

I shrug, "It's an assistant coaching position for the Manticores. It's not like I'll be running drills and getting hip checked. I'll mostly be on the sidelines."

"Still. You're more important than this job. Okay?"

My eyes fall closed and I take a deep breath. "Yeah, you're right. I'll be careful, I promise."

Before I can offer Ash anything to drink or ask him to stay for dinner, he says, "I need to head over to that open house."

"You weren't kidding?"

Ash laughs, and his dark blue eyes twinkle with mischief. "You really think I would pass on the opportunity to be Robbie's neighbor? It will annoy the shit out of him, so you bet your ass I'm making an offer on that house."

I laugh. "Yeah. Yeah, it will."

"All right, I'll see you at Thanksgiving most likely, unless we get a day or two before then and decide to come visit. You know how schedules can be."

"Yeah. Tell Eli I say hi. Oh, and—" I break off, biting the inside of my cheek. Why is it so hard to ask for help? "Can you give me your therapist's number?"

"Marge? Hell yeah. She's the best. She does video calls now, so you don't even have to go into her office."

I shake my head at Ash, knowing I'll miss him until Thanksgiving. "Sounds great, man."

ALICE

I TAKE my third attempt at parallel parking in front of my apartment building, but the angle is all wrong. Again.

Whoever invented parallel parking deserves a spot in the darkest, deepest parts of hell.

"Ugh," I groan, frustrated. My hands smack the wheel, and I look closer at the car parked behind me. The damn SUV is overhanging into my spot, which means I definitely won't fit in the tight space.

I turn the volume up on my favorite Taylor Swift song and take a lap around the building, trying not to think of all the papers I have to grade tonight. By the time I get back, there's an open spot across the street and I take another four tries to park the Jeep that my brother, Robbie, sold to me last year when his daughter was born and he needed to upgrade to a minivan.

The traffic slows down enough for me to jaywalk across the street, and I sneer at the Texas-plated red SUV. I balance the new potted plant I bought in one hand and open the door to the apartment building with the other.

I'm mentally chewing out the owner of the SUV when I run into a brick wall.

"Al, I'm so glad I caught you on my way out."

"Ash?" I ask, looking up at one of my favorite people in the world—after my brothers and Eli of course.

"Hey, I need to tell you something," he says, pulling me to the side of the lobby and sitting me down on one of the chairs. Ash sits on the coffee table, facing me, and the poor thing creaks under his weight.

"Damn, look at you all sexy and fit," I say, and wink.

"Yes, yes, I look amazing—"

"And your hair is longer—"

"I know, I'm hot. Listen—"

"What's the rush? Come up to my place and we can chat for a bit. Sorry I didn't come see you at training camp this year."

"Al, listen to me—"

"Ooh, I need to send you a manuscript of my book too—"

"Jordan's back."

My smile instantly falls. *Fuck.* I knew he was coming back because his sister told me a few weeks ago, but I thought I had more time to come to terms with the fact that he'd be back. Here, in my life. The place he ran away from and left me heartbroken.

"Oh." That's all I muster to say as I chew on my bottom lip.

Ash reaches out with a thumb and stops my ministrations. His look is one of sadness but also understanding.

"I'm sorry, babe."

I shake my head and force myself to smile. "Hey, it's fine. I knew he'd be back eventually."

"There's more." My smile falls again and Ash grimaces. "He's subletting my apartment."

I gulp. "You mean, the one across the hall from mine?"

"That's the one."

"Yay!" I weakly wave my free hand in the air.

"Are you gonna be okay?"

I sigh and run a hand through my shoulder-length blond hair. My curtain bangs fall back into my eyes and I blow them out of the way.

"Your haircut looks nice," Ash says, tapping my shoe with his.

I tap his back and give him a small smile, "Yeah. I'll be fine. It's not your job to look after everyone, you know?"

"Sure it is. It used to be Robbie but now that he's a dad, his priorities have shifted. With good reason."

"Oh, and you thought it should be you? You think you have what it takes to be the *dad* of the group?" I tease him.

Ash mocks his affront. "Naturally."

"Ha! Good one, bud."

His phone pings and he swears. "I'm sorry to cut this short, Al. I need to look at a house for sale."

"Is it the one across the street from Robbie?"

"Yes!! You've seen it?" he asks, excitement written all over his face. *Oh, this boy is trouble.*

"I didn't go inside, but if I could afford to buy a house, I'd totally buy that one," I say, thinking of the pretty white ranch-style home. I may have stalked the hell out of it on Zillow.

"I have big plans," Ash says, grinning like a fool. I shake my head at his antics and kiss his cheek.

"Good luck, Ash. Thanks for the heads up. Kick ass this season, yeah?"

"Anything for you, Al."

I watch him leave the apartment building and square my shoulders on my way to the elevator. My heart beats fast as it approaches the third floor.

What am I going to say to him?

What is he going to say to me?

The elevator doors open but my body refuses to move. The doors close again and I shut my eyes tight, trying to put him out of my mind. But it's pointless.

When I open my eyes, the man I've been in love with for almost a decade is standing in front of me, hands tucked in the pockets of his dark blue jeans. His eyes are wide and his mouth opens like he might say something. For a moment I want to fling myself into his strong arms and go back to that night before the trade.

Before he broke my heart.

Before he ruined me.

Tears spring to my eyes and I hate myself for being so

weak around him. I've thought about this moment so many times. I promised myself that I would be on top of the world when I saw him next. That I would keep my head held high and make him feel as small as he made me feel when he ditched me in January with no explanation.

But I can't. Because even after everything, I still care about him. I still want what's best for him. But that doesn't mean he can just waltz back into my life and expect things to go back to normal. *Again.* I might be able to *forgive* the past, but I can't *forget*.

I inhale deeply and take a determined step out of the elevator.

"Alice." His deep velvety voice almost stops me in my tracks. *God, how I've missed that voice.*

It takes all my confidence and willpower to say, "Excuse me," as I sidestep him and walk over to my apartment, not sparing a look behind me.

CHAPTER 20

August

ALICE

I SHUT the door to my apartment and rest my forehead against it, closing my eyes. How many times did I imagine him coming back? *Too many to count.* And now that he's here, I feel like I'm that awkward version of myself—running into him on the lakeshore. How many times has he come back into my life only to disappear?

I don't think I can take it again.

I've spent the majority of my life pining after him, only to briefly get a glimpse of what it would be like to be a couple. But in the end, I was left with a broken heart. At first I thought my feelings were unrequited so I pined silently, wishing that he saw me as more than Robbie's little sister. It was one thing to love him from a distance and suffer when I saw him date someone else. It was a completely different kind of pain to have Jordan and know what he *tastes* like, what he *feels* like, only for him to end it between us like it meant nothing.

I wipe the tears off my face and harden my resolve for what's to come. Now that he's back, he'll be in my life. We're practically family, after all. But that doesn't mean I want to see him every day, and he'll quickly learn that.

My phone buzzes and I take it out of my back pocket. The message from Ash makes me smile the tiniest bit.

> ASH
> don't think I forgot about your book i'll stop by later tonight to take a peek …
>
> ALICE
> Aw, you're my biggest fan, Ash.
>
> ASH
> don't you mean your only fan?
>
> ALICE
> Wow, rude.
>
> ASH
> just kidding, love you blondie

I can always count on Ash to put a smile on my face. Once I change into my casual outfit of sweatpants and matching purple sweatshirt, I put the flowers I picked up at the farmers market in a vase with some water and grab my laptop.

What better way to let out my feelings than writing about them? After all, my romance novel inspiration came from my failed relationship with Jordan, so there's a bright side to all this pain.

I never thought that my writing would be good enough to publish, but after taking a few creative writing classes, joining a group of local writers, and getting lots of feedback on my short stories, I decided to take a stab at it and write a full novel. I dedicated most of my summer to writing it, and now that the school year has started, I'm back to teaching middle schoolers and figuring out how to publish my book in my spare time.

As a reader, I tend to pick up romances more than other genres, so when the time came for me to sit down and write an outline, I knew exactly what the story would be about. A second chance romance featuring Elissa, a small-town flower shop owner who is hopelessly in love with her brother's best friend, Jackson. The two of them dated in high school, but through a twist of fate, Jackson had to leave town and take care of his elderly father in Colorado. This left Elissa heartbroken, but they got the chance to reunite when Jackson's dad died and he moved back to town.

Unlike real life, my characters do get their happy ending. They say to write about what you know, after all. One night, I felt bold and posted the premise of my novel and an aesthetic board to my social media, where I have tens of thousands of followers. After that, people were practically begging for the whole story. *My* story.

So here I am, a year later, with a final manuscript in hand and anxiety about publishing it. Even if no one reads it, this story means so much to me, and it helped me process all of my feelings for Jordan. In a way, it's really helped me begin to heal.

There'll always be a Jordan-shaped hole in my heart.

JORDAN

. . .

MY FEET REFUSE TO COOPERATE, so I just stand there in front of the elevator contemplating every decision I've ever made. Alice is clearly still mad at me for not being able to come to town earlier this year, when Valerie—Robbie and Olivia's daughter—was born.

After being traded and moving to Texas, I shut everyone in my life out. All my friends and family, and especially Alice. I thought that getting a clean break would be easier for the both of us. But the truth is, as soon as I was on my own, I missed all of them. My family. And Alice—I missed her the most.

Without realizing it, I had cut out the brightest light in my life and was left agonized in the gloomy darkness.

I tried to briefly explain why I couldn't make it that weekend, but I downplayed my injury, not wanting any of them to pity me, not when they were celebrating the birth of Robbie and Olivia's daughter. Besides, Alice was too mad to hear me out. I had made a promise to be there, for Robbie, for Olivia—for Alice, and I broke that promise. I'm sure my injury seemed like an excuse, but the extent of it was much more complicated.

Robbie seemed understanding enough, and we've kept in touch on a semi-regular basis since then, though he does seem to have a lot on his plate now that he's a dad.

And the truth is, I never told anyone how bad my injury really was, except for Ash. When he and I reconnected last November, he was going through therapy, and I confided in him about how lonely and depressed I was feeling away from my family and friends. He not only encouraged me to find a therapist, but he made me a priority, calling as often as he could to check in and make sure I was taking care of myself.

I get a twinge of pain in my hip and grit through it,

making my way to the car to collect the last of my belongings.

Now that I'm back for good, I need to fix things between us. Not just with Alice, but with the rest of my friends too. And maybe, just maybe, I can win Alice back, one way or the other.

As much as I wanted to write off our story as something casual, things between us were so much more. Seeing her now is bringing back all the feelings that I didn't let myself show back then. Even though I refused to acknowledge them, the truth is I loved her. I still do.

One thing that people have said about me is that I'm stubborn as hell. If I put my mind to something, I accomplish it. No matter what.

And I'm going to get her back.

CHAPTER 21

August

JORDAN

THE RED, white, and black Manticores logo looms above me as I enter the arena through the main office and head to the front desk.

"Good morning, how can I help you?" the young woman at the front desk says, looking up from her computer screen.

"I'm Jordan Hill, the new assistant coach. I need to pick up my badge and equipment," I say, cracking my fingers, expelling some of the nervous energy I feel.

The young woman beams at me and stands up, extending a hand. "Nice to meet you, sir, we're so excited to have you. I'm Molly." I gently take it, and we shake hands quickly. I hope she doesn't mind the sweat.

I bite back my grimace and say, "Nice to meet you,

Molly. Do you know where I'm supposed to go to pick things up?"

"Oh, right. I can take you," she says, spinning around and leading me down the hallway, past some of the conference rooms and pictures of former players that have moved up to the NHL. I spot Ash and Eli's pictures framed next to each other and smile, snapping a photo and sending it to the group chat.

Molly looks back at what's got me distracted and smiles. "They're legends around here, you know? You all are."

"How do you mean?"

She points at another picture on the wall at the end of the hallway, one from training camp three years ago, all of us gathered on the ice in our red and white jerseys. Our first line is kneeling down, big smiles on our faces. Robbie is at our core, Ash and Eli to his right, me, Tripp, and Tony, our other defenseman, on his left. "That was the dream team," she says, and I swallow the knot in my throat because she's right. We were the dream team.

"Coach Brian never shuts up about you guys. He says everyone should aspire to play like you all did."

I snort, remembering how much coach Brian used to yell at us about our consistency and performance. Knowing that he speaks highly of me and my past teammates eases some of my nerves.

"Hey, Jordan. Good to have you back," a feminine voice says, and I look up just in time to see Malia walking down the hall with a yoga mat in hand. Her hand goes up and I high-five it as she walks by me.

"Good to be back. How is volleyball coaching?" I ask, knowing that since they moved back from Quebec a couple years ago, she's taken over as head coach of the Thunderbirds, the same team she started her professional volleyball career with.

"It's peachy! Can't wait for the season to start in January. You should come over for dinner, Alex will be grilling tonight," she says in a rush.

"Oh, sure, that'd be nice," I say, not expecting the invite, even though I probably should have. Alex is about as friendly as Robbie under the surface, even though he seems intimidating at first. And Malia has been nothing but nice from the first moment I met her. I still remember the holiday gala eight years ago when she bid on Robbie at the charity auction to make Alex jealous.

"I'll see you later," I say, and she waves at me on her way out.

"Here we are, this is your office, Coach," Molly says a moment later, gesturing to a small room with a window, a desk with a computer, and two chairs.

I smile like a fool and take a seat in the chair behind the desk, spinning around. The wall to my right has a whiteboard with markers and there's a small filling cabinet in the corner of the room as well.

"Holler if you need anything," Molly says, and waves on her way back to the front desk.

My badge and tracksuit are neatly stacked on the desk in front of me, along with a booklet. I leaf through it and find my computer login and the schedule for training camp.

A knock at the door startles me and the deep chuckle coming from the man leaning on the doorframe brings me back in time.

"You haven't changed one bit," Coach Brian says, smiling, even though it's mostly covered by his thick mustache.

"Tell that to my bum hip," I joke, making my way to

shake his hand. He surprises me, wrapping me in an awkward hug instead and patting me on the back.

"I'm glad you're okay, kid. You had me worried there for a bit."

"You had time to check up on me? Don't you have enough hooligans to keep in line?" I try deflecting.

"You've always been my favorite and you know it," he winks playfully. "Ready to take on a new challenge?"

I blow out a breath, nodding. "I am. To be honest, I've been going a little crazy without hockey for the past seven months."

Brian looks at me, no traces of amusement left on his slightly wrinkled face. "That injury—I wouldn't wish that on my worst enemy. I'm surprised you're not taking more time to recover, but selfishly I'm glad you're back. I could really use you to oversee the defense development, especially the penalty kill."

"Really?" I ask, stunned. I hoped he'd have me working with the defensemen since that's my expertise, but I didn't expect him to put this much trust in me.

"You're one of the most principled and patient people I know. Even as a player, you were always putting in the work, watching the tapes and giving me suggestions, for fuck's sake. I may have seemed annoyed at the time, but trust me, your judgement was appreciated."

I feel my cheeks are on fire from the praise and I look down, fiddling with the badge I put on earlier. "Thanks, Coach."

"It's Brian now. And don't expect me to kiss your ass all the time, this job is hard. At the ECHL level, it's all about attendance and the fun of it, drawing people in, showing them what hockey is. At the NHL, it's all about winning, the stakes are higher than ever. But here—" He stops, shaking his head. "At the AHL, it's all about the development. Sure, we want to fucking win, but we've got the top prospects in the palm of our hands, and we're the ones responsible for shaping them, molding them into the players they eventually become."

Brian pauses, letting me take this all in. It's definitely more than I expected, but the idea of helping players develop doesn't scare me away. If anything, I want to see them succeed.

"So, do you still think you're up for the challenge?" he asks.

"Abso-fucking-lutely," I say with no hesitation.

ALICE

I BREATHE through the pain and hold the plank position like the instructor tells us to. Why did I think a hot yoga class at eight in the morning was a good idea? Sweat pours in rivulets to the mat in front of me and I close my eyes, counting down the seconds until I can collapse back down. Hopefully never to get up again.

"You may now bring your knees to the mat and transition to child pose," the instructor says in her low, sultry voice. At first I found it soothing, but now, at the eleventh hour of the class, I just find it grating. I'm hot, I'm sweaty, everything hurts.

I do my best not to whimper in relief when the class is dismissed. I wipe down my mat and roll it.

"What did you think?" Malia asks from my right, and I glare at her. She just smiles wide and shakes her head at me, her short dark brown hair with highlights barely touching the tops of her shoulders now that she got a haircut.

"Personally, I loved it," Olivia pipes up from my left, and I turn my incredulous gaze on her instead. Traitors, both of them. If my friend Megan could make it to this godforsaken yoga class, she'd be on my side for sure. Instead, she's enjoying the last week of summer break at the beach.

"You know, when I suggested a girls' day, I meant getting brunch and maybe getting our nails done, not sweating like pigs and then going out in public."

They both laugh at my antics and I sigh, realizing that of course they'd want to work out first thing in the morning. They're both athletes.

"Good thing the arena is right next door, and I have access to the women's locker room. We can go shower and change into our spare clothes there before getting brunch," Malia offers, and I grumble. "What?" she asks, her hazel eyes sparkling with amusement.

"You and your logic. So infuriating," I joke, lightly punching her shoulder.

"I like that plan. The sooner we get food, the better," Olivia says with a smile.

HALF AN HOUR LATER, we're showered and dressed in a variety of summer outfits. I'm wearing a strapless dress with cherries and bows printed on it, the hem of it hitting just above my knees. I've got a matching pink claw clip pinning my wavy hair up, and as much as I wanted to wear some strappy heels, I didn't want to get blisters walking all over downtown, so I opted for a pair of white Birkenstocks instead.

Malia looks cute in her green romper with spaghetti straps, her tanned legs looking longer in her platform white sneakers, even if she's only an inch taller than me. Olivia opted for a simple white dress and black sandals, her long brown hair braided down one shoulder.

"Look at us, we need to take a picture before we get to the restaurant," I say, pulling out the phone. The three of us fit into the frame and I snap a few photos, realizing that there's a wall of hockey pictures behind us. I spot Ash and Eli's next to each other and open the group chat to tease them about it. That's when I realize there's an unread text from Jordan. And he's sent the same exact photo. *Shit, is he still here?*

"You okay?" Olivia asks, her hand squeezing my shoulder gently. "Your face fell when you looked at the phone. Is everything good?"

I try to smile, but Olivia knows me too well by now and her green gaze pins me to the spot, asking me to spit it out. "Jordan is back and—" I take a deep breath and look around the hallway, making sure he won't just appear out of nowhere. "I guess I'm struggling with the fact that I'm just supposed to accept it."

Olivia nods thoughtfully and rolls her lips. "Maybe we need to talk through it more over some mimosas."

"I second that," Malia interjects, leading us back down the hallway. As we pass one of the glass-door conference rooms, I look over and see Jordan. He's fully immersed in the game tape he's watching, but at the last second, his head turns to look at me. I stand there and blink a few times while his gaze roams up and down my body.

I do my best not to shiver from the attention and only

break out of my trance when Malia waves at the group of men.

"Good luck with training camp," she yells at them as they wave back. I take one more peek at Jordan. His chocolate brown eyes are still pinned on me, and I hold my head high as I walk away.

THE WALK across the street is a short one and we luckily get one of the last patio tables at The Arcadian. I settle next to Malia on the comfy couch while Olivia takes up a wide patio chair on the opposite side.

The summer brunch menu at my brother's restaurant is different from what they usually serve, but my mouth waters as I read over the Monte Cristo sandwich description.

"Hey guys, long time no see," Gen says. They are one of the regular bartenders here at The Arcadian, and they also pick up random shifts when needed, so we do in fact see them all the time.

"Gen, that French 75 you made me the other day with the lavender was divine," Malia says, bringing her fingers to her lips in a "chef's kiss" gesture.

"Want another one? I've got elderflower this time."

"Yes, please. You can experiment your drinks on me anytime," Malia says. "And I'll also take the baked avocado, please."

"Guys, I don't know what to order. How is this possible? I always know what food I want," Olivia says, flipping the menu back and forth.

Gen laughs and offers, "Want me to surprise you?"

Olivia gasps and smiles deviously. "Obviously, go crazy."

"Okay, I really want the Monte Cristo sandwich with glut—" I begin, but Gen cuts me off.

"Gluten-free bread, I got you girl."

"Has anyone ever told you that you're the best? And apparently a mind reader too?" I laugh and hand over the menus as Gen tucks them under their tattooed arm.

"Multiple times, yes. I mostly hear it from you, though."

"Good. Oh, I also want a mimosa."

"Me too," Olivia says.

"Actually, there's a mimosa bar inside, you two can make them however you want. I recommend adding in the peach juice."

"Let's do it!" I tell Olivia, and we head over to the bar.

When I'm done garnishing my drink with a fresh slice of peach, Olivia startles me by saying, "Listen, about Jordan."

"Oh no, can we please not ruin this day by talking about my ex?" I whine.

Olivia gives me a gentle smile. It's her 'mom' smile, the exact same one she gives Val when she eats too much applesauce. "I know it's hard to have to all of a sudden share the same building and even be at dinners with him again. But maybe you two need to have a conversation and find a way to move on."

I take a big sip of my drink and let her comment sink in. "It's not that I don't want to move on, I just—I've loved him for so long, and then he ditched not just me, but all of us. Twice!" I say, holding up two fingers in front of her face.

Olivia tries not to smile at how dramatic I'm being, but it slips anyway. I deflate a little and say, "You're right, though. I need to be a mature adult about this. I think I just need to adjust to him being here on my own terms, you know. I can't just flip a switch and pretend everything is fine."

"I get that. I'm not asking you to, I just want you to be happy. If that means having a tough conversation with Jordan, you know I have your back. If it means dating someone else, I can also support you there. I just don't want to see you go back to being mopey old Alice," she says, twirling a strand of my hair.

I grab her drink and place them both down on the nearest table, enveloping her in a hug. "You're my best friend, and I love you, you know that?"

"Duh, of course I know. Who else would watch a *Lord of The Rings* marathon with you in one day? That's true love right there."

"Thanks for the advice," I say, pulling back.

"Anytime. It gets me free babysitting, so I can't complain," Olivia says, and I cackle all the way back to our table.

CHAPTER 22

September

ALICE

I MANAGED to avoid Jordan for almost a month and a half, but I'm running out of excuses. I've skipped family dinners, claiming I had to put finishing touches on my book. I've also skipped visiting training camp, instead volunteering to babysit Valerie so Robbie and Olivia could have an extended kid-free weekend away.

The eight-month-old baby is staring at me with her wide green eyes as I change her diaper, giggling as I tickle her sides. I want one so bad, my ovaries might actually explode. But seeing as I don't have a serious relationship, and the one person I've ever loved is the exact person I've been avoiding recently, I'll stay content babysitting my adorable niece.

"Who's the best baby in the whole world?" I singsong,

and little Val flaps her arms at me to pick her up. I do so and hold her with one arm, snapping a selfie with the other and sending it to the group chat.

> **ALICE**
> We're about to have the time of our lives watching Disney movies.

> **OLIVIA**
> Aw, my favorite girls. :)

> **ROBBIE**
> Make sure she eats enough.

> **ROBBIE**
> And make sure she doesn't pull on Caramel's tail too much, he scratched her the other day.

I roll my eyes at my overprotective brother. I think out of the two of them, he was the one most reluctant to leave Val alone with me for the weekend. Olivia's had to make a few trips already for a referee camp this summer, and she's prepared to be gone during the season too, as her job will take her all over the Midwest.

My brother, however, takes the job of stay-at-home dad very seriously.

> **ALICE**
> Okay, dad. She's in good hands, don't worry. Enjoy your weekend.

My phone pings again, but it's not the group chat this time. It's a text from Jordan.

> **JORDAN**
> I hope you didn't skip this weekend because of me.

I scowl and leave it on read, just like all the texts he's sent me since January. For a while there, he got the hint, leaving me alone. But ever since he moved back, he's started to pester me again. He makes it impossible for me to move on, and I dread the day that I'll actually have to talk to him again in person.

> **JORDAN**
> I'm not staying at the cabin.

I roll my eyes and think about texting back, but I'm worried that once I do, he'll find some way to burrow himself back into my life. I've got enough to deal with as it is, the last thing I want is to let him in again.

JORDAN

EVERYONE ELSE HAS GATHERED HERE for a bonfire—Ash and Eli, Robbie and Olivia, even Alex and Malia are here, alongside my sister and Michael. My nieces are already asleep in the basement, and the whole cabin is full. Even though the place is crowded, Alice's absence is palpable. Or am I the only one feeling it?

"I really like the guy, he'd be a great fit for running the program here," Alex says, taking a sip of his IPA and adjusting the black baseball cap on his head.

Robbie throws another couple logs in the fire and nods. "I agree, he's dedicated and seems to genuinely want to give back to the community and help kids."

"What are we talking about?" Ash asks, carrying a tray of fruit and cheeses, placing it on a table by the cooler.

"Alex and Robbie are enamored. Got themselves a

boyfriend," Malia snickers, making fun of the guys, who have been constantly talking about this new guy—Jason.

"Oh yeah, what's he like?" I ask.

"Har-har," Robbie says, sitting in the hammock next to Olivia. "We've been talking about expanding the youth program. The community here has always shown up for us at training camp, and it would be a good spot to try a pilot program."

"Jason's one of the guys we've been interviewing to run the local program, maybe even coaching the kids," Alex supplies, pulling his wife into his lap. "I think he's got what it takes, even if he's a little young at twenty-one."

"You know who else has got what it takes?" Ash asks, squeezing my shoulders. "This guy. Congrats on your first day as assistant coach, man."

"Thanks," I mumble, peeling the label off my beer and avoiding everyone's eyes.

"You looked amazing out there," Robbie says, and I lift my gaze to him. He nods and I crack a smile. "It's good to have you back."

"It's good to be back," I say, and bite back my emotions. I don't deserve these guys. Not after keeping them in the dark about my injury and reason for retiring. Even though Robbie and I have kept in touch, I couldn't bring myself to burden him with my sob story. Not when he became a dad and had so much on his plate already. But I promised myself I would be honest from now on, no matter how hard those conversations would be.

"There's actually something I've been meaning to tell you all," I say, clearing my throat and standing up. Looking around the fire, everyone's eyes are on me. I catch my sister's gaze and give her an apologetic smile, knowing I've kept her in the dark too.

"I haven't been entirely upfront with you all about the reason I came back. That injury I got in January, when I was supposed to meet you all at the hospital—well, it wasn't just a broken leg," I say, glancing at everyone, catching their confused looks.

"The hit landed me in the hospital for something much worse. I had a fractured hip"—I grimace just thinking about it and how dark and miserable it felt in that lonely hospital room—"and recovery was a bitch, honestly." I laugh, looking at the sky and blowing out a breath. This is harder to share than I thought.

Ash pats my back and nods at me to keep going, so I do. "It took about five months to recover, but I'm still dealing with a lot of pain. I may need a hip replacement if I want a chance for the pain to go away completely, but even then ..." I trail off, looking at my friends.

"Why didn't you tell us when it happened?" Robbie asks, shock and disappointment written all over his face.

Fuck, I hate seeing that expression aimed at me. "I wasn't going to ruin one of the greatest nights of your life."

"Why didn't you tell us after?" Eli asks, even though I'm sure he knows a lot more than he leads on since Ash was flying to Texas on a regular basis to check on me during my recovery.

I shake my head. Because I was embarrassed, because I didn't want to be pitied. "Because I didn't want to be a burden on any of you. You've all got your careers and you're kicking ass—"

Tangela stands up so quickly that her chair falls backwards. She gives me one tearful look and heads inside the house, Michael trailing after her. I run a hand over my short beard and consider following her to explain myself.

"Does Alice know?" Olivia asks, a contemplative look

on her face. When her green eyes meet mine, I *know* that she knows about my past with Alice.

"No, she doesn't," I say, my shoulders dropping. "And I want to tell her myself, if you don't mind keeping it to yourself a bit longer."

She purses her lips but gives me a curt nod and I relax.

"I'm sorry, I should have told you guys. But more than that, I should have trusted that you'd all have my back when I needed you."

Robbie takes a few steps towards me and wraps me up in a big hug. I cling to him tightly and let my tears fall. "From now on, we'll be honest with one another, all right?" he says, and I nod, relieved. Getting this reaction from Robbie gives me hope that Alice might forgive me too.

"I should go talk to Tangela," I say, preparing myself for a well-deserved lecture.

THE CABIN IS quiet as I make my way down to the basement in search of my sister. My nieces are snuggled up together on one of the beds, but the other is left untouched. I frown, wondering where my sister ended up.

The bathroom door is open and the sauna is off, so I make my way back upstairs and look around the other rooms. Nothing.

The front door swings open and I spin around, hand over my heart. "Man, you scared me," I say to Michael as he watched me intently.

"She's really mad at you," he says, tucking his hands in the pockets of his basketball shorts and toeing off his sneakers, leaving them by the door.

"I know, I'm sorry," I offer, and attempt to walk by him. Michael and I have never really been close, but we've had amicable visits and short conversations about the weather and hockey. So I'm surprised when he takes a step towards me and wraps me in a hug.

After a beat of hesitation, I return the embrace and pat his back, unsure what prompted this reaction. "You good?"

"Yeah," he says, straightening up and crossing his arms over his chest. "I'm just glad you're okay, even if you did hide your injury from everyone. I've been around hockey my whole life, I've seen how brutal something like that can be," he says.

I don't know how to reply, but Michael smiles and pats my shoulder on his way to the basement. "Go talk to her."

The breeze picks up and rattles the wind chimes as I walk to the end of the porch where Tangela is leaning against the railing, staring out into the darkness of the trees. I mirror her stance and let our shoulders brush against one another.

The silence stretches on for so long that I feel a churning in my stomach and try to blink back the tears that threaten to fall.

"Why did you keep me in the dark?" she asks quietly. My hands grip the railing and I let my head drop back when I realize how hurt she is.

"I just couldn't—"

"No, Jordan," she says firmly, turning to face me with a stony expression on her face. Her dark brown eyes gleam with tears and I reach out to hug her, but she sidesteps me.

"Tangy ..."

"I need you to listen to me, okay? I know that growing up, our parents never really made us talk about our feelings and we learned to bottle things up and pretend that everything was fine. And I know you've always been anxious and introverted and mostly kept to yourself, but Jordan, we're your family. We're supposed to share the bad things too. We're supposed to lean on each other through tough times," she says, taking a deep breath and wiping away a tear.

God, I hate this.

"I'm really disappointed that you didn't think you could lean on me for this. I'm your big sister, I'm supposed to have your back. So don't tell me that you couldn't bother to pick up the phone and call. You simply didn't want to."

I swallow and shrug, knowing she's right. Growing up, we were always there for one another, but at some point I decided that she didn't need me anymore. That I didn't need her. Finding my voice, I say, "Sometimes I just feel left out. You married into this amazing, wonderful family and I just tagged along. I thought I belonged with the Manticores, but when I got traded, I think something in me broke. It made me feel unworthy—of my job, of my friends, my family. So I took the cowardly way out and ran away. And I figured everyone would be fine without me."

"You fucking fool. I wouldn't even be here if it wasn't for you. If you and Robbie didn't become best friends. And we were all devastated when you left," she says, lightly punching my chest. "Asshole."

"Really?"

"Yes, really. We had some really depressing family dinners without you there. I can't believe you've kept all of this inside for so long. Is that still how you feel? Like you don't belong?"

I reach out for a hug, and this time my sister lets me embrace her, turning so that her cheek is over my heart. "No," I say softly. "I've been seeing a therapist and I'm on antidepressants, which has helped a lot. There's always gonna be some part of me that is doubtful, but I think being back here, amongst all of you—it's helping."

Tangela nods against me and hugs me tight. "I'll always be here for you, no matter what. Please don't push us away again."

"I'll try my best," I say with a small smile.

CHAPTER 23

November

ALICE

THANKSGIVING COMES TOO QUICKLY. I had to sit through so many family dinners in the last couple of months, pretending like everything was fine, and that I was oh-so-happy Jordan was back in our lives. But I'm not a great actress, and there's only so much faking I can do around him.

His pestering has increased from texting to leaving me notes on my door. And when those went unanswered, he started leaving lemon scones and hot tea at my doorstep each morning. It's infuriating how hard he's trying. And while I eat the delicious, thoughtful, and confusing treats, I'm still not ready to let him in again. I've been burned too many times.

Except this is one of my favorite holidays, and I refuse to hide in a corner and avoid him all day. I'm peeling potatoes at the kitchen counter and watching Val in her high chair out of the corner of my eye when Jordan walks in through the back door at my parents' house.

He's looking good as always in a sweater that I've seen him in before and my eyes flick over his biceps, expecting the material to be stretched tight around his muscles, but it actually looks loose. Has he lost weight?

I subtly let my eyes roam over his frame, and I frown when I realize that he does seem to have gotten skinnier. He runs a hand over his short beard and smiles at my mom as he hands her a bouquet of flowers. I roll my eyes. *What a kiss-ass.*

Jordan looks my way, and we stare at each other for a long moment. He takes a step towards me and I turn my attention to the potato in my hand.

"Hey, Al," he says, both his arms tucked behind him.

I look up and narrow my eyes at him. "Hi."

"I like your dress," he says, nodding at my favorite green sweater dress with the oversized sleeves. I had to pull them all the way up my forearms to peel the potatoes and his eyes seem to be glued to the spot on my right arm where I got a little bookish tattoo.

"Thanks," I mumble, wishing he would just go away. I want to stay angry at him, because if I don't, I'll just end up pining after him for the rest of my life. It's not like I can just cut him out of it.

Jordan leans into the kitchen island, holding himself on an elbow and reaching from behind his back to offer me a single white rose. "Got you something."

I frown down at it, noticing all the thorns have been

picked out. *Stupid, thoughtful Jordan.* With a loud sigh, I snatch it away from him, adding it to a glass of water. When I look back at Jordan, he gives me a lopsided smile and walks over to Val, kissing her head and feeding her some mashed bananas. I swallow hard, watching him be so incredibly good and sweet with her. I expected Robbie and Olivia to be more angry that he just ditched us for the better part of a year, and that he didn't meet his niece until he moved back. But oddly everyone has been fine with him coming back and picking things up like nothing ever changed.

So why am I still so hung up on it?

JORDAN

WE WATCH the football game in the Elliots' large living room, and for the first time in years, I feel like I'm finally home. I missed this so much.

I don't care that the kids are loud and running around the entire house, and I don't mind that we don't all fit at the table so we have to squeeze around. I just want to be here with all of them.

Alice looks at my plate from across the table and I follow her gaze, wincing at the small amount of food there. Ever since my recovery, my diet and lifestyle have changed a lot, and I definitely don't have the appetite of a professional hockey player anymore.

She raises an eyebrow at me but I just shrug, not wanting to explain all that right now. I'm just happy she's not outright avoiding me today. Baby steps.

"Olivia, are you reffing the Manticores game tomorrow?" Alice asks.

"No, I have the weekend off for once." Olivia smiles, bouncing Valerie in her lap.

"Speaking of tomorrow, I need some help at the furniture store. I'm getting some new bookshelves for my bedroom." Alice turns to her father. "Dad, are you busy?"

"Sorry, honey. I have plans with some old friends that are in town."

"Michael?" she asks, looking at her older brother.

"Sorry sis, I promised the girls I'd take them to the trampoline park," Michael says.

"Ash? Eli? You got plans?" The two of them look at one another with wide eyes, whispering something to each other.

Ash clears his throat and says, "Sorry, Al. We have some plans we can't get out of."

Alice frowns, her shoulders slumping. Before she can turn her head to Robbie, I say with too much enthusiasm, "I can take you."

She freezes, glancing at me and then quickly away. "Oh, I don't want to bother you, I'm sure you've got work since your team has a game tomorrow," she says, trying to wave me off.

"Morning skate is early, but then I'm free for most of the day. I can meet you there at ten if that works," I insist, knowing she won't refuse me in front of her whole family. Not when she doesn't have a good enough reason to.

With a deep inhale and a forced smile, she says, "Sure. Thanks, Jordan."

LATER, once everybody is stuffed full of turkey and pies, I pull her aside and tell her, "Look, I know you're still not ready to hear me out, and that's okay. But I really want to be here for you, and I won't let you down."

"Okay," she says after a beat, crossing her arms and nodding. "I'll see you in the morning then."

CHAPTER 24

November

ALICE

THE CALL GOES straight to voice mail for the third time as I pace around the furniture store, drawing the attention of everyone around me.

He didn't come.

Jordan promised he'd be here to help me, and he didn't come. My eyes burn with unshed tears, and I do my best to keep them at bay. I refuse to cry in front of all these people who are just trying to get their Black Friday deals.

My phone vibrates in my hand and hot anger takes over as soon as I see Jordan's name on the screen. "Where the hell are you?" I bite out, moving to a corner of the store.

"Alice," he says quietly, and pauses for the longest time. "I'm sorry, something came up and I can't join you today."

I scoff and shake my head even though he can't see my disappointment. "Can't or won't?"

Jordan exhales and I can't tell if he's exasperated with me or disappointed in himself, but I don't care. He promised me this one thing. After telling me again and again how he wants to make things right, now he's bailing at the last second.

"Al, I'm so sorry, I will make this up to you—"

"Don't bother. I won't be counting on you any longer," I say, and hang up the phone. A tear escapes me, and I cover my mouth to stop myself from sobbing in the middle of the store. I glance at the bookshelf that would have been perfect for my bedroom and decide to let it go. There's no way I could unload this thing by myself and bring it into my apartment, even if I did manage to get it into my car.

I make my way out of the store without drawing any more attention to myself and rest my head on the steering wheel once I make it into the Jeep. My phone buzzes and I glance down at it.

ASH

how is furniture shopping going?

I love Ash to death, but this is not the time to check up on me. I wipe my tears and call him.

"Hey," he tries to say enthusiastically, but I can tell he's tired as hell.

"You sound awful," I snort.

"Rude," he mumbles.

"I'm sorry, I'm just being bitchy because Jordan bailed on me."

"What do you mean?"

"He just called saying he *can't* come help me. Like he

went on and on about how he wants to make things up to me and that he won't let me down again, and then he just fucking bails. I'm so over it."

Ash is quiet on the other end for too long and I pull the phone away from my ear just to make sure I didn't accidentally hang up on him. "Ash, are you still there?"

He sighs, and I can picture him pinching the bridge of his nose. "He still hasn't told you, has he?"

"Still hasn't told me what?"

"About his injury," Ash says quietly, and I can hear him shuffle something in the background.

Injury? Did Jordan get injured recently? Coaching? My mind runs through all the details of last week and even yesterday. He seemed fine at dinner.

"What injury?" I finally ask.

"The one from January, when he shattered his hip."

My eyebrows pinch in confusion as I try to think back. That can't be right, he had a minor injury in January, which was why he couldn't come home when Val was born.

"I was the only one who knew at the time how bad it really was," Ash says, and takes a deep breath, "and it was really bad, Al."

My shoulders drop and I close my eyes. Fuck, why didn't he say anything?

"What happened?" I ask, not completely sure that I want to know.

"He was pretty brutally checked. There's a video out there but I don't recommend watching it. He violently crashed into the boards and was taken off the ice on a stretcher and then ended up with a hip fracture and a concussion."

I can't help but vividly picture everything Ash is telling

me, and it makes me feel sick to my stomach. As someone who's grown up with hockey, I know a thing or two about injuries, especially after Robbie had to get through two torn ACLs. But this, this sounds so much worse somehow.

"Is that why he retired?" I ask, and immediately feel dumb. Of course that's why.

"Al, it took him five months to recover and he's still in pain most days. That was a career-ending injury."

"What do you mean he's still in pain?" I ask, and my voice wobbles, more tears gathering on my lashes.

"Fuck, I really shouldn't be the one telling you all this. He—he's got something called post-traumatic osteoarthritis, it's like chronic pain essentially. Unless he gets a total hip replacement, he's gonna have to deal with that pain for a long while."

"Why doesn't he get one?" I squeak out.

Ash snorts. "Have you met Jordan? He's the most stubborn guy I know and up until recently, he hadn't even told his family how bad the injury was, let alone accept anyone's help or advice."

"But if he's in pain—" I try to argue, but Ash cuts me off.

"He thinks doing his physical therapy is enough, but that's just the bare minimum. I know what he's like, and most of the time he feels like he's a burden to others, so no matter what you say he's not going to listen."

"Fuck, Ash. I was so rude to him. I told him he's not someone I can count on," I say, chewing on the corner of my lip. God, I'm such an idiot.

"Damn, ruthless."

"*Ash!*" I cry out.

"Sorry, sorry. Look, I'm sure he'll look past you being rude. But maybe you should check on him. If he truly bailed on you, he must be having a bad flare."

"You think he'd want to see me?"

"Probably not, but you have a spare key." Ash goes quiet for a moment. "Sometimes he just needs some tough love and someone to stick by him even when he wants to push everyone away."

I nod even though he can't see me. "Thank you for telling me."

"Just ... take it easy on him, Al."

"I'll try," I say with an eye roll, and Ash laughs, almost like he could see me.

"Love you, blondie."

"Miss you, goldfish."

THE RADIO IS PLAYING Christmas music and normally I would be all for it, but my mind keeps straying to Jordan. Is he okay? *Please let him be okay.*

I go to my apartment first and change into leggings and an old comfortable navy blue sweater before grabbing the key to Jordan's apartment from my junk drawer. I fiddle with it for a moment, contemplating if he even wants me there, but decide to follow Ash's advice and give Jordan a dose of tough love.

Walking into his apartment, the lights are all off, blackout curtains pulled tight. It's so dark and quiet that for a moment I wonder if he's even home. But his car was in front of the building, so he must be here. I quietly pad over to his bedroom and push the door open.

"Jordan?"

The lump on the bed moves the tiniest bit and I bite my lip in worry.

"Jordan, are you okay?" I ask again.

"Alice?"

I let out a breath and move to the bed, not knowing what to do, but wanting to make sure he's okay all the same.

"I'm here," I say, flipping the nightstand light on and getting on top of the comforter, grabbing the edge of it and pulling it down to reveal Jordan. My eyes are still adjusting, but I can clearly see his pained face. My hands move of their own volition and cup his face, my thumb stroking his short beard.

"How are you here?" he asks with a resigned look on his face, eyes tired and heavy.

"I used the spare key. I know it's only supposed to be used in emergencies, but this kind of seemed like one." I ramble on until Jordan pulls his arms out of the comforter and caresses my wrists.

"I—" he says, but swallows hard, eyes closed tight. He's going to tell me he doesn't want me here, seeing him like this. *Too bad.*

"Don't even try to tell me to leave. I'm so mad at you right now, I could actually punch you, if you weren't already in pain. Jordan, why the hell didn't you tell me?"

His brown eyes roam my face as his thumb continues to stroke my wrist. "Tell you what?"

I huff in frustration and pull my hands away, lying down beside him. Maybe if he's not looking at me straight-on he might actually tell me everything himself. "Why didn't you tell me the real extent of your injury?"

"You talked to Ash?" he hedges.

"Yes, but I want you to tell me."

"I don't—"

"None of that bullshit. You said you came to Grand

Marquee to get back in our good graces. If you want us"—I say, stopping myself before continuing—"if you want *me* to let you in again, you have to be honest."

Jordan's fingers find mine on top of the comforter and he squeezes my hand in his. He's quiet for so long that I think this might be the end of it all. He won't open up, and I can't chase him again knowing he won't—

"You're right," he says quietly. "I'll tell you everything."

JORDAN

THE PAIN HAS BEEN EXCRUCIATING. I usually keep my medication nearby, but I got hopeful, not having a flare in a few weeks. When it got too painful to even stand, I had no choice but to lay here motionless until the pain subsided.

The shittiest part was having to call Alice and tell her I couldn't help her go furniture shopping today. I've let her down so many times in the past but the fact that I couldn't even get out of bed today felt like a slap in the face. *I can't even be there for those I love.*

What do I have to offer anymore? I'm a washed-up, depressed hockey player with a bum hip and no real prospects in life besides coaching. *I feel so useless.* I wouldn't be surprised if all my friends gave up on me. I feel like giving up on myself most of the time.

I wince at the negative thoughts and remember what my new therapist said—I need to spend more time with supportive people, pulling the curtain to give them a glimpse into the darkness lurking beneath.

And Alice—she's here and she's not taking no for an

answer. Maybe it's time to let her see everything rather than hiding the ugly parts of myself.

"Things were bad once I moved to Texas. I was miserable there, Al," I say, shaking my head but keeping her hand tight in mine, like that small act can give me the strength to push through this. "I didn't know anyone, and you know me, I'm always so fucking anxious in new places." I laugh bitterly and shake my head again, thinking back on how much I actually hated it there and how much I missed home.

"Hockey helped, it kept me active and social enough out on the road, but at the apartment, the depression was getting worse. At some point I stopped responding to group chats. It was too hard to think about everyone here when I felt like I was aimlessly drifting." I take a deep breath and turn my head slightly to look at Alice. She's listening intently, looking at the ceiling fan above us, giving me the space I need to get this all out.

"Ultimately, I stopped answering calls too. My sister was the only one I'd check in with, mostly because I knew she'd freak out and hop on a plane to see me if I went too long without contact."

Alice's lips tilt at the corners and I want to keep her smiling all the time. She's a ray of sunshine and I'm a fucking tornado, ready to wreck everything in my path.

"It went on like that for the two years I was there, until the injury."

I'm quiet for so long that Alice turns towards me and pins me with her cornflower blue gaze, giving me an understanding look. She wants me to keep going, but I don't know if I can.

"Ash said the injury was really bad," she says softly, and I openly gaze at her face. She's got a small amount of makeup on, and her shoulder-length hair is loose and wavy. A few strands fall in her face. I reach out and tuck them behind her ear, the way I know she would. That small smile returns to her face and I face the ceiling again, closing my eyes.

"It was awful. I blacked out for a bit so I don't remember much between when I was hit and when the stretcher was brought out, but everything hurt. I was taken to the hospital and by the time I fully realized what was happening, I was starting to panic. They told me surgery was required, and ..." I trail off, chuckling.

"What?" Alice asks, confused as to why I'm laughing.

"I'm basically a robot now, metal plates, screws, and all."

Her hand grips mine tighter and she digs her nails into my palm. "That's not funny."

I turn my head towards her and—yep, she's trying really hard not to laugh. I smile and say, "It's a little funny."

She bites her lip, and my eyes track the movement. I want her so badly I don't even know what to do with myself sometimes.

"What happened after the surgery?"

I shrug. "Recovery was a bitch; it took five months for me to get my body back in shape, but I'm still not at my best. There was a lot of physical training involved, but I really struggled with my mental health."

"I'm so sorry. That's an awful thing to go through on your own," she says.

"If it hadn't been for Ash, I honestly don't know how I would've gotten through it all. He heard about the injury from an old friend of his that played on my team, so he flew down to see me, stayed with me when I was at my worst, and found me a therapist. So I wasn't completely alone."

"Why didn't you tell us or ask for help?" Alice asks.

This is the question I don't know how to answer, but I land on the next best thing.

"I didn't want to bother anyone."

"Oh, Jordan," she says, and drapes her free arm over my chest, her nose landing in the crook of my neck. I turn my head and inhale the sweet coconut scent of her hair. God, I've missed her so much.

When I try to move so I can better hug her, the pain comes back in full force, and I hiss through my teeth. Alice's head snaps up and she pulls back. I want to tell her it's fine, that I'm okay, but I'm so very clearly not.

"Can you do me a favor?" I ask, dreading that I have to ask for anything when I should be the one being there for her, helping her with her new bookcase instead.

"Yeah. What's wrong?"

"I couldn't get up earlier, so I didn't take my meds. Can you bring them, please?" I ask, and fist the comforter so tight, I might hurt my fingers.

"Of course, are they in the medicine cabinet?"

"Yes. And water, please."

Alice rushes out to the kitchen and comes back with a tall glass of water that she hands me before running to the bathroom. I take a couple big gulps of water while I wait for Alice to come back out. She takes longer than I expect so I call out, "Al, everything okay?"

I hear the cabinet closing and Alice comes out, walking slowly with all my medication.

"I, um—" She looks down at the bottles in her hand, blinking fast. "I don't know which one you need."

"That's okay, I'll show you," I say, taking the bottles from her as she kneels back on the bed. "The red bottle is for the pain. I usually take one tablet three times a day, but I can take two now since I didn't before."

Alice keeps looking down at the bottles, and her voice wavers as she says, "What about the others?"

I point at the blue bottle first, then the yellow one. "That's my antidepressant, and the other one I have to take to prevent stomach problems. I've been on all three since the injury."

"Oh," she says as she watches me take them. "Thank you, for telling me."

I finish the water, and my stomach lets out the loudest growl. I wince as I lay back down and think about how I want to reply, but Alice springs back up off the bed.

"I'm gonna go make you some food. You probably didn't eat anything."

"It's fine, you don't have to."

"Shut up and let me help," she yells out as she heads towards the kitchen.

I let out a small laugh and bask in how much lighter I feel now that I'm not keeping anything from Alice. This feels like a huge step in getting her back, but my doubt creeps in. What if she only feels bad for me?

I don't have time to spiral further because Alice comes back with two plates of Thanksgiving leftovers, the smell of cranberry and turkey already making my mouth water. I sit up and lift the comforter so she can join me. Alice assesses me for a moment and smiles, handing me a plate and getting her legs under the comforter, pulling it over her lap.

We eat in silence, stealing glances at one another. When we're done, Alice stacks the plates and places them on her nightstand. I expect her to go back to her apartment now, but she surprises me by scooting down and getting comfortable next to me. She turns onto her side and laces her fingers with mine again.

She looks like she belongs.

Alice moves closer and rests her forehead on my shoulder. "Is this okay?" she asks.

"Yes," I say, but it's an understatement.

It's better than okay.

It's perfect.

CHAPTER 25

November

JORDAN

I WAKE UP RESTED, the pain having subsided after Alice brought me my medication. The room is still shrouded in darkness, and I reach for my phone that's face down on the nightstand.

I have a lot of missed calls and texts from work, and I quickly type out a message that I'm feeling better and that I'll be able to be in attendance at tonight's game. Alice stirs next to me and when I turn my head, I find her watching me with a soft expression. I'm still worried that she's only here because she feels bad for me.

"How are you feeling?" she asks, giving me a small smile, her bangs falling in her eyes. I reach out without thinking and brush the dark blond strands away, my fingertips lingering on her forehead, my thumb brushing back and forth on her cheek.

Alice's eyes fall closed, and she gives me a content sigh. I fight the urge to kiss her and pull my hand back, pulling the blanket off me.

"Much better. Thank you," I swallow hard, pushing myself off the bed and trying to stretch. There's some lingering pain, but not enough to incapacitate me the rest of the day.

"Shouldn't you rest more?" she asks, sitting up in my bed, looking adorably rumpled.

I shake my head, twisting my body in another stretch. "I have a game to coach tonight."

"Are you still in pain?"

The concern in her face stops me in my tracks and pulls at my heartstrings. "I'm always in pain, but this is a manageable level." Her face falls and her eyes shine with tears. Fuck.

"J, I'm so sorry," she says, a tear falling down her cheek and landing on the comforter. I swallow hard and reach out a hand. When she takes it, I pull her to the edge of the bed and give her a hug.

"I'll be okay, I promise," I say, trying to put her at ease.

"I just wish you'd told me sooner. I wish I could help more," Alice says helplessly, hugging me harder.

"There's one thing you can help me with ..." I trail off, not sure if it's the best idea to have her this close, but she wants me to let her in, to let her help me, so I have to try.

"Anything," she says, pulling back and wiping her face.

"I need help with my stretches," I say, blushing at the request. I almost expect her to laugh it off, but she takes the task very seriously, jumping off the bed.

"Do you have a yoga mat?" she asks, looking around the

room, peeking in my closet, like she might find some hidden equipment there.

I smile. There's the Alice I know. "No. I just lay on the floor usually."

She whips back around to stare at me. "Are you crazy? You need to use a mat. It will help with your joints, not to mention it's more comfortable."

I raise an eyebrow at her. "Okay, miss *expert*. I'll get one."

"Let's go to my place, I have one there," she says, grabbing my hand and dragging me with her across the hall.

"How did you get into my place, again?" I ask, trying to remember if she's mentioned it already. Alice unlocks her door and we enter her much brighter apartment, and—wow. This is the first time I'm seeing it since she moved in, and it's so overwhelmingly *her*. The furniture is mostly white, from the coffee table to the TV stand to the bookshelves along the living room wall. There are plants and flowers everywhere, some real, some not, and a giant plush chair by the window, getting plenty of natural light.

"I mentioned it earlier, I used the spare key I have for emergencies," she says, peeking at my face for a reaction. I don't let her see how glad I am that she even cared enough to use it.

"Good to know," I say, looking around the place more. The apartment is a mirror of my own, with the same style of kitchen counter and modern appliances.

"You have one too, by the way," she says, and my attention returns to her as she's tucking her hair behind both ears.

"A spare key?"

"Yeah," she says, biting her lip. "A spare key to mine. It's in your junk drawer."

"Oh, I thought it was a spare for my own."

"Nope," she laughs. "You know Ash and Eli, they practically lived at each other's places even when they weren't together."

"Did they tell you they got the house?" I ask, following her into her bedroom. The decor reminds me of her old apartment she had in college. I glance at her bed and the pink bows on her sheets, and remember that first time she kissed me. I was such a fool to turn her down.

"Yes, I'm so excited. Robbie is going to lose his mind when he finds out they're moving in across the street," she says in a muffled voice, entering her closet and digging around for the yoga mat.

"It'll be great," I say, looking around the room more, stepping closer to the full-length mirror on the wall that's directly across from the bed. I wonder if she ever watches it as she's touching herself.

I groan and scrub my hands down my face. What is wrong with me? She held my hand in bed for a day and now I'm a fucking horndog for her. This is what I get for not getting laid in years.

"Okay, found it," she says, coming back out with a rolled up purple mat. "Let's set up in the living room."

ALICE

JORDAN BARELY FITS on the mat, and I bite back a smile. I make a mental note to order him a proper mat that he can use for stretching—one that won't have his long legs dangling so far off it.

"What kind of stretches do you usually do?" I ask, putting my hair up and pinning it with a claw clip.

Jordan looks up at me from where he's lying on his back and gestures for me to get down too. I kneel next to him and wait for instructions, but he just stares at me. After a beat, he says, "Maybe this is a bad idea."

"Why?" I frown.

"It's just—you'll have to touch me," he says, cheeks turning pink as he looks down at my hands, which are gripping his thigh. Huh, when did that happen?

"Well, good thing you don't have cooties." I snort and he cracks a smile.

"Okay, let's start with some hamstring stretches then," he says. "You'll have to push my leg and keep it straight at first. Then push it while my knee is bent, so I can stretch the glutes too."

I giggle at the word glutes, and he rolls his eyes at me. "Okay, I think I got it," I say, moving to kneel in front of him, taking hold of his left leg first and holding it straight, bending it towards him.

Jordan grimaces but doesn't make a sound and I quickly stop. "What's wrong?"

"Just ... go slower," he says, breathing through his nose.

"I'm sorry, did I hurt you?"

"S'fine, I'm just a baby when it comes to pain." Jordan smiles, but it doesn't ease the tightness in my chest. I hate seeing him in pain. No matter how strained our relationship is, I would never wish him harm.

I run one of my hands up to grab his ankle, the other one landing on his muscular thigh. Even though he hasn't played hockey in close to a year, he's still got the strong legs of a professional player. Gently, I start to push, leaning my body into the movement. When I think I've gone far enough, I stop.

"More," Jordan says in a ragged voice, and I suck in a

breath. This is way too intimate of a position, but I can't back out now. He inhales and exhales deeply through the burn, lifting his arms up over his head. The movement makes his T-shirt ride up and I'm met with a familiar glimpse of his brown skin and the curly black hair that trails down to his athletic pants.

I blink and avert my gaze, finding a spot on the carpet next to his head to stare at instead. Jordan's eyes catch mine for a brief second and I pray he didn't see me looking. After about a minute, I switch over to his other leg, doing the same exercise.

His sexy grunting does something to me, because all I can think about is drawing out these sounds from him in a much more compromising position. I'm relieved when he sits up to do some other hip stretches, and I leave him alone while I make us coffee.

I'm in my head when he comes to the kitchen, a soft look on his face. I hand him my favorite mug that says "smut reader" on it and smirk as he flushes at the sight of it.

"Thank you for the coffee and for all the help today," he says, taking a sip and leaning forward on the kitchen island.

"Anytime," I say, taking a sip of my own.

"How is your book going, by the way?" he asks, and I groan.

"Who told you about that?"

Jordan frowns at me but says, "Everyone is talking about it. You know that, right?"

My mouth opens but nothing comes out. I've been pretty excited to publish my first book, but I didn't expect anyone would actually care that much about it. My family has always seen my reading as a hobby rather than a large part of my life. I figured the same would go with my writing.

"Are they?" I ask shyly.

"We're all so proud of you for going after your dreams," he says, brown eyes boring into mine with so much love and sincerity.

"Thanks," I say, breaking the contact. "The book is going well, for the most part. I just need a cover. And maybe more time, since teaching is taking a lot of it at the moment."

"Can I read it?" he asks, and my head snaps up to his.

"No!" I say, louder than I mean to. I would die of embarrassment if he read my book. "I mean, not yet. And since when do you read romance?" I recover, looking at him skeptically.

Jordan shrugs, giving me a small smile. "I've read a few."

"Really?"

"Yes, really." He rolls his eyes, finishing the last of his coffee and rinsing the mug.

I want to ask him more. Which ones did he read? How did he pick them? Were they smutty? My cheeks burn but before I can ask any of my asinine questions, he says, "I should head out if I want to get to work on time."

I nod and walk him to the door. "Take it easy, yeah?"

"I will, and—" He stops himself, looking down at his feet and fidgeting, cracking his knuckles.

I get the feeling asking for help is still not something he's comfortable with, so I give him a break and say, "Hey, Jordan? If you need a stretching partner, let me know."

His eyes find mine and he gives me another devastating smile, his shoulders relaxing. "I would love that."

CHAPTER 26

December

ALICE

HOLIDAY SHOPPING IS one of my favorite things. I know people usually dread it, but I think it's the perfect time to connect with the community. And fine, maybe it's also a great time to do some people watching.

This year marks the first time Grand Marquee has ever had a Christkindl market, and I walked the eight blocks over so I didn't have to deal with the overcrowded parking. My cheeks are numb from the cold, but my smile is wide as I take in the parking lot of the Downtown Market that's been transformed into a winter wonderland.

There are over thirty vendors here, from food trucks to jewelry makers to local bath and body shops and more. The log cabin-style booths all have signs at the top with the business's name and garlands surrounding it. In the center of the parking lot stands a massive Christmas tree, lit up in multicolor hues.

I bounce on my feet in giddy anticipation, ready to meet new people and find some gifts for my friends and family. My first stop is the hot cocoa stand, where I order the largest size they have, topped with whipped cream, a toasted marshmallow, and lots of melted chocolate.

I pick up the cutest toys for my nieces, a handmade blanket for Robbie, and custom engraved ornaments for Ash and Eli. When I spot a hand-knit book sleeve, I immediately think of Olivia and how she always complains her books get damaged in the luggage when she travels.

My parents are getting what they always do—a short story. Ever since I was fifteen and discovered my passion for writing, I shared it with them in the form of a holiday gift. It's become a tradition at this point, and I've written them lots of different stories—a thriller about a woman getting stranded in a snowstorm, a fluffy romance about childhood friends, and even a fantasy about elves looking for a missing Santa Claus. This year, it's a murder mystery set in the 1900s.

The only one I'm struggling to find a gift for is Jordan. He's always been hard to shop for. He already has everything he wants or needs and it's impossible to surprise him. Even though I already got him a yoga mat as an inside joke, I do want to find something nice for him.

Something has shifted in our relationship ever since Thanksgiving. At first I thought that maybe I gave in too fast, that I should have held on to my anger. Because what if he does it again? What if he picks up and leaves, *again*, and leaves me behind? I don't think I could take it.

I've seen him almost daily since that night—at the coffee shop down the street when we leave for work in the morning; at family dinners, which have become more frequent recently; and even at the gym on the first floor of our apartment complex.

He hasn't asked for more help with his stretches, and part of me is disappointed. Not because I don't get to put my hands on him again, although that is a huge downside, but because I thought he was making progress in asking for help.

My phone buzzes and I pick up the call.

"Hey, Roro," I say, smiling at my brother's old nickname.

"Hey, Al. I need to ask you a favor," he says, jumping right in.

"What's up?" I ask distractedly, running my hands over a soft red scarf.

"Can you babysit this weekend? We have a fundraiser for the Blue Line Brigade and it's all hands on deck," he says in a rush.

"Robbie, of course. Are you okay though? You sound stressed."

My brother sighs, and I take a seat on one of the benches that just opened up. "Yeah, this week has been a lot, honestly. I thought Olivia would be home this weekend, but her schedule got mixed up. And—" He trails off, sighing.

"And what?" I ask, frowning and gripping the phone a little tighter.

"Honestly, I feel like I'm failing," he eventually says in a sad voice.

"Are you kidding? You're, like, the best, Robbie. You're an amazing dad, a great entrepreneur, a great husband. Why would you think you're failing?"

"I don't know. It's just hard when she's gone for longer

periods of time," he says quietly and my heart sinks. Robbie always puts up such a great front, being there when everyone else needs him, but he struggles asking for help just like the rest of us.

"How about I take Val for the whole weekend? That way you can focus on work and get some rest too."

"I can't do that to you. Just a few hours would be—"

"Please, please, please. You know I don't see her as often as I want."

Robbie laughs, though I catch the reluctance in his tone. "Are you sure?"

"Yes. I'll come get her."

"Thank you. You're the best."

When I get to Robbie's house, I find him napping on the couch and Valerie quietly playing in her living room crib. The cats run up to me, meowing for attention and I smile, giving each one a pet.

"Hey, baby," I coo at Valerie, picking her up and snuggling her to my chest. She babbles incoherently at me, and I kiss the top of her head. I step over the pile of toys on the floor and grab a nearby blanket with one hand, draping it over Robbie. He's out like a light, and I take a moment to really take him in. He looks tired, and his dark blond hair is sticking out in all directions. I sit next to him, rearranging the pillows and propping his head up on a fluffy blue one.

Val is content playing with my hair and a random toy she found, which she has a death grip on, so I turn the TV on low volume and let my mind wander to all the things I could be doing to help my family more. By the time Robbie wakes up, I have a plan in mind. I just hope he's willing to accept the help.

. . .

JORDAN

THE FOOD IS PRECARIOUSLY close to falling out of my arms, but I manage to readjust at the last second, pressing the button to the third floor with my elbow.

"Wait," a familiar voice says from the hallway, and I stick a leg out to stop the door from closing.

Alice's flushed face comes into view as she's pushing something into the elevator. I peek around the mountain of bags I'm holding and notice she has Val bundled up in her stroller, a variety of luggage dangling from the handles.

"Thanks," she breathes out, sounding winded.

"Everything okay?" I ask, facing her.

"Yeah, I'm babysitting for the weekend," she says, peeking down at Val and smiling. The baby giggles and waves her little arm up at Alice and I can't stop the grin that overtakes my face. Alice is so good with kids, and I've imagined more than once what starting a family with her would be like.

My cheeks redden at the thought, and I quickly look away. "I'm babysitting too, for the night," I say.

"Really?" She perks up at the thought of seeing Katie and Lory, and my stomach does something it hasn't done in a while—it *flutters*.

"Yeah, they're watching a movie right now, I just stepped into the lobby to get the delivery."

"Uncle of the year," she sing-songs, stepping closer and peeking at the bags. "Wow, you went all out."

I laugh, looking at all the pizza, salads, and mac and cheese I ordered, not knowing what the kids like nowadays. "I like to give them options," I say.

Her stomach growls right as we get to our floor and I

hold the elevator door open once more. "Well, if you have any leftovers, you know who to call," she jokes.

"Why don't you join us? The girls like hanging out with Val and I have way more food than we all could eat," I say with as much nonchalance as I can, trying not to show her how much I want her to come over. How badly I want to spend more time with her.

Alice stops in her tracks, and I can see her pondering it. My eyes are drawn to the way her teeth sink into her lower lip, and I wish she were biting me instead. *Fuck*, I'm jealous of her pretty lip.

After a moment, she nods and gives me a shy smile. "That would be nice, actually."

"All right then, come in," I say, grinning as I open the door and hold it for her.

"Aunt Alice," Katie and Lory exclaim in unison and run up to hug her, fawning over Valerie in the process.

"Wow, no 'thank you, Uncle Jordan' for bringing back food?" I tease them, placing the bags down on the kitchen island. As I start opening up the containers, Alice moves to the cupboards, pulling out plates and forks.

"Girls, food is ready! Who wants pizza?" I ask, and they both reply enthusiastically.

"Um, actually," Alice leans in to whisper, "Lory can't have tomatoes. She's been getting rashes from them."

I look down at her and frown. How did I not know that? Have I not been paying enough attention since I've been back?

"Oh, I didn't realize," I say, sullen.

"It's okay. It's not something super common, but tomato sauce is not the best for her," Alice says, shrugging one shoulder in a "what can you do" gesture.

I nod and swallow down the disappointment, promising

to myself that I'll do better next time. "Hey Lory, how does some mac and cheese sound? It's even got the crumbles I know you like," I say, picking the six-year-old up and swinging her from side to side. Her giggles tell me I haven't completely messed up her dinner, and that she will in fact not throw herself into a fit of crying over the pizza.

"Yummy," she says once I'm done playing with her.

"That's right," I say, and set her on the couch, handing her a plate of food.

When I get back to the counter, Alice is staring down at a pizza box, mouth open like she might ask something.

"Everything okay?" I ask, opening up the box.

She blinks down at the pizza and pins me with her blue gaze. "You got a gluten-free one?"

My cheeks heat and I look down at the thin crust pizza, grabbing a few slices and placing them on a plate. "Yeah," I mumble.

"For me?" she asks in disbelief.

"Yeah, I was hoping you'd come hang out if pizza was involved," I say, sliding the plate in front of her and glancing at her face. Is she upset or relieved that I took the liberty?

"Thanks." She smiles, stepping closer to me and giving me a quick hug. "Thanks for remembering."

"I remember everything about you," I whisper into her hair before she pulls away and heads over to the couch.

AFTER A WHOLE MARATHON of Disney movies, all three girls are asleep. I carry Katie to the bedroom while Alice takes Lory and we tuck them in my bed, closing the door softly behind us.

"I think this is one of the most successful sleepovers yet," Alice whispers, looking at me over her shoulder. She changed after dinner and she's in her softest pajamas, looking adorable and comfortable in my apartment. Another flash of longing runs through me and it's so powerful that I stop in my tracks for a moment, closing my eyes tight against the vivid image of her like this every night. What would it feel like to have this version of her—soft and gentle and soothing—forever?

"You should stay the night," I blurt out, and she stops walking in front of me. I stop just before barreling into her, placing my hands on her shoulders to steady myself.

"Oh?" she asks, leaning into my chest for the briefest moment. She quickly recovers and turns to face me, and my hands fall back to my sides.

"I just mean, the girls will want to see you in the morning. And I can make breakfast," I add lamely. *Idiot*. Why would she spend the night when she can sleep in her own bed across the hall?

"Where would I sleep?" she hedges, looking over at the couch.

"The couch is big enough, I just need to pull it open. I'll grab some sheets."

"Um, yeah. Okay," she says, tucking her hair behind both ears.

"Really?" I ask in a daze. I didn't actually expect her to say yes.

"Yeah. A sleepover. It will be fun." She nods quickly, flashing me a small smile. "Plus, if Val wakes up in the middle of the night, I can just let you take care of her."

I shake my head. "You just don't want to do the hard work, I see."

"Hey, kids are exhausting."

"True. But they're so cute."

"Agreed," she says, looking down at Valerie in her crib.

"Do you want kids some day?" I whisper as I pull the couch out and cover it with sheets.

Alice comes over to help and gives me a questioning look. "Of course. The more the merrier."

"I think I would want at least three," I say, surprising even myself. I've never thought much about having kids. At least not until I retired from hockey and realized that I don't have much going for me. Most guys in their early thirties already have a wife and kids, but I was always too focused on my career. And truthfully, I was always too in love with Alice to even notice anyone else.

"I think you'd be a great dad," she says softly, laying down on one end of the couch, pulling the blanket we used as cushion on the floor earlier on top of her.

I grab a comforter from the linen closet and cover her with it instead. I think about saying something else—how she'd be a great mom, how I wish for her to have the best in life, even if that's not me. But when I bend down to whisper it, her eyes are closed and her breathing is even.

She's asleep.

My hand reaches out and brushes the hair off her forehead. Leaning in, I press a lingering kiss to her warm skin. "I think I'd be even greater with you by my side," I whisper at her temple.

CHAPTER 27

December

ALICE

I WAKE UP INSIDE A FURNACE. Or is it a sauna? I feel a bead of sweat rolling down the bridge of my nose and I scrunch it a few times. I try to move my arm, but it's stuck in the heavy blanket I'm cocooned under.

The blanket moves and I—

Wait, the blanket moves? My eyes fly open and the first thing I notice is a silver necklace resting against a white shirt. The same white shirt Jordan was wearing last night while we had a movie marathon and took care of the girls.

My nose is precariously close to the hollow spot at his throat, and I can feel every breath he inhales and exhales, ruffling what I'm sure is an incredible case of bed hair. My eyelids flutter closed once more as I bask in the closeness.

Jordan's arms are around me, one draped over my shoulder, the other pinned under me.

This can't possibly be comfortable for him. I should move. I should put some distance between us, not just because I'm overheated, but because I told myself I wouldn't do this again. It's bad enough for my bruised-up heart that I've let him in again, even just as a friend.

But we have never been able to be just friends. From the moment I met him, I knew I was going to fall head over heels in love with him. And I think deep down, he knew it too. This thing between us is too raw, too real. It's stolen glances at the dinner table and subtle touches between friends. It's fond memories at the cabin and hot kisses in the snow. It's steady hands on my waist and warm lips against my forehead. It's ordinary moments made extraordinary by the man holding me.

I blink back the tears that threaten to spill and burrow myself deeper, enjoying this moment for as long as I can. I don't know where we stand anymore, but I do know that my attraction to Jordan is still as strong as ever.

Valerie's soft cries pull me out of my comfortable nap, and I gently push back on Jordan's chest to check on her. He turns on his back but doesn't wake up and I breathe a sigh of relief, not wanting to deal with the awkwardness of waking up tangled in each other and having to—god forbid—talk about it.

My niece's face is pinched with big fat tears at the corners of her eyes, and I pull her into my arms, hugging her tight. "What's wrong, baby? Were you lonely?" I ask quietly. After a quick diaper change and a bottle, she's all smiley and happy once more. It's astounding how much she takes after Olivia. She, too, is hangry most of the time.

I place her in the high chair I brought over from my

apartment last night and peek into Jordan's bedroom to check on the girls. They're both still asleep and sprawled out in the king-sized bed. I smile and pull the blanket up to cover them. My gaze snags on a picture on Jordan's nightstand and my fingers involuntarily reach out to grab it.

It's a picture of us at Robbie and Olivia's wedding, walking down the aisle together. It doesn't look like one of the professional pictures from that weekend and I bring it closer to my face for inspection. I'm smiling wide, looking down at the bouquet in my hand, while Jordan's head is turned my way, a soft look on his face. Another piece of my armor cracks and falls from where it's encased around my heart.

Even after everything I had put him through—ignoring him, not being willing to hear him out, he was still looking at me like I meant the world to him.

More than that, he keeps the picture on his nightstand.

Does he look at it every night?

Is it a constant reminder of what we could have had?

I swallow the lump in my throat and tiptoe out of the room. Jordan is still asleep on the couch, lying face down on his stomach after having rolled out of the blanket. His arms are clutching the pillow above his head, and his long legs are sprawled, one socked foot dangling over the edge.

I bite my lip and allow myself one more glance, roaming over his muscular thighs and his firm ass before deciding on making breakfast.

I'm quiet as I pull blueberries, milk, and a carton of eggs out of the fridge. I land on making pancakes, knowing the girls will love it as much as Jordan. When the microwave beeps, I take the butter out and look over my shoulder. He's still asleep and as much as I want to enjoy his conversation, I'm glad he's getting some rest. He needs it. Especially now that I know how much pain he deals with on a regular basis.

With my back to the living room, I flip the last of the pancakes and scramble a few eggs, adding them into the pan opposite the bacon.

"That smells so good." Jordan's deep voice comes from somewhere behind me, and I turn just in time to see him stretching with a sleepy expression on his face. I stare open-mouthed, barely holding on to the spatula, as he closes the space between us and leans in, peeking at the stove and the stack of pancakes on the plate next to it.

"Blueberry. My favorite," he says, giving me a dopey smile. His freckles are stark in the morning light, and I trace the pattern over his nose and cheeks with my eyes. I want to kiss those freckles. I want to sink my teeth into his bottom lip and taste that dopey smile.

Instead, I clear my throat and take a step back, until my spine meets the edge of the fridge. Jordan looks at me like I've grown another head, but I save the moment by saying, "Want some orange juice?"

"Sure," he says, and I busy myself pouring us juice and stacking food on our plates.

JORDAN

I'M NOT sure what changed between last night, when Alice made her way into my arms, claiming to be cold, and this morning. One moment, she was pinning me with her gorgeous blue eyes, her gaze searching, and the next, she was focusing on everything other than me.

Does she feel this pull between us too?

After breakfast, I offer to keep an eye on all three kids while she takes a shower. As much as I want her to stay, she runs back to her apartment and comes back wearing a matching set of pink sweats, her shoulder-length hair damp from the shower.

"Your turn," she says, making herself comfortable on the couch, placing a book next to her and perching her laptop on her thighs.

"Okay," I chuckle, grabbing a towel out of the linen closet and heading into the bathroom. My shower is quick since I don't want to leave her alone too long. I crave being with her, next to her, around her. I'll take every ounce of attention she's willing to give me.

Once I step out of the shower, a towel wrapped around my waist, I realize I didn't bring any clothes in here with me. I groan and screw my eyes shut.

Shit.

The door creaks as I open it slowly and poke my head out, looking towards the living room. Alice's gaze snaps to mine and she smiles, trying not to show her amusement.

"Everything okay?" she asks with a raised eyebrow.

My cheeks are on fire, and I look down at the floor of my hallway in embarrassment. "I forgot to grab clothes."

Alice laughs breezily, throwing her head back against the couch. "Want some help?" she asks once she finally calms down.

"No!" I yell out, groaning once more and holding my towel with both hands. "Can you just look away?"

"Sure thing, hotshot," she says, winking at me, and my dick twitches at the old nickname. I bite my lip and look out once more, making sure she is indeed not watching.

I rush down the hall and duck into my bedroom, but her light chuckle follows me all the way into the closet.

BY THE END of the day, we've stuffed ourselves with leftovers and junk food, watched three movies, and even played a couple of card games.

The girls are asleep once more but before Alice can make herself comfortable on the couch, I say, "What if we take the sleepover to the bedroom?"

Her wide eyes meet mine and she blushes. Hard. I didn't mean anything by my comment, but a smirk still plays on my lips. I like where her mind is at.

"I just mean—it's a king-sized bed, we can all fit. And Val's crib is portable."

"Right, of course. That would be good," she says, nodding and trying to convince herself.

She tucks Katie and Lory in on one side of the bed and we place Val by my side, so we can easily reach her if she wakes up. I bring in her laptop and book and she takes them both with a shy smile.

I don't have time to wonder what she's thinking about because she makes herself comfortable in the middle of the bed, getting back to her screen and sitting up against the headboard.

Reluctantly, I slide in next to her and mirror her position, scrolling on my phone and looking at some team reports. The room is quiet except for the sound of the girls' breathing and Alice's fingers flying across the keyboard.

I wonder what she's writing. I'm dying to know what her book is about and if she'd ever let me read it. Taking a shot in the dark, I whisper, "Is that your book you're working on?"

"No, I'm putting some finishing touches on the story for my parents for Christmas."

I smile, happy that they still have that tradition. "What genre is it this year?"

Alice slowly turns her head to look at me and grins. "Two words: murder mystery," she says, wiggling her eyebrows.

I bite my lip, looking down at her. She smells so good, I want to wrap her up in my arms and get drunk on her coconut shampoo.

"This is my book, by the way," she says shyly, tapping a manicured finger on the pink book sitting between us.

I gasp, startling her. "You mean, I could have been reading it this whole time?"

"I never said you could read it," she says, but I can tell she's just teasing.

"You won't have a choice. Once it's published, I'll buy a whole case of them," I whisper back.

"Better put your money where your mouth is, hotshot."

"You know I will," I say, my gaze dipping to her lips and the curve of her smile.

"We'll see." That's all she says as she gets back to her typing.

When I look over at her again, her head is slumped against her chest and her arms have gone slack. I put her computer to sleep and place it on my nightstand and I grab her book, planning to do the same.

Except I don't. Instead, I read the back of it, and then I read the dedication, the author's note, and the prologue. And by the time my eyelids are closing shut, I'm halfway through the book. I'm dying to know what happens to the characters and if they get their happy ending, but sleep wins over this time.

When I lie down after turning the light off, Alice stirs and drifts closer to me, her head finding the spot between my shoulder and chest. I curve my arm around her and pull her closer, letting my fingers tangle in her hair.

I fall asleep inhaling her sweet scent and muttering, "I hope we get our happy ending."

CHAPTER 28

December

ALICE

I'VE BEEN WORKING on my next novel and even though the story will end up being quite emotional, all I can think of at the moment is: *SMUT*.

I really need to get laid.

Seeing Jordan the other day in nothing but his boxers sent me into a horny frenzy. Why does he have to be so damn good-looking?

The frustration builds and I delete another paragraph. Nothing makes sense for this character. I've tried writing her into a hookup scene, I've tried the one bed trope, but the chemistry just isn't there. It needs *more*. She's sexy and strong and she wouldn't just have sex with the first guy she meets. But maybe ... maybe she could reconnect with her older brother's best friend.

Ugh, this again?

I shake my head and slam the lid of my laptop shut. I stand up and pace my living room for a minute before dejectedly plopping down on my soft, oversized reading chair. Pulling my phone out of my sweatpants, I start looking for inspiration. "How to spice up your sex life," I type into the search bar.

The first article that pops up is something that no one in the history of existence should ever read, so I move on to the next. My eyebrow lifts up, and I click on it. This one talks about everything from experimenting with toys, to acting out fantasies, to exploring erogenous zones. My eyes widen and I quickly exit out. Maybe I'm not quite this adventurous yet.

Before I can turn off my phone for good, something catches my eye. "Five reasons why you should do a boudoir photoshoot."

An hour later, I finally come out of the rabbit hole I went down. I put my phone away and turn on my computer, inspiration hitting me all at once. Maybe my character is curious enough to get some boudoir shots and send them to her brother's best friend—I mean, her childhood friend.

Except the more I write, the more I realize I have no idea what I'm talking about. After a couple glasses of wine and a lot of frustrated groans, I get back on my phone and start searching for boudoir photographers in the area. I grab the bottle to top off my glass and realize that it's empty. *Huh, when did that happen?*

I get a notification from the app that connects me with photographers in the area and it looks like Sam is available tomorrow.

Well, don't mind if I do.

I WAKE up in my reading chair the next morning with drool on my face and a pounding headache. Did I really kill a whole bottle of Riesling by myself and pass out?

My phone buzzes and I squint at the message on the screen. Apparently, Sam will be here tonight for our appointment. What appoint—

Oh.

Oh, shit.

No, no, no.

Please, please, dear God or whoever is out there, please give me a sign that I didn't book a boudoir photoshoot. My phone dings again and when I tap the message, I see a receipt for a non-refundable payment.

Fuck.

I scramble out and run a hand through my messy hair. There's got to be a way out of this. This Sam person will understand. Right? It was just a drunken mistake.

I groan and decide to call the one person who would not judge me for this.

"Hello, *lapsi**." Normally his nickname for me—*kid*—would irritate me, but I'm too distressed to care.

"Eli, help me!"

His voice changes from amusement to concern in an instant. "What happened?" Eli says, his Finnish accent coming out like it does when he's angry or serious.

"I think I did something really stupid," I say, choking on

---

* Lapsi = kid

the words. I think I might actually cry. What was I *thinking*?

"Are you safe?" he asks.

"Yes, I'm not in any actual danger, Eli. I'm just freaking out."

"*Helvetti**! You almost gave me a heart attack."

"Sorry," I mumble.

Eli sighs and says, "Okay, tell me. What happened?"

I wince. Eli and I talk about everything, so I shouldn't feel embarrassed about this, but I think that maybe this might be crossing the line. He's like a brother to me after all, and it's not like he gives me details of his and Ash's sex life, so why should I bring up mine?

"Al?"

"Okay, just please don't think of me as weird after I tell you," I say but don't give him a chance to reply. "So, I was writing a chapter last night and it got smutty, but I wasn't getting the flow of it right, so I ended up researching boudoir photoshoots and I may have gotten drunk on a bottle of wine and accidentally booked a photographer." I rush out the last of the words and hold my breath in anticipation.

Eli chokes and sputters on whatever he's drinking, and after a long moment he sighs so loudly that I can almost feel it in my own bones through the phone. "What the fuck?" His accent makes it sound more like *watdafok* and I grimace.

"Sorry, TMI, I just don't know what to do. Apparently, I paid $300 for someone to come take pictures of me in my lingerie."

"Jesus, Al. Can't you cancel it?"

---

* Helvetti = hell

"No, apparently it's nonrefundable. And I don't have that kind of money to just throw around."

"I'll pay for it, just cancel if you want."

"No, I'm not gonna take your money," I say, a little annoyed that he would offer but grateful at the same time. Annoying older brother figures, always there ready to protect.

"Okay, so ..."

I wait for him to continue, and when he doesn't, I supply, "So ...?"

"So do it."

"What??"

"It sounds like your drunk subconscious was telling you to do some research. For your book, of course. So do it," he says, matter-of-fact. Um, who is this person?

"Eli, are you feeling okay? Aren't you usually against impulsive decisions, especially ones that are made under the influence?"

"Usually," he muses. "But I don't know, maybe you should get outside of your comfort zone. I've recently found that it's good for you."

"Hm, interesting. I mean, you're not wrong, this would be a good research opportunity."

"Problem solved, then?"

I sigh and accept my fate. I guess it is.

"Sounds like it. Are you coming home for Christmas?"

"Most likely. Depends on the game schedule."

"All right, love you. Say hi to Ash for me."

"Love you too, *lapsi*. Ash will have a field day when I tell him about this." Eli chuckles.

Of course he will.

I NERVOUSLY PACE around the apartment, tidying up pillows and fixing my hair and makeup every five minutes. Sam texted that they are running a few minutes late and as if I wasn't nervous enough, now I have even more time to overthink this whole thing.

The silky black robe I have on does nothing to keep me warm, so I rub my arms with my palms, warding off the chill that threatens to overtake me. I would turn the heat up, but I don't want to be all sweaty for the photoshoot.

There's a knock at the front door and I jump up, startled. It takes me longer than it should to walk the few steps over there and open it.

"Alice?"

"Um, yes?"

"I'm Sam," the guy in the hallway says, and I blink at him a couple times. Why did I assume Sam was a woman?

"Right, nice to meet you, Sam," I recover, opening the door wider to let him step inside. I poke my head in the hallway and look around, praying that Jordan has practice today and that he's not anywhere near my apartment when I'm taking racy pictures with a complete stranger.

Except, maybe I should be worried that I'm in my apartment with some random person, one I didn't expect to be of the male sex when I decided to go through with this plan.

"Can I get you anything?" I ask, adjusting my robe and making sure it covers everything.

Sam looks me up and down with an inscrutable expression and says, "No, I'll start setting up lighting. I assume we're doing this in the bedroom?"

My brain short-circuits at the word "bedroom," and I just stare at him, wide-eyed and, frankly, a little panicked. What is he expecting to do?

He sighs, annoyance showing on his bearded face as he *tsks* at me. "The photoshoot location—in the bedroom or somewhere else?"

Oh. Right. "Of course, um, I think I'd prefer the living room. I basically live in that reading chair anyway," I mumble nervously. I get that I have no clue what I'm doing, but this guy is giving me weird vibes and I feel uncomfortable.

"Great," he says, and turns away, opening up his bag and pulling out various cameras and tools for adjusting lighting.

I awkwardly stand behind him and try not to fidget. What the hell am I supposed to do now?

"Do you have any ideas for poses?" he asks, looking over his shoulder.

"I've never done this before, so not really."

"Clearly."

Excuse me? My mouth drops open and I almost ask what he means by that, but decide it's probably best not to engage.

"I'll guide you through the most popular poses and if you want to freestyle, you can."

Freestyle. Boudoir. Poses.

What the hell did I get myself into?

"Totally," I say, feigning confidence. "How long is the session?"

"Hour and a half," Sam supplies, messing with the camera settings.

I send a quick text to Eli, letting him know the session is about to start. Just in case this guy decides to murder me or something, Eli can send for help if he doesn't hear from me soon.

"Ready when you are, princess."

I cringe at the nickname, but hide it by turning to my kitchen island and placing my phone there, face down.

Walking over to the reading chair, I stiffly sit on the edge of it, looking up at Sam.

He smirks at me and that uneasy feeling in my stomach returns. "Got any music?"

I nod and point behind him at the device mounted on the wall. Sam connects his phone to it and plays some sexy pop playlist he probably found on a streaming service. I wince when he turns the volume up way higher than I normally would in the apartment.

Thankfully it's the middle of the day on a Friday and most of my neighbors are at work. I hope.

He readies the camera and takes a few test photos while I fidget with the bracelets I impulsively put on while I was getting ready. Sam frowns at me and lets his camera drop, the strap keeping it from falling from around his neck. He approaches and leans in while I try to keep distance between us. After fluffing some pillows, he pulls back and grabs my shoulders. I stiffen at the unwanted contact but if he notices my discomfort, he doesn't acknowledge it.

"Lean back and prop yourself up on your elbows."

I only follow the instructions when he releases me, and I let out a shaky breath. My robe rides up my thighs and I squirm under the camera lens.

"Cross one leg over the other and prop it up," he instructs, and I reluctantly do it.

I thought this photoshoot would be sexy and empowering, but so far I'm cold, uncomfortable, and the farthest away from feeling attractive.

Sam gets annoyed with my pouting and stiff posture as he guides me around various simple poses in my reading chair. "All right, let's try something else. Plant your feet on the floor and straighten your spine."

He takes a couple more pictures, but he seems to grow more and more frustrated. *Me too, buddy.* His next command is what sends me into a spiral. "Take off the robe and spread your legs."

"Excuse me?" I stammer out.

He sighs and rubs his temple with one hand. "If all you're gonna do is sit there awkwardly with a robe on, then what's the point of even doing this? Who would ever find this sexy?" He says "this" while pointing at me with such disgust that I immediately feel stupid and small for doing this. I knew this was a bad idea.

I swallow hard, blinking away the tears that threaten to spill and start to take off the robe. Sam takes pictures while I do it and I can see his gaze roaming over my chest where the tops of my breasts are spilling out of the pushup bra.

Sam asks me to open my legs up again, but I ignore him, readjusting my hair and fidgeting with my bracelets some more. He groans in frustration but takes some more pictures in the same pose. I keep my legs firmly closed together the whole time and don't hear what he says next due to the loud music.

"You really need to open up those pretty legs of yours." He speaks up, but the music cuts out abruptly, so it sounds more like he's yelling it at me. We both look over to the speaker on the wall and—

Fuck.
Fuck.
Fuck.

A very intimidating, very angry Jordan is staring menacingly at Sam, the speaker cord dangling from his hand.

"Or what?" he says, voice deep and darker than I've ever heard it.

Sam takes a visible step back from me and swallows.

"This is a private session," Sam tries to say, and Jordan chuckles, dropping the cord and taking a few slow steps forward.

I'm frozen to the spot, and I don't even dare look for my robe that got discarded on the floor somewhere. My eyes are glued to Jordan, and I wonder what he'll do. Would he punch Sam for me? Protect my honor?

Am I into this?

I shake my head, and Jordan glances at me. His expression is not one I can decipher, but I hold his gaze nonetheless, trying to communicate how uncomfortable this random guy is making me.

Jordan's jaw clenches and he turns back to Sam.

"This session is over. Leave."

"Whatever, this is the worst photoshoot I've ever done anyway. Thanks for the free money," Sam says bitterly, and tries to get past Jordan, but he doesn't get far.

Jordan grabs Sam by the collar of his shirt and pulls him close to eye level, which is a ridiculous sight—Sam, five foot eight, on his tiptoes in front of J.

"I don't care who you are or why you're here, but you better leave."

I bite my lip to keep from laughing and slowly stand up, finding my robe and throwing it back on to at least cover my almost-naked butt.

Sam scoffs and picks up his tools, shoving them in his bag as fast as possible. Before he can put his camera away, Jordan snatches it away, pulling out the SD card.

"Hey, that's my property."

"Not anymore," Jordan says, shoving the camera back in Sam's chest.

Sam cowers in front of Jordan's glare but turns to me and says, "I'm gonna bill you for that."

"You're never going to speak to her again. And you're going to lose her number too, while you're at it," Jordan says, reaching in his pocket and pulling out a hundred-dollar bill from his wallet.

Frankly, Sam doesn't deserve any more money for being such an asshole, but I don't want to make the situation worse.

I'm grateful for Jordan as he kicks the nasty photographer out of my apartment, but I'm dreading the silence that follows. Jordan's back is to me, and I can see his muscles shifting underneath his white T-shirt as he takes in heavy breaths, the fists at his side clenching and unclenching.

I've seen every version of Jordan throughout the years—happy, sad, depressed, neutral, excited, angry—but never furious Jordan. I take a step closer and my heels clack against the hardwood floor. Jordan's shoulders stop moving, almost like he's stopped breathing. Is he mad at me? Disappointed?

I can't stand his anger pointed at me, so I bite back my tears and rush forward to hug him. My arms go around his torso, my hands curling into his soft shirt, my head between his shoulder blades.

"J, I don't know why you came, but I'm so glad you did." I squeeze him harder whispering, "Thank you, thank you." I expect him to turn around, hug me back, or at least acknowledge what I said, but he doesn't.

"J?" I say, and slowly drop my hands, thinking maybe I've crossed the line with a hug.

Jordan hangs his head and turns around to face me, a sad smile on his lips. "You haven't called me that in a really long time," he says in a gruff voice.

He's right, of course, but I'm not sure how to respond, so I stay rooted to the spot.

"What were you thinking?" he asks with a deep sigh.

"I wasn't. Clearly," I mumble.

"There must have been a reason for it," he prods, and I keep my gaze glued to his collarbone, where a silver necklace is stark against his brown skin.

"Al?"

"I was doing research," I say, embarrassed that he found me in this situation and had to intervene because I clearly wasn't looking out for myself.

"For what?"

"A new book I'm writing."

"Hm," he says as his pointer finger reaches for my chin and tilts my head up to meet his gaze. The look in his brown eyes is indecipherable and I don't know if I want to lose myself in it or hide as fast as I can.

My feet stay planted to the floor, though, so I guess I'm not running. But is being so close to him really a good idea? I still don't know how I feel about him being back in my life, even after our recent heart to heart. I swallow hard and Jordan lets go of my chin only to reach down, down, down.

What is he doing? Why am I not stopping him?

Just when I think he'll pull me in, I feel his knuckles brush against the sliver of skin accessible through my corset. His deft fingers work quickly and when I look down, I see he's tied my robe around my middle. The tops of my breasts are still showing, but the rest of me is decently covered.

I can feel the blush on my face spread over to my chest,

and I *know* Jordan notices it as his eyes bounce over the spot.

"Did it help?"

"What?"

"The photoshoot. Did it help with your book?"

I shake my head, still entranced by his proximity. "No," I whisper.

"Be careful next time," he says, teeth grinding as he looks back at the door that Sam was kicked out through.

This time, I'm the one to reach out and take his face in my hands. Some of the tension in his body is gone and he lets me bring our foreheads close together. Our noses brush and I find myself saying, "There won't be a next time if you help me finish it."

CHAPTER 29

December

JORDAN

I THINK my brain stopped working because all I can do is stare down at Alice. For a moment, I'm lost in the cornflower blue of her eyes as I map the seemingly endless galaxy I see there. Her hands are soft but unwavering as they hold my head in place, our noses still brushing.

It takes almost too long for me to process what she just said. *There won't be a next time if you help me finish it.* Fucking hell. How can I ever say no to this girl?

The self-doubt I struggle with creeps back in and I close my eyes tight, letting out a long exhale. I expect her to back away, take my reaction as a rejection, but she doesn't move.

"J?" she asks, and I can't believe how much I've missed her calling me by that silly nickname. The way she says it, tentative and raw, makes me think of our time at the cabin, when there was nothing else except for this—two bodies, two hearts, and nothing but time to explore each other.

But that's in the past, and up until today I thought she was completely over me, or at least pretending to be. But right here and now, it feels like she might let me in again.

I open my eyes and Alice meets my gaze head on, no hesitation on her face.

"What exactly are you asking?" I ask, voice hoarse as my hands find her hips and dig in to help me ground myself.

Alice swallows and tips her head more, our lips inches apart. "I want you to take the photos."

I contemplate the request for a moment and try not to let my disappointment show. I should tell her no. I should kiss some sense into her and tell her how much I missed her in the last couple of years. I should tell her I've never felt this for anyone else, no matter how hard I tried.

Instead, I say, "Okay."

Alice straightens up, clearly taken by surprise and I fight every instinct I have to not take it back. If this is what she wants, if this is what will get her to trust me, this is what I will do.

"Really?" she asks, amusement brightening up her eyes.

"Yes," I say tightly, and step back from her, pulling my phone out and opening up the camera.

"Okay," Alice says, still thrown for a loop.

"Lead the way."

After looking around and fidgeting with her robe she looks at me wide-eyed and says, "We should move to the bedroom." She walks past me, and I can't help but admire her thighs and the way her heels make her calves pop. I breathe through my nose and subtly adjust my cock as I follow her into the room. This girl is going to ruin me.

She places her phone on her charger and the speaker

attached to it starts playing something soft and melodic in the background. I stand in the middle of the room, wondering how the fuck I'm going to get through this as Alice saunters over to the bed and perches at the end of it.

"Well?" she says, raising a dark blond eyebrow.

I bite the corner of my lip at her shenanigans, but don't say anything for fear that she'll stop this little roleplaying session. I'm too into it to care that it might not be such a great idea.

Walking closer to the bed, I aim the camera at her from a higher angle and start snapping pictures. Alice's confidence grows with each click as she pushes her breasts together, making her cleavage irresistible. She follows up by crossing one leg over the other, her head tipped up to look at the camera seductively.

I hope she doesn't look at my crotch because I'm already fucking hard. My hands start to shake a little as she spreads her legs open and takes off her robe. Alice's body is a fucking work of art. Her waist is narrow, but her thighs are thick, and her ass is—fuck, I don't even know. She's soft in all the right spots and I can't help but stare down at her through the camera.

After a second, she reaches out and steadies my hand, bringing me out of my reverie. Fuck, what am I doing? *What are we doing?*

"J?"

"Sorry," I say, snapping a few more pictures and trying to pull my hand out of hers, but she doesn't let go.

"I have an idea, if you really want to help," she says, voice sultry.

All I can do is nod and Alice guides me, taking my hand and placing it on her chest. My thumb involuntarily brushes the swell of her breast, and I can feel her heartbeat kicking up.

"Take the picture," she says, holding my wrist in place. I snap at least three and the corner of her lips tick upward.

Fuck, I like this smug, confident version of her. More than I should, considering she might not want anything to do with me outside of this moment.

She guides my hand lower before stopping suddenly. My eyes snap to her face, making sure she's okay. I expect her to panic and push me away, but her eyes go wide and she says, "I have another idea."

I swallow hard and nod as Alice trails my hand up her chest and spreads my fingers around the slim column of her throat, her eyes not once leaving mine. I break the trance we're in so I can look down at the phone and reposition the camera, stepping closer to her in the process.

Alice's legs spread wider as I step between them and she arches her back, letting me guide her, my hand wrapped around her throat.

Fuck if this isn't the hottest thing that ever happened to me.

I take a few pictures, and Alice lets go of my wrist, letting me guide her this way and that, taking different pictures from various angles. I switch the setting to video and ask, "Do you trust me?"

She smirks and says, "You wouldn't be giving me a hand necklace if I didn't trust you, J."

Something in my chest loosens at her words. She does trust me. I'll take it, even if that trust is just with her body and not with her heart.

I hit the button to start recording and gently tighten my hold on her throat. Alice's eyes widen but there's determination there, rather than fear. She wants to see what I'll do next.

My knee pushes her thigh further out as I place it on the bed and I slowly push her down until she's laying on the mattress, back still arched as I hover above her.

I take a close-up video of her as my hand lets go of her throat and roams down her chest, fingers tangling in her corset, pulling at the laces. I don't go further, but end the video, placing the phone next to her on the bed. Leaning in, I whisper, "Anything else you want?"

My tactic to scare her off and slow this madness down doesn't deter her. Alice takes hold of my hand that's still tangled in her laces and starts pulling. I can't help but stare as the material starts to get loose and her breasts spill out. I don't know if I want to flip her over and smack her fine ass for being a brat or if I want to bury my face in her tits.

You should do neither.

Common sense threatens to take over, but Alice has other plans and I'm nothing but putty in her hands.

"Give me what I want, just for tonight," she says, one hand brushing my short beard.

"And what do you want?"

"You."

"To do what?" I ask, teasing her as I gingerly brush my fingers over her nipple.

Alice gasps and arches into me more. "To make me come."

I close my eyes and press my forehead to her chest. *To make me come.*

Not *to love me,* or *to spend the night.* She wants this to be purely physical and I know I should leave, but I can't. Not when she just said she trusts me with this. She trusts me again for the first time in years, and I'm not going to let her down.

"J?" she asks, voice wavering in confidence. I lift my head up and don't give her the chance to say anything else. My tongue flicks her nipple and she arches into me, hands gripping my back, my head. I lick and tease her sensitive peaks until she's writhing under me, but I'm far from close to letting her come.

I'm a starving man and the only thing I crave is the taste of her skin. My hand twists her other nipple and I alternate between licks and soft bites and grazes of my teeth.

"Fuck, J," she pants out, "I need more."

I pull away as soon as she says it and her wide blue eyes are on me in an instant. I push her further into the mattress and snake an arm around her waist. In one swift move, I flip us over so she's on top and I think I might have made a huge mistake, because I can feel her grinding on my cock.

My fingers dig into her thighs and stop her right as she's about to kiss me. I need some kind of distance between us, because if she kisses me, I already know I'll be a goner.

I reach under her thighs and lift her off me enough to scoot down the bed and position myself at her entrance. She smells sweet and floral and as my nose grazes her underwear, I realize she's so fucking *wet*.

Alice whimpers as she hovers above me. "What are you doing?"

"I'm feeling hungry all of a sudden."

"I don't think—" She doesn't finish the thought as I run my tongue over the soaked underwear, relishing in the way she gasps and shudders above me.

Fuck, my body remembers how responsive she is and all my blood rushes to my cock. My fingers dig into her soft flesh and I drag my beard along her thigh.

"Don't think what?" I say, hiding a smile into her skin as I give her a nibble.

Alice's leg shakes and she clears her throat before saying, "I don't want to hurt you."

I laugh and reach up with both hands, tearing her lacy underwear and throwing it on the floor. "You won't," I say, and run my tongue through her slit, flattening it against the sensitive bud. "Now fucking sit."

When she hesitates, I grab a hold of her ass and pull her fully onto my face. Alice gasps but she slowly relaxes as I take my time to lick and tease her, my hands kneading her plump ass.

"More," she says, moving her hips as my lips wrap around her clit and suck. *"Fuck, J."*

I bring her to the edge again and again, my fingers digging into the soft flesh of her thighs. As much as I want to draw this out, I can't. She feels and tastes too good and I bury my face in her sweet pussy as she comes on my tongue, riding out her pleasure, shaking until she's ready to collapse.

ALICE

MY HEART THREATENS to beat right out of my chest as I pant and try to get my legs to stop shaking.

Jordan trails more kisses along my thigh, his short beard giving me the sweetest friction. I'm sensitive and sore *everywhere* but I want more. I need more.

I didn't expect to sit on his face after he helped me get rid of that creepy photographer, just as I didn't expect him to take my racy photos and wrap his hand around my throat.

I wonder what else he's willing to do. How far he's willing to take this.

Maybe I'm a filthy fucking liar, because even though I told myself I wouldn't want anything casual or fleeting with Jordan again, the truth is, in this moment, I'd take anything.

Feeling bolder after the mind-blowing orgasm, I thread my fingers through his curls and pull, dragging his mouth away from the spot on my thigh he's found so fascinating. For a brief moment, our eyes connect and I'm taken aback by the pure unadulterated desire I see there.

His lips part but before he can say anything and break this moment, I guide his mouth back to my clit. Jordan closes his eyes and moans, his tongue roughly brushing my most sensitive spot. I hold his head in place with both hands and move against his tongue.

When his eyes open again, I watch him admiring me, writhing and moaning on top of him, drowning in the pleasure of having him devour me whole. I roll my hips, feeling like I might actually come again.

Jordan lifts me off and flips me onto my back, and I land on the mattress with a thud. Kneeling by the side of the bed, he grabs my ankles and roughly pulls me to the edge of it. I yelp and grin at the look on his face.

He looks like he wants me. He looks on the verge of losing his goddamn mind.

Do it, I silently beg him with nothing but a look.

There's no one else for me but you. Go ahead and ruin me.

Jordan's eyes flare in understanding and he positions my legs over his shoulders, then slips both hands under my ass, pulling me into his face.

The moment his mouth is on me again, my eyes roll to the back of my head and my muscles contract and shift. My ankles hook at his back and Jordan takes it for the encouragement it is. His tongue laps at me as he grunts and presses himself into the bed, searching for friction.

"Fuck, J. Your mouth feels so good," I say, fisting the sheets at my side and arching my back as much as the position allows.

Jordan moves his mouth down by just a little, his tongue dipping inside of me. He hums contentedly and draws lazy circles inside me, and I feel like I might burst.

"Good boy," I say, clenching harder around him. "I want you drenched in my cum."

Jordan pushes himself further into the side of the bed with a grunt, his tongue returning to my clit, nipping and flicking while he pumps a single finger inside me. That's all it takes for me to fall apart, crying out his name over and over again.

My head is facing the full-length mirror across the room, and I watch us unabashedly for a moment. He stays like that, face buried in my cunt, his beard scraping against me, ragged breaths warming me up. The hands at my waist squeeze once, twice, before his thumbs dig into my flesh. The pressure grounds me, makes me feel like this is real. That I didn't just imagine it.

I hope he leaves bruises behind. I want to feel him for days.

I run my fingers through his hair and after what feels like an eternity, his grip on me loosens, fingertips trailing down my thighs as he pulls away, looking at me with so much intensity. I should look away, I should put an end to this, but instead, I reach for the collar of his shirt and say, "Your turn, hotshot."

Jordan swallows but doesn't say anything, and my

stomach drops. Was this too much? Did I read things wrong?

"I—" he says, running a hand down his face, closing his eyes tightly. When he opens them again, the look he gives me is resigned. Remorseful, even.

Fuck.

"I can't," he chokes out.

I blink, taken aback by the sudden change. Did I do something wrong?

"Why?" I whisper, but I can tell he's not going to respond.

Jordan looks away from me, his gaze snagging on my ripped underwear on the floor.

"I'm sorry," he says, standing up and wincing. He presses his hand flat against his hip bone and steps away from the bed. *Away from me.*

I grab the discarded robe and throw it back on, fastening it as I follow him. As he reaches the front door, I breathlessly ask, "Are you okay? Is it your hip?"

"It's nothing," he says, avoiding my eyes. "I just—need to go." With another wince, he leaves the apartment, leaving me more confused and bruised than ever.

CHAPTER 30

December

JORDAN

I CAME in my pants like a fucking teenager. What the hell is wrong with me? I've barely been able to get hard in the last year since I started taking my antidepressants, let alone get myself off. But one night with Alice and I completely lost it.

She didn't even touch me, and I bucked against her mattress, thinking about nothing except the sweet taste of her against my lips.

I lean against my door and knock my head back against the wood. *Fucking embarrassing.* She probably thinks I'm pathetic. I couldn't even tell her. I just had to run away.

Peeling off my clothes, I throw them straight in the washer and jump into the shower, letting the hot water seep into my bones. Maybe it'll scrub off the feeling of fucking this up.

I'm pretty sure this was my one chance at getting Alice back. Things have been good lately, we're talking again, looking out for one another. And I just had to fuck it up.

I turn the water off and stand there in the shower until I'm cold and shivering, my forehead pressed to the cool, dark blue tile.

Idiot.

With a groan, I finally pull back, frustration building higher when I realize I don't have a towel. I yank open the door to the hallway and I see Alice at the last possible second. I don't have the chance to stop myself from barreling into her, so she ends up plastered against my wet and naked chest.

On instinct, my arms fly around her shoulders to steady her, and she yelps in surprise. Her nose is pressed against my chest, her small hands landing on my waist.

We stand there for a long moment, looking at one another with wide eyes. Her lips pull to the side in the smallest grin as she says, "We have got to stop meeting like this."

I exhale an amused breath and step back, only to realize that I'm buck fucking naked. My gaze drops to her robe, which is covered in water splotches, the material turning see-through.

"What are you doing here?"

She sighs, a tad exasperated, and crosses her arms. The see-through part rides up and I can see her stiff nipple poking at the fabric.

I swallow and slowly bring my hands down to cover my already hardening cock. Alice notices anyway and looks down at my hands, but she doesn't linger on my dick.

Instead, her wide eyes turn glassy and she takes a step towards me, lips parted.

"J," she utters my favorite nickname, hand outstretched, her fingertips grazing the long and ugly scar at my hip.

Every instinct I have tells me to turn her away, to not let her see the ugliest parts of myself. But my body doesn't move. I stand as still as I can and close my eyes at her touch. She's gentle, tracing the length of the scar with her thumb, leaving goosebumps in her wake.

When I open my eyes again, her blue gaze is already on me. "I need you to tell me why," she says, frowning.

"Why what?"

"You said you can't do this. With me. Why?"

My eyebrows scrunch together. I never said that. Did I? I was so focused on the fact that I came in my pants that I didn't even realize what came out of my mouth.

"That came out wrong. I just—" I blow out a breath, my fingers twitching to take her back into my arms. Instead, I keep them firmly in place to hide my ridiculous boner.

"No more secrets, please," she whispers.

I bite my lip and nod. "I can't do this without making a fool of myself. I haven't had an orgasm in months, and I came in my pants like a horny teen."

Alice looks at me, slack jawed, and shakes her head. "Wait, months?"

I blush and look away towards the safety of my bedroom. Maybe I can make a run for it still, get out of this conversation. She follows my gaze and narrows her eyes at me, blocking the way and crossing her arms.

My shoulders deflate and I groan. "Yes, months. I've had a hard time because of my medication. Happy?" I snap, even though I don't mean to.

Alice blinks and drops her arms back down. "Oh.

Okay," she says with a slow nod. "That's understandable. Why would that make you look like a fool?"

"Did you forget about the part where I came in my pants?" I snort.

She shrugs, leaning on the wall with her shoulder and adjusting her legs, crossing one over the other. "I think it's hot."

My gaze drags down her body, from her chest to her thick thighs and soft legs. By the time I look all the way down, I realize she's still wearing the black heels from earlier. I bite my lip, wanting those legs wrapped around me again.

"I also think you should finish what you started. I never pegged you for a quitter," she teases, her pupils darkening as she looks at me in all my naked glory.

My jaw clicks and I let my hands fall to my sides, so she can see how much she's affecting me. I'm fully hard again and she looks at me with so much desire that all my shyness dissipates. Alice undoes the loop of her robe and slowly turns around, letting the silky material drop off her shoulders. It lands on the hardwood floor of my hallway, and I can't take my eyes off her plump ass.

"Good boy," she says with a look over her shoulder as she heads towards my bedroom.

ALICE

I EXPECT to be the one leading since Jordan seems to be struggling with his confidence, but as soon as I reach the bed, his arms come around me as he pulls me against him.

His front is plastered to my back, and I shiver at the naked feel of him against my ass.

My head falls back against his chest and Jordan slowly caresses my hair away from my neck with a finger, his lips ghosting my skin with a kiss. My eyelashes flutter closed, and I tilt my head more, exposing the soft flesh at my neck. He wastes no time, peppering me with kisses and soft bites followed by soothing licks.

Jordan keeps a hand splayed across my stomach, his hot and hard erection pressing further into me. His other hand finds my breast and pinches my nipple, drawing a whimper from my lips. "More, J," I say, placing my hand on top of his and squeezing harder.

He follows my direction and brings both hands to my breasts, giving me just the right pressure to drive me crazy. I reach back and grip his cock, moaning at the feel of him in my hand. I missed him. All of him.

"I won't last long if you touch me like that," he groans into the crook of my neck, teeth scraping my sensitive spot.

"Hm, we'll see." I step out of his embrace and grin, turning us around and pushing him down on the bed. Jordan lands on his elbows, looking up at me like he can't believe this is happening again.

"Move up and lay against the headboard," I instruct, feeling giddy when Jordan eagerly obeys. He props himself against the pillows and fists the sheets at his side as I slowly crawl between his legs.

"Fuck," he says once I reach him and hover over his body. My left hand leaves a trail of goosebumps from his collarbone down to his hip. My eyes snag on the scar and a pang of sadness hits me, but I try to not let it show. I wish he would have told me about his gruesome injury. I wish he would have let me help him.

Jordan swallows and cups my face, tearing my gaze away from his scar. "I'm sorry," he says, voice gruff.

I smile and shake my head. "It's okay, J. Really." I lean in and capture his lips with mine. He sighs into the kiss, and I press into him harder. My nipples graze the black hairs on his chest and I moan, my teeth sinking into his plump bottom lip.

His arms come around me, but I pin them back to the mattress, giving him a wicked smirk. Jordan frowns, but it quickly fades as I kiss my way down his body, my tongue poking out to taste all the dips and valleys of his chest and abs, all the way down to his cock.

I press a sweet kiss to the leaking head and it twitches, making me smile. Jordan is breathing hard and watching me with so much intensity that my toes curl in my heels. I sit up and lean back to take the shoes off, but Jordan stops me with a rough command. "Leave them on."

My spine straightens and I look back at him in surprise. His jaw is clenched, his eyes bouncing from my legs to my breast and back to my face. There's a slight blush forming on his cheeks, and I smile. "Okay, hotshot. Whatever you want."

Jordan raises an eyebrow at me and I grin wider, returning to his cock and licking him from base to tip in one go. His rough exhale is stark in the quiet room, and I waste no time, taking him in my mouth as deep as I can.

"Jesus, fuck," he says, and I choke on a laugh, his dick deep down my throat. I pull off of him and clear my throat. "Are you okay?" Jordan asks in concern, one hand reaching down to brush a strand of hair out of my eye.

"Peachy," I say, bringing my mouth close to him again and spitting on his cock. It's Jordan's turn to make a choking sound as his fingers tighten in my hair. "What do you want, J?"

"Fuck, I don't know. Anything. *Everything*," he says, chocolate brown eyes boring into me, and I get the feeling he's not just talking about just sex.

"You want me to fuck you with my mouth?" I ask, and swallow the head of his cock again, hollowing my cheeks and sucking hard, letting go with a pop. Jordan groans but doesn't respond. "Or should I ride you until you buck and come inside me?" I say in a sultry voice I don't recognize.

"Baby, when did you get such a filthy mouth?" Jordan says, panting as I move to take one of his balls in my mouth, licking and sucking gently. "Actually, don't tell me. I can't handle thinking about you with anyone else," he says, holding my face with both hands as I make my way up once more and bob my head on his cock again and again.

When I come up for air, his thumbs caress my cheekbones and I admit, "There was no one else." Jordan lifts my head so he can look at me. Does he think I'm lying?

"What about the guy you brought home for Christmas that one time?" he asks, jaw clenched and eyes sad.

I burst out laughing and his expression relaxes. "I never even kissed him. I brought him to see if you'd be jealous. Or if you were truly over me after you left," I say, pressing a kiss to his stomach, making my way back up to his mouth.

"I could never get over you," he says, tipping his head to kiss me, but I pull away at the last second.

"There was no one else for you either?" I ask, needing to hear him say it.

Jordan slowly shakes his head, his eyes boring into mine. "No. I was too busy pining after the love of my life to even try loving someone new."

I suck in a breath and feel tears pricking the back of my

eyes. *The love of my life.* I've imagined him confessing his love for me so many times, but we were always a case of right people, wrong time. I never allowed myself to believe that he'd still feel the same way after all these years.

Jordan brushes a tear from my face and pulls me into a hug. I land on his chest and bury my nose in the hollow of his throat. *My favorite place to be.*

His fingers massage my scalp with one hand and rub my back with the other, and I relax in his embrace. "You're the love of my life too," I whisper.

Jordan squeezes me harder and gently flips us around so he can hover above me. "Do you want to stop? We can take this slow and talk through everything before we jump into anything physical."

"It's a little late for that. You made me come twice with your mouth today." I grin, and he chuckles. "Plus, I want to make you feel good too," I say, nipping at his bottom lip and running my tongue along the seam. He lets me in, taking control of the kiss and rubbing himself on me.

"Okay," he mumbles, taking a nipple in his mouth and leaving hot, wet kisses behind. "I have one condition though," he says, reaching down and guiding his cock to my clit, rubbing back and forth and making my eyes roll to the back of my head.

"Anything," I say in a lusty haze. I'll give him anything. *Everything.*

"Eyes on me, baby," he says, and I snap them open, looking down where the head of his cock is positioned at my entrance. Jordan slowly spreads my legs open further and brings them up to my chest. I inhale sharply as the tip of him prods my entrance. "Let's go on a date," he says, right before he slams into me with a groan.

"Fuck," I moan, locking my arms around my knees,

loving this position. He pulls out almost all the way before he repeats the motion, hitting nice and deep.

"Fuck yes? Or fuck no?" He smirks, cupping my breast with his left hand and finding my clit with the thumb of his right hand. The pressure is almost too much, but Jordan is on a mission to fuck me into this mattress.

"Yes, hotshot. I'll go on a date with you," I manage to say between moans as Jordan buries himself to the hilt inside me. I'm almost there but he has other plans, flipping me over in a swift move and covering me with his large body.

"I want to come on your ass," he growls in my ear, biting my lobe and pulling back, snapping his hips against me again and again, one hand holding me down, pressing at the small of my back. I use the pillow to muffle my screams, but Jordan yanks it away from me. "I want to hear you scream my name, baby."

"Fuck, J, I'm almost there."

"Me too," he says, panting hard and reaching between me and the mattress to rub my clit. I squeeze my eyes tight as my orgasm hits me hard. My toes curl, my legs shake, and my mouth is yelling out his name. Jordan groans and swears, pulling out at the last second.

I watch over the curve of my shoulder as he touches himself in long slow pulls, his hot cum landing on my ass and back. Jordan's head is thrown back and he's panting hard. When his eyes open, they land on the mess he made on me and he blushes. I grin at him and bite the corner of my lip. "So who's planning the date?"

CHAPTER 31

December

JORDAN

"SO LET ME GET THIS STRAIGHT," Robbie says, frowning down at the applesauce that Valerie just flung on his shirt and all over the floor. "You want to date my sister?"

I pick up the crying baby out of her high chair and bounce her in my arms a few times until she calms down. Robbie turns the faucet on and runs hot water over a rag, cleaning up the mess on the floor and his shirt. I clear my throat, trying to remain calm, even though I'm freaking out about what Robbie thinks of me dating Alice. Eventually, I say, "Yeah. I want to date Alice. I figured you should know."

"I'm confused," he says, throwing the rag in a small basket by the hallway. "I thought you two were already dating." Robbie faces me fully now, hands resting on his hips. His look is incredulous, and I'm stunned by his words.

I stop bouncing Val and she stops giggling. I stare at my best friend and notice there's still some applesauce on his face.

Shaking my head I say, "No. I mean, there was something between us at some point, but let's just say it was never the right time."

I hand over puffy-cheeked Valerie and she immediately rests her head on her dad's chest. Robbie sighs and kisses her forehead. I can tell he's tired and maybe a little overwhelmed at times, but ever since he started asking for help babysitting, he's been looking a little better. "So why are you telling me now? Are you asking for my blessing?" he asks, lips twitching in a genuine smile.

Shaking my head, I reach out and swipe the applesauce off his forehead. He laughs and mumbles a thank you. "I just wanted you to know. I'm here to stay and I'll make up for all the lost time and heartbreak I caused her."

Robbie's gaze narrows on me in assessment. I hold it, letting him see the sincerity in my statement. "You better. She was really devastated when you left. I don't think I've ever seen her like that before. Not that she told me any of this," he says, walking Val over to her playmat in the living room and taking a seat on the couch.

"How did you know, then? That there was something going on?"

"I'm not blind, man. I saw the way you two acted around each other. We all did. It was just a matter of time until you two finally figured it out. I just want to make sure that you won't break her heart again," he says.

"I promise I won't. She's always been the one for me and even when I was gone, I was never out of love with her. I was just too afraid to take a chance, and I worried too much about what our families would think."

Robbie gives me a confused look and I laugh. "Yeah, I

see how stupid that was now. This time, I'm here to stay and I won't let anything come between myself and Alice again." The vow I make is not only for Robbie, but for myself too. I'll do anything to be in her life.

"I'll hold you to that," he says, and pats my shoulder.

"WHERE ARE WE GOING?" Alice asks as soon as she opens her apartment door, giving me a wide smile. She's wearing her signature pink lipstick and my favorite dress—the green sweater one that shows off her ass.

I smirk and swing my hand around from where it's hiding behind my back. She gasps at the bouquet of white roses I hold and gingerly takes it from me. With her nose buried in them, she says, "Thank you, but you didn't have to go through the trouble."

My hands grip the door frame as I lean in and steal a kiss, whispering against her lips, "I'm just making up for all the dates I never took you on."

"Aw, J," she says, motioning for me to go inside while she adds the flowers to a jar of water. As soon as her hands are free again, I spin her around and place them around my neck, pulling her in and swaying in the kitchen. "What are you doing?" she giggles.

"Dancing with you," I say, not able to contain my grin. "I want to fit a thousand little moments in this one date," I say against her lips. "You deserve the best."

"Have you been reading more romance novels?" she asks, eyes narrowing on me. "You're giving off cinnamon roll vibes."

I laugh and kiss her forehead, spinning her around and

catching her right back in my arms. "What does that mean?"

"Nothing, don't worry about it," she says, blushing.

"Hmm, well I haven't been reading anything lately. Except for your book."

"What?" she pulls back, her blue eyes widening.

"That night we were babysitting and you fell asleep while writing, I put your laptop away and started reading the copy you had of your book. I got halfway through it before you took it home the next day," I say, biting back my smile at her shocked expression.

"Oh," she says, chewing on her lip. "What did you think?"

I tilt my head in thought and look towards the living room, spotting the book on the coffee table. "I think I need to know if Elissa and Jackson get their happy ending."

Alice's expression softens, her lips pulling into a small smile. "They do," she whispers.

"Shh, spoiler alert," I laugh, placing my hand on her mouth. She giggles and fists the side of my coat, pulling me in for a kiss. When she pulls back I say, "I want to finish it. It's really good."

"Yeah?" she blushes, looking up at me through her lashes.

"Yeah."

"I guess you can borrow it," she says, rolling her eyes and pulling away to get her coat on. "If you tell me where we're going."

I grin and shake my head, giving in. "I booked us a cooking class."

Alice gasps and clasps her hands in excitement. "Oh my god, yes! I've been wanting to go to one forever."

"I know," I say, squeezing her hand and leading her out the door.

ALICE

THE COOKING CLASS is at one of the local Italian restaurants. The addition in the back is used primarily for catering purposes and teaching beginner classes. Our instructor, Chef Roman, walks us through the space and gives us a little bit of history about the place and what we'll be making.

"Each couple can get situated at one of these tables." He gestures to the stainless steel tables, which have an assortment of ingredients and tools on them.

I pick up the little pizza cutter and smile excitedly at Jordan. I feel like he hasn't taken his eyes off me this whole time. Ever since he showed up at my doorstep with flowers, he's been absolutely perfect. I blush thinking about how he admitted to reading my book. When I peer over at him, he's grinning, looking delectable in a dark red sweater that complements the green of my dress.

I know he wants this day to be perfect, but I also need him to know that I'll take all the versions of him. I want him completely. Desperately.

"And today we will be making ravioli from scratch. After the class, you can move to the main restaurant, where a table has been reserved for each couple to enjoy a three-course meal. Are you ready to begin?" the chef asks with a smile, and we all nod.

It's hard to concentrate on anything Chef Roman is saying as my eyes keep straying to Jordan and the way he rolls up his sleeves. Or how his deft fingers tie his apron. Or how his chocolate eyes find mine, making sure I'm having a good time.

"Miss Alice?" someone says, breaking me out of my reverie as I imagine Jordan's fingers wrapped around my throat.

"Hm? Yes," I say, quickly straightening up.

"I was told you have an intolerance, so I took the liberty to create a special blend of flour, all of it gluten-free."

I blink, looking over at Jordan, who is swirling a glass of wine and sniffing it, completely ignorant of my inner thoughts and how much I want to jump his bones right now for something as trivial as remembering my food preferences.

"Thank you so much," I say, facing the chef again. "I appreciate it."

"No problem."

Jordan takes a sip of his wine and cringes. My laugh startles him and he schools his expression, handing the wine to me. "Do you want to try it?"

"I want to know why you made that face," I say, taking it from him and taking a sip. Jordan watches me intently the whole time and frowns when I place the glass on the table.

"It tastes like chalk," he whispers, looking around to make sure Chef Roman doesn't hear him. I laugh and grab his hand in mine, running my thumb over his knuckles.

"It's a dry red wine, of course it tastes like chalk. Do you want to ask for something else?"

"No, I'm good," he says, shrugging it off. "I'm not a big drinker anyway since it doesn't mix well with my medication."

I squeeze his fingers and he gives me a smile, one meant

just for me. One that says, *I have a thousand things I want to experience with you.*

"Okay. Ready to make some delicious herb and cheese ravioli?"

"So ready," he says, leaning in and kissing my forehead.

We start by mixing the flour with water, oil, and an egg, making sure it's ready to knead. I pull my two rings off, realizing at the last second that I don't have pockets in this dress. Jordan holds his hand out and I place them in his palm. I expect him to put them in the pocket of his jeans, but instead, he pulls his silver necklace out and unclasps it, adding my rings to it before refastening it behind his neck.

I smile at him and kiss his bicep, since that's all I can reach. I dig my hands in the dough just to have something to do. Just so I don't grab him and make out with him in front of the people in this class.

I try to move a strand of my hair with my shoulder, and when that doesn't work, I try to blow it away from my face. Jordan's hand reaches out and tucks the hair behind my ear. Leaning in, he says, "Want me to take over now?"

"Sure, my arms could use a break," I say, laughing. Jordan's hands come down on top of mine and he has us both kneading the dough once, twice, until Chef Roman's next instruction breaks us out of it. I pull my hands away and grab the glass of wine, taking a few sips.

Jordan's shoulder touches mine as he puts all his power into it. When he picks up the rolling pin and lifts his sleeves even higher up his forearms, I have to cross my legs where I stand. How am I going to make it through dinner when I can barely make it through this class?

BY THE TIME the dessert comes out, all I can think about is Jordan's hands on me. Not only did he look sexy as hell rolling out the ravioli, but he continued to be the perfect date, pulling out my chair in the restaurant, holding my hand as we talked about the most random, trivial things.

"What do you want for Christmas?" he asks out of the blue, as he takes a bite of the gluten-free tiramisu.

I take my time answering, sipping on the dessert wine I ordered. I'm a little tipsy and I'm sure it shows as I've been giggling and smiling nonstop. "I don't need anything, J." He raises a thick dark eyebrow at me, and I roll my eyes. "I mean it. I have all the books I need, my release date is set, I'm happy with all I have," I shrug.

"I'm sure you can think of something," he says, licking cocoa powder from the corner of his lips.

"A bigger place to live? I truly don't know," I say.

"Why a bigger place?"

I grab his hand and steal his next bite of tiramisu, relishing in the way his eyes track my lips as they wrap around the spoon. When I lean back in my chair, I say, "I like the apartment, but I'm running out of space for bookshelves. And it would be nice to have an office and a desktop to use for writing."

"Okay," he says, watching me intently as he polishes off the last bite.

"What about you? What do you want for Christmas?"

His response is immediate, and it makes me crack up. "A PS5," he says.

"Okay, nerd." I smile and run my foot up the inside of

his leg under the table. Jordan chokes on his water, flustered. He grabs my ankle with a firm hand and rubs at the exposed skin.

The waitress comes over to clear the rest of the plates and I grin as Jordan looks everywhere but at me. "Can I get you two anything else?" she asks.

"Just the check, please," I say, amused.

"It's actually all taken care of. Part of the cooking class," she explains, and I thank her again.

"Can we please get out of here?" I ask Jordan, tapping his knee with my foot where he still has my ankle prisoner.

"Fuck, yes," he groans in a low voice, and lets go of me.

I put my coat on and I expect Jordan to be up and ushering me out the door, but he's still in the chair, head in his hands. I lean in, concerned and ask, "Are you okay?"

His head comes up and his nostrils flare, his eyes boring into me. "I need a minute."

I grin at him across the table as he stares at the ceiling, mumbling something.

"What are you saying?"

"I'm naming as many hockey players as I can think of."

ONCE WE LEAVE THE RESTAURANT, Jordan keeps a hand on me the whole drive home and my smile hurts my cheeks, but I can't stop. He's burrowed himself into every little corner of my life and now that he's here and he's putting in the effort, I can't help but think that my happy ending is coming.

CHAPTER 32

December

JORDAN

ALICE'S HAND grips me and I groan my approval, even though I should probably stop her. My alarm hasn't gone off yet, but as I squint at the clock on my nightstand, I see it's almost 7 a.m.

"Are you awake yet?" she asks sleepily, smiling into the crook of my neck. I shake my head and she giggles, trailing her hand down and cupping my balls. *Fuck.*

"I need to get to work," I grumble, stopping her hand and turning over to face her. She looks adorable in one of my oversized shirts and nothing else. Her bottom lip pops out in a pout, and I kiss it quickly. "I'll make it up to you, I promise," I say, trailing a few more pecks down her jaw and neck.

"Fine, I'll allow it this time," she says, pulling me back

into a deeper kiss. For the first time in a long time, I finally feel like I'm right where I belong. I may be terrified of fucking this up again and losing her for good, but I can't imagine not trying. I can't imagine a world without her in it.

It's on the tip of my tongue to tell her how much I love her, but something holds me back. I want her to know I'm all in before I start making promises.

We break apart when my alarm goes off and I put on my coaching tracksuit, ready to head to practice.

"Did I tell you how sexy you look in that, *Coach*?" Alice says, running a finger down my bicep.

My eyebrows raise and I fight a smile as I look down at her trying to seduce me. As if she needs to. If I didn't have to get to work, I'd be on her in an instant. "No, tell me," I tease.

"Well, your ass especially is fucking fabulous," she says, squeezing one of my cheeks.

I laugh and tip her head back to kiss her. "You are a devious little thing, aren't you?"

"Yeah, but I'm *your* devious little thing."

I groan against her lips and use all my willpower to step away from my perfect girlfriend. "I'm sorry, I really do have to go. Will I see you at the game?"

"I'll be there. I'm bringing a friend from work."

"Okay, have a good day molding those young minds," I say, and wrap her in a hug.

"Have a good day yelling at grown men on skates."

"I don't yell," I scoff, grabbing a red Manticores winter hat and putting it on.

"Whatever you say, hotshot," she says, biting her lip.

I walk backwards out of my own bedroom, admiring her naked legs and thick thighs that I wouldn't mind having wrapped around me again.

"Practice is going to be pure torture when all I can think about is my sexy girlfriend," I say with a wink, hearing her laughter echoing in the hall as I leave my apartment.

When I get to my car, I send Ash a quick text, thinking of an idea for Alice's Christmas present.

JORDAN

> I have a huge favor to ask and you're not going to like it.

ALICE

THE ARENA IS PACKED by the time we get to our seats. Happy hour with Megan usually involves more than one drink and long-winded conversations about our crappy coworkers, none of which I mind. But I knew I had to cut it short today, which is why I invited her to see the game with me.

"So, I finally get to see the elusive Jordan in the flesh," she says, pulling her beanie further down her ears to ward off the cold.

"You've seen pictures at least."

"Yeah, but it's not the same. I need to get a good read on him, you know? Really see what his vibes are if he's here to stay for good this time."

I sigh, feeling bad that Megan got the brunt of most of my complaints and heartbreak over Jordan. She's seen me cry at work in between classes and in the break room. "Things are different now," I say, a touch defensively.

"I'm not suggesting otherwise. I just want you to be happy, Al," she says gently, squeezing my hand.

I squeeze hers back and say, "We're figuring things out. It's a good thing, I promise." I'm not sure if I'm trying to convince her or myself. The truth is, I could tell Jordan was holding back today and all I want is for him to be open with me and be able to say what's on his mind.

Right as my mind starts to wander, the announcer welcomes the Manticores to the ice, and I stand up, cheering. The seats Jordan has reserved under his name for the season are right by the home bench, so if I lean into the railing and pop my head over, I can see the players in the tunnel.

Tripp, the team's new captain since Robbie retired, sees me and waves enthusiastically. I wave back and smile, reaching my hand down for a high five as they start getting on the ice.

The coaches and staff are the last ones to come out and I watch Jordan as he confidently takes his place behind the bench, looking like a million bucks in his charcoal grey suit that looks like it was tailor-made for him.

"Hey, hotshot," I yell over at him, earning a glare from the nearest security attendant. All the coaches turn over to look at me at the same time and I bite my lip, laughing.

I wave at Jordan and turn around, showing him the jersey I'm wearing. It's his old one with the number 20 stitched under "Hill". It's well-worn and frayed at the cuffs, but it's my favorite one. And now I have a reason to wear it again. Now I have a reason to come to games again.

When I turn back around, I expect Jordan to be embarrassed, maybe sporting a blush on his pretty face, but instead he's grinning from ear to ear.

Hand over his heart, he throws his head back and closes

his eyes. When he looks back at me, all I see on his face is pure happiness. I blow him a kiss and he winks at me, just like he did this morning as he was walking away in his sexy-ass tracksuit.

I swoon and decide I've made enough of a scene for now. When I turn back to Megan I find her regarding Jordan with a curious expression on her angular face. She usually looks stoic, but there's some softness to her now. "What?" I ask her, not sure I want to know what she's thinking.

"I get it now," she says as we continue to stand and turn to face the flag for the anthem.

"Get what?"

"That man is head over heels in love with you."

CHAPTER 33

December - Christmas Day

ALICE

SOMEONE IS TRYING to kick in my apartment door. The pounding comes again, and I rub the sleep from my eyes, wishing my hangover would just disappear.

Robbie's fundraising gala for Blue Line Brigade was last night, and I may have had a little too much fun, dressing up in my fanciest dress, drinking mimosas with Olivia and Malia, and having a blast bidding on the auction.

I even won a basket of Manticore goodies after adding all my raffle tickets to it. I smile at how much fun we had last night. Jordan and I danced together a handful of times, and even managed to steal a few moments together, kissing in the hall or taking a short walk for a breath of fresh air. And at the end, we left the gala and headed to the Arcadian for drinks, hanging out well into the night with Alex and Malia.

Jordan and I have not found the time to go on more dates since that night a week ago, and while I was a bit disappointed we didn't get to see each other as much, we've both been busy. At least I managed to see a home game and catch him in action as the assistant coach. I loved seeing him so confident behind the bench, making good calls and helping lead the team to a 4-1 victory.

Between that game, finalizing everything for my book to get published, and babysitting the kids as our siblings prepared for hosting the holidays, I haven't been able to get my hands on him as much as I wanted to.

The pounding on the door persists—or is that the pounding in my head? I peek through the peephole and see a fit chest and a dark red beard. I roll my eyes and fling the door wide open. "Ash, what the hell? Don't you know my head is killing me?"

"It's an emergency," he says, barreling past me.

I straighten up at that and spin on my heels. "What? What happened?" I ask, panicked.

"I have to pee," he says, running down the hall.

Groaning, I fall on top of the couch and regret even getting up this morning. Ash comes back out and pokes my cheek, but I swat him away with a glare. "To what do I owe this visit?"

"Aw, that's no way to greet your best friend," he teases, laying down beside me. I scoot over, making space for his six-two ass.

"You're not my best friend," I mumble, turning my head to see his expression. He snickers and scowls at me and I grin, poking him in the side. "Eli's my best friend. Followed by Olivia, then Robbie, then—"

"Bullshit." He laughs and elbows me.

"What are you really doing here?" I ask.

"I'm supposed to keep you busy as Jordan sets up your Christmas present."

"What did he get me?" I question, skeptically.

"Yeah, I'm not falling for that. C'mon, get dressed and we'll go get some coffee on the way to Robbie's house," he says, standing up and dragging me by my arms. When I don't cooperate, he throws me over his shoulder and walks me to my bedroom. "Don't think I won't dress you like a doll," he says, and I relent.

"Fiiine, I'll get dressed," I say, walking into the closet and pulling out my favorite holiday sweater that has a fluffy cat in a Santa suit on it. I pair it with a comfy pair of red leggings and walk back out, ready to go.

"Cute," Ash smirks. "Jordan must love your wardrobe choices."

"Hey, don't make fun of my sweaters," I pout.

"I didn't mean it in a bad way," he shrugs. "Y'all are nerds, so it makes sense."

"Speaking of us, together. Has he mentioned anything to you?" I ask, looking at him through my mirror as I put on my tree-shaped earrings.

Ash leans back on his elbows, raising an eyebrow at me. "Like what?"

"Like, if he thinks we're serious or if he thinks we're casual?" I ask, voice going higher on the word casual. As much as I want to believe that Jordan is all in, there's still some doubt in the back of my mind that at the next opportunity, he might leave me behind.

"Al, are you kidding? He's crazy about you. He even made me give up—" he stops himself from finishing that thought, jaw clicking shut.

"Made you give up what?" I ask, eyes narrowed.

Ash mimes zipping his mouth shut and throwing away the key and I groan. "I just—I trust him, but I just wish things would move a bit faster, you know? I mean, we did just go on our first date a week ago, but I feel like we should be further along in this relationship." I frown and pick at my nails. "I don't know what I want."

"You want some kind of commitment, it sounds like," Ash says, wrapping me in a hug. "Which is understandable. I know it's not your forte, and it's not mine either, but just be patient, yeah?"

I nod against him and sigh. "Yeah, you're right."

WE PULL into Robbie's driveway and I'm shocked to see that everyone's cars are already here. Did I miss the memo about when Christmas brunch was supposed to start?

Ash turns the engine off and grins over at me. I smile back, not sure why he's so chipper. "Everything okay?" I ask, hand on the door handle, ready to make my way inside.

"Oh yeah. Can I show you something across the street, though? Before we join everyone?"

"Across the street?" I whip my head around, looking over at the house that was for sale for the past six months. Realization hits me like a brick—this is the house he bought for him and Eli. "You got the keys already? Show me!" I squeak out, and open the car door enthusiastically.

Ash is unusually quiet as we make our way across the street and approach the front door. I laugh, noticing the Christmas wreath on the front door. "When the hell did you have time to decorate?"

He smirks over at me but doesn't answer, sliding the key inside the lock and pushing the door open, gesturing for me to go in first. My curiosity is piqued, and I take a few slow steps inside.

From what I can see in the hallway, the place is similar to Robbie's ranch-style home, all modern flooring and crisp white walls. I lean against the wall as I take off my shoes and notice part of a fireplace in what seems to be the living room. "Ash, this place is amazing. Are you excited?" I ask and he nods, offering me his arm.

I take it with a raised eyebrow, and he leads me towards the room with the fireplace with what I now notice is a large TV above it. *Wow, they moved things in here fast.* As we round the corner, a large cream-colored sectional is taking up the majority of the living room. It resembles my own couch at the apartment, and I smile.

I'm too busy gawking at the large windows on the other wall and how much natural light the place has, that I don't notice movement in the kitchen until Ash spins me around.

"Surprise!!" a chorus of voices exclaim. My hands fly up to cover my mouth and I jump up, more than a little startled.

"Guys, what the hell?" I ask, looking around the kitchen and noticing that my entire family is here. My mom and dad, huddled in a corner, each holding a glass of eggnog; Michael, Tangela and the kids next to them. Robbie is grinning at me, his elbows resting on the kitchen island, which is covered in trays of food and mugs for wassail. Olivia is holding Val and her green eyes sparkle as she gives me a Cheshire Cat grin.

"I feel like everybody is in on something except for me," I say warily as Ash walks over to Eli and puts his arm around his boyfriend. I frown when I realize Jordan is not here.

"You'll catch on soon enough, *lapsi*," Eli says, and looks behind me at the fireplace.

I spin around, taking in the living room again. There's a variety of plush pink pillows on the couch and a decent sized coffee table with a pastel multi-colored rug underneath. On top of the table is a framed picture and a stack of papers and I narrow my eyes, looking between them and my traitorous family that won't tell me what is going on.

As I approach, I realize the picture is the same one that Jordan has on his nightstand, the one of us walking down the aisle at Robbie's wedding. My hand shakes a little as I reach for the papers and quickly open them up.

"It's a deed," I say, dumbfounded. I skim through the unfamiliar words until I get to the transfer of ownership.

From Ashton T. Meyers to Jordan L. Hill and Alice M. Elliot.

Tears prick my eyes and I suck in a sharp breath, not quite believing my eyes. Did he just—

"Merry Christmas," Jordan says from behind me in that sultry deep voice of his.

JORDAN

ALICE IS FROZEN in her spot and my stomach drops, thinking this may have been a huge mistake. When she told me a week ago that all she wanted for Christmas was a bigger place to live, I thought of the perfect gift. Maybe it was a little *too* presumptuous to assume she wanted me to move in with her, but it felt *right*. We've wasted so much time, and all I want is to spend my life with her. I'd like that to start as soon as possible.

Everyone is quiet behind me, and I glance at them, shrugging. They all give me similar looks, not knowing what to do next. At least I wasn't the only one who thought this was a great plan. Everyone was looped in on it, and I even had to bribe Ash to sell me this house. I may owe him my firstborn and possibly my soul, but that's a problem for the future.

I clear my throat, tapping Alice on the shoulder where she's still looking down at the damn papers. "Do you not like it?" I whisper, brushing a strand of hair behind her ear. "There's still time to return it, those papers haven't been filed yet," I joke.

Alice turns around and stares at me, a single tear forming at the corner of her eye and falling down her cheek. I step closer and cup her face with my hands, catching it. "Why are you crying?"

"Did you really buy us a house?" she whispers, her blue gaze locked on mine, an emotion I can't quite figure out swirling in the depths of her eyes.

"I did. If you want it—" I say, biting my lip. "If you want me, I'm all yours."

She shakes her head and blurts, "I got you a yoga mat. I couldn't find a PS5."

I laugh and brush her cheeks with my thumbs as Alice blows out a breath and gives me a slow smile, one that takes over her whole face and lights up her eyes. "Yes, of course I want you. And the house," she says, leaning in like she might kiss me, but stopping at the last second.

Her eyes roam around the kitchen, where her family is looking at us. She bites her lip and says, "We haven't really told people that we're dating."

"Oh please, we've all known for ages. Just kiss already," Robbie says, rolling his eyes at us.

I chuckle and my lips meet hers in a pressing kiss. Alice sighs happily against me and puts her arms around my waist.

A chorus of "Finally!" and "Took them long enough," and "Woot!" comes from the kitchen and we break apart, laughing. My lips find her forehead in a long, promising kiss.

We spend Christmas in a mostly unfurnished home with all the people we love squeezing together on the couch, watching our favorite holiday movies and drinking festive drinks. Alice sits between my legs, her head resting on my chest, and I know deep in my bones that I'm finally home.

PART 4
UNTIL I FOUND YOU

CHAPTER 34

Two Months Later

JORDAN

MY HANDS GRIP the steering wheel and I get honked at again as I struggle to park the car. The pink balloons are taking up the entirety of the backseat, blocking my view. If it wasn't for Alex and Malia's help, I probably couldn't have fit them in the car at all.

But today is Alice's book release, which means I'll put up with all the balloons, and the cold weather, and the rude drivers on the road, if it means I can surprise her with the best day ever.

I manage not to pop any balloons and make my way to the back of the bookstore. I knock exactly three times as instructed and wait.

The door swings open and I peek around the balloons to

see a grinning Ash. "Jordie, you made it," he whispers, and holds the door open for me to enter.

"Stop calling me that," I whisper back, and look down the hallway for a glimpse of my girlfriend. I catch a glimpse of blond hair and her pink cherry bow-patterned dress and I smile to myself.

"Aw, you're such a simp," Ash says, and punches my shoulder.

"You're one to talk. What's that on your wrist, huh?"

He smirks, looking cocky with his dark red hair that's getting longer than usual. His most recent tattoo peeks out of his jacket and he grins down at it.

"It says Eli ... in cursive," I deadpan, answering for him.

"Yeah, well—welcome to the simp club."

"Is everyone here?" I ask, taking a few small steps into the bookstore.

"Oh, yeah. Alice is distracted by Olivia and Malia, so all I have to do is send the text and everyone will come in."

It took some coordination, but we managed to get all our friends, family, and even coworkers to come support Alice for her big day. Her teacher friends, her mom's bookclub, and even some of the Manticores and their wives and girlfriends, were happy to come out.

"Okay, let's do it," I say. Ash sends the text and leads me over to Alice's table.

The conversation dies down as we approach, and I place the balloons on the floor by her table. I smirk down at it, seeing that she's got goodies laid out next to her books, and a pink tablecloth. God, she's so fucking cute.

"Surprise!" I yell out, holding out the bouquet of flowers for her.

"J, these are so cute! Thank you," she says, rushing to give me a hug. Her voice sounds wobbly and I give her a squeeze before tilting her head up to better see her expression.

"Are you okay?" I ask, noticing her glassy eyes.

"Yeah, I'm just so happy," she says with a laugh.

Thank god. I didn't want to kick anyone's ass today for making her cry.

"You're amazing and I love you," I say, stealing a quick kiss.

She doesn't get a chance to reply because the next moment, all our friends, families, and coworkers walk into the store, taking up the small space of the first floor. There are easily forty people here, and Alice is stunned.

"Oh, J. Did you do this?"

"I figured everyone needed to hear about your amazing book. Now's your chance to tell them."

A tear falls down her cheek and I catch it with my thumb. Alice gives me her most radiant smile and kisses me on the cheek. "I love you so much, hotshot."

I bask in the happiness that radiates from Alice, stepping back and letting her sell books with the help of Olivia and Malia. When I spot a stack of flyers on the table, I grab them and head outside.

Ash, Eli, Robbie, and Alex are all outside chatting and I narrow my eyes as I step in their direction. The conversation stops abruptly, and my eyebrows fly up.

"Talking about me?"

They all look at me with a mixture of apprehension.

"Okay, what's going on?" I ask, crossing my arms over my chest.

"When are you gonna propose?" Ash asks bluntly, and I choke on air. Wow, they really were talking about me.

"None of your business."

"But you will, right?" Eli asks, frowning.

"Of course. What has gotten into you all?" I ask incredulously.

"Well, we just thought you might propose today," Alex says, hands in his pockets, the picture of nonchalance.

"And take away from her accomplishment? Hell no."

"That's—a really good point," Robbie says, nodding.

"Did you all seriously think I was going to propose to my girlfriend on her book release day, and then back out of it?"

"Well ..." Ash ponders.

"A little," Alex admits, shrugging.

"*Kyllä*," Eli mutters in Finnish.

"Sorry," Robbie says, wincing.

"Wow, unbelievable. Just for that, you're all gonna stay out here and help me hand out these flyers," I say, passing them out to each of my friends.

"Excuse me, ma'am, do you like romance books?" Ash yells after a middle-aged woman and Eli swats at him, saying, "Subtle, *hani*."

"So there will be a proposal?" Robbie asks me quietly.

I roll my eyes and whisper just for him to hear, "She already said yes."

EPILOGUE

Two Years Later

ALICE

MID-OCTOBER MAY NOT HAVE BEEN the best time for a wedding in terms of weather, but it sure is gorgeous at our cabin. The changing colors of the leaves painted a beautiful mosaic on the drive up, and I smile thinking back on the wedding pictures we took yesterday at Sleeping Bear Dunes.

Our friends are here for the weekend, which is a feat considering Ash and Eli still play in the NHL and Olivia had her first game in the same league recently. Robbie and Alex were more than happy to come up and spend some extra time here as they met with their business partner, Jason, who now oversees the Traverse City branch of Blue Line Brigade.

Malia has led the Thunderbirds to two PVF championships as the head coach for the volleyball team, and she's happily agreed to be one of my bridesmaids, alongside my old work friend Megan and, of course, Olivia. My rock. My maid of honor.

The air is chilly, but not cold enough that we'd need coats. Yet I still bounce on my feet, waiting around the building for our cue.

"Nervous?" my dad asks, a glossy sheen to his blue eyes.

I blink and roll my eyes. "Not even a little bit." I smirk, and he pats my hand where it rests on his forearm.

"I'm surprised you guys didn't elope the day after he got you the house." He laughs and shakes his head in wonder.

"That's the day he asked me to marry him," I say, smiling as I think back on that Christmas Day. After everyone left, Jordan gave me a tour of the rest of the house. The finished basement where we ended up building a custom gaming table and housed hundreds of board games; the four-season den that ended up being my office; the bookshelves he custom-ordered; and the two bedrooms, one of which was fully furnished. After he spent hours touching me, telling me how much he loved me, how he couldn't wait to start a family, he asked me to marry him. He asked me to go down to City Hall with him so we could elope.

But I had one request before we gave in and started on forever. I begged him to reconsider getting a hip replacement. We weighed all the pros and cons together and he eventually agreed that it would be the best thing for his health in the long run. Even though the recovery was tough and he had to take a leave of absence, we got through it together. And now, a year later, he's back to coaching the Manticores and spending some of his free time with Robbie's organization.

"Did he?" my dad asks, his mostly gray mustache twitching.

"I wanted to make sure he was happy with his health and progress before we took that step," I say.

"Smart cookie."

"And you're good to go," the emcee says, waving us down. I take a deep breath, and my dad leads me as we turn the corner and face the crowd of people standing and smiling at us. I smile back as we walk down the aisle, but my eyes never stray away from my almost-husband. He looks stunning in his maroon suit—a color that turns his eyes a pretty shade of amber.

My heart races as we approach, and Jordan reaches out for me. My left hand grazes his right palm and he squeezes my fingers, bringing them up to his lips and pressing a kiss to my knuckles. His thumb rubs over the princess cut engagement ring he put there the day after his surgery.

The ceremony moves quickly, and soon the minister asks us to say our vows. Olivia hands me my notebook and I blow out a breath, trying to steady all my overwhelming feelings. I don't mind being the center of attention, having done a few author events by now and advertising my books. But this is different—it's personal. All our loved ones are here, witnessing the promise Jordan and I are making to each other.

"J, from the moment I face-planted into your arms twelve years ago, I always hoped we'd make it here," I say, the laughter from the crowd steadying me. "It's no shock that I've written your name next to mine in every notebook, and every scrap of paper, wishing I could manifest our love. What was an unrequited, one-sided crush turned into stolen glances and late-night conversations. And when life tore us apart," I say, blinking back tears and looking up at

Jordan, "I thought I'd never have that kind of connection again. I'm so glad that I was wrong," I say with a wet laugh. Jordan wipes a tear away and reaches out a hand that I gladly take before continuing.

"I always knew what we had was special, that you'd be in my life one way or another. And I promise to always have your back. I promise to love you, to cherish you, to let you be the passenger princess, to always let you win at games—"

Jordan laughs, his bottom lip wobbling. "Sore loser," he whispers thickly, but it's loud enough for our wedding party to hear and crack up.

"I promise to be yours until death do us part. I love you so much," I say, letting a tear drop and handing the notebook back to Olivia. She takes it and dabs at my wet cheek with her sleeve as more chuckles rise up from the crowd of guests.

"Jordan, you may read your vows now," the minister says, and Jordan gives me a big smile. His fingers tighten around mine again as he grounds himself to me. He doesn't reach for a piece of paper, but rather speaks from the heart. My heart melts at the significance of it, knowing that he still deals with anxiety most days, and that speaking in front of all these people can't be easy.

"I'm not great with words, as you well know. I often bask in the silence around me, content to just be around you. I love watching you grow and want you to know that I'm so incredibly proud of everything you have accomplished. You inspire me every day to be the best version of myself.

"You've been my rock these past few years and I can't imagine my life without you. I may not be perfect, but I'll try my damn hardest to never let you down, to never make you feel small. You light up my whole world and if death were to part us, I promise I will find you in the next life, so you can be my beacon once more," he says through tears, eyes never straying from mine.

"I love you, Alice."

"I love you too, J."

My heart might burst out of my chest if I can't kiss him soon. I look at the minister, antsy to get this going.

"Repeat after me," he says, walking us through the rest of the ceremony. Jordan and I grin at each other, our hands swaying together in front of us. Mine shake as I place the rose gold band on his finger, but his hands are steady in contrast.

"You may now kiss the bride."

JORDAN

"THANK GOD," I say, cupping my wife's face and capturing her lips in a bruising kiss. I don't care that we have an audience, I need to feel her against me. I need to know she's mine. *Forever*.

Alice lets out the smallest moan against me and I smile into the kiss. I can't wait to get her out of this dress and into my lap. In one quick movement, I swing us around and dip her, our mouths still fused together. Everyone cheers and hollers as we come up for air and rush up the aisle.

"You have no idea how much I want you out of this fucking dress," I growl in her ear as we get inside the venue at one of our favorite wineries here in Traverse City.

"I think I have some idea," she says as she runs a hand

over the bulge in my pants. I grunt and she leans into me, peppering kisses to my clean-shaven jaw and scraping her teeth down the side of my neck. I shudder and keep her at arm's length right as more people start walking into the venue.

"You are a menace," I whisper, twirling her, admiring the way her dress billows with the movement. "A gorgeous little menace."

"I'll be so good to you later," she promises, a smirk playing on her lips.

WEDDINGS HAVE NEVER BEEN something I looked forward to. I've always found it draining, especially things like this—talking to so many people, one after the other with seemingly no break. But the look of pure happiness on Alice's face makes all of it worth it.

After our first dance, we eat the first course of our meal and sit through some thoughtful and hilarious speeches from our families and friends as Olivia and Ash take the stage with loving messages and hilarious memories.

By the time everyone leaves, our feet hurt from dancing, our cheeks hurt from smiling, and our hearts are full.

"Ready to get some rest?" I ask Alice as she leans into my side in the elevator up to our room at the venue. My hand wraps around her shoulder and I kiss the top of her head.

"I have other plans," she says, wiggling her eyebrows at me seductively.

"You barely slept last night, let's get you in some comfy

pajamas and you can do filthy unspeakable things to me tomorrow," I chuckle.

The room is dark as we enter, and I turn the light on the dimmest setting. Alice is still a little tipsy from the shots she did earlier, and I steady her on her feet, my palm splayed against her back.

"Did you have a good time?" she asks, yawning.

"The best," I mumble against her forehead, gently turning her around and getting to work on the buttons of her dress. My fingertips graze her spine with each pop of a button and my mouth leaves a trail of kisses behind, covering up the goosebumps forming on her skin.

I kneel down as I kiss the last spot at the base of her spine and my hands trail up her calves and legs, all the way to her garter. While her dress is short and stops at her knees, there's plenty of layers I need to get through, so I throw the material over my head and kiss the inside of her thigh before dragging the garter down with my teeth.

Alice moans above me and mumbles something incoherent. I chuckle and pull myself out from under her dress. "Arms up, baby."

She does as instructed and I lift the dress off her, making sure it doesn't snag in the braided crown atop her head. Gently, I set it down on the couch and return to my wife. Her eyes are half closed, but a smile still takes over her pretty pink lips. I kiss her cheek and reach behind her to pop open her push-up bra. It falls to the floor with a thud and I run my hands down her sides, my thumbs hooking into her lace panties, and pulling them off too.

I take a second to admire her while she's naked and soft. *God, she's perfect.*

"Sit here for a second," I say, leading her to the side of the bed. She does as she's told, looking at me through half lidded eyes as I take off my suit and under-layers. I leave my boxers on, and she frowns. "Don't pout, baby," I laugh, reaching over on the bed and dragging her pajamas closer to me. "Arms up one more time."

Alice gives me her cute-but-infuriated look, which just makes her resemble a grumpy cat, but she listens anyway. I pull her silky shirt down her torso and instruct her to stand.

She wobbles again and I steady her with a hand on her hip. As I drag one side of her matching pants onto one leg, her hands find purchase in my hair, and she scrapes her nails on my scalp in a soothing motion. "I married the best man today," she says, looking down at me with a soft look in her eyes.

"I married the love of my life," I respond, swiftly kissing her lips and redirecting my attention to pulling all the pins out of her hair.

"I should brush it," she says, taking a step towards the bathroom, and I blindly follow. I pull the rest of her hair out of her braids and brush it over a few times, tying it in a low ponytail at the back of her neck.

I spot the makeup wipes on the counter and take a few out, remembering her nightly skin care routine. With one hand, I tip her chin up so I can better see what I'm doing. With the other, I press the wipe to her face and rub in gentle circles until all the foundation comes off. I grab a few more wipes and run them over her eyelids and mouth.

By the time I'm done, she looks like my everyday Alice again—just as gorgeous and smelling faintly of coconut. She smiles at me, and I allow myself one more kiss. She opens up and chases me with her tongue, tasting like the cherry cake we shared for dessert.

I sigh and pick her up, bridal style. "I think I was

supposed to do this earlier," I say, walking her to the bed and setting her down.

She laughs and keeps her arms around my neck as I pull the covers on top of us. "We'll figure it out. Together," she says, and I press one last kiss to her forehead before she falls asleep in my arms.

"Together." I smile, letting sleep pull me under.

THE END.

ACKNOWLEDGEMENTS

We meet again.

What a wild ride this past year and a half has been. And to think it all started at a hockey game...

It's funny how inspiration can hit you sometimes, and for me it was as easy as seeing a female referee on the ice and wondering why we don't have more women in the hockey world. That led to countless hours of research and writing to finish the first manuscript of The Love Penalty. And as soon as I had finished Robbie and Olivia's story, I knew I had to write a book for each couple in the friend group.

Ash and Eli's story in Bar Down took me the longest to write, not only because I was experimenting with different story structures, but also because I wanted to get their story right.

Alex and Malia's story came next. The novella was a pure passion project, and one that I didn't think would see the light of day. And yet, the more I wrote, the more I realized that they play an essential role in the found family, and especially in Alice and Jordan's story.

And that brings us to this book's protagonists. For those who know me in real life, you've probably noticed little bits and pieces of myself in each character I write. But I have to admit that Alice is by far the one I resonate with the most. And let's face it, we're all a little nerdy and bookish at heart.

Delay of Game was the hardest book to write for a number of reasons. And one of those reasons is that it deals with the miscommunication trope (*ew, Stef, why did you do that??*). It's hard to write a second chance romance where both protagonists clearly still love and care about one another even after they've been ripped apart. While the miscommunication trope is not my favorite, I felt that it was necessary for their story (sorry not sorry).

(*Okay, we get it, can we move on to the part where you give thanks?*)

Before I get too sappy, I just want to say thank you to everyone that has picked up the Grand Marquee Manticore series and read it. This (fourth book) would not exist without your support. So from the bottom of my heart, THANK YOU!

This book is the last one in the series when it comes to the main four couples. Who knows, maybe I'll write a few spin-offs one day, but for now, it's goodbye.

Thank you to my developmental editor, Kay—I could not have refined Jordan's character arc without you. Your support and feedback has meant so much to me.

To my copy editor, Erin—I'm so sorry about all the commas you had to add. I promise I will do better self edits next time.

Annie & Rachel — thank you for always replying to my unhinged messages. I don't know that I could do this whole author thing without amazing friends like you.

Maddi — that stretching scene was all for you. You're

welcome. (*But seriously, thanks for being the most supportive friend and outstanding PA*).

To my alpha readers, I don't know what this book would even look like without your input. Thank you for always being down to read my terrible first drafts.

And to my family & my lovely husband, thank you for giving me the support I needed this last year to pursue my passion (*I'm sorry I was on my phone so much*). We need another vacation where I'm not writing. Or editing. Or organizing a book convention.

Okay, that's it for now.

See you soon with more stories.

- STEF

ABOUT THE AUTHOR

Project leader by day, romance author by night, Stef C.R. lives in West Michigan with her husband and not one, not two, but three cats. When she's not working or writing stories, she spends her time reading fantasy and romance, endlessly cheering on the Red Wings, Charles LeClerc, and listening to Noah Kahan.

ARE you looking for romances with happily ever afters? Then let's escape into the world of swoony MMCs and unforgettable heroines together. Find more information at stefwritesstories.com!

www.ingramcontent.com/pod-product-compliance
Lightning Source LLC
LaVergne TN
LVHW011944060526
838201LV00061B/4204